16 Marsden Place

Rachel Brimble

OMNIFIC PUBLISHING
DALLAS

Omnific Publishing
10000 North Central Expressway, Dallas, TX 75231
www.omnificpublishing.com

First Omnific eBook edition, June 2013
First Omnific trade paperback edition, June 2013

The characters and events in this book are fictitious.
Any similarity to real persons, living or dead,
is coincidental and not intended by the author.

Library of Congress Cataloguing-in-Publication Data

Brimble, Rachel.
   16 Marsden Place / Rachel Brimble – 1st ed.
   ISBN: 978-1-623420-20-8
   1. Contemporary Romance — Fiction. 2. Neighbors — Romance.
   3. Divorce — Romance. 4. England — Romance. I. Title

10 9 8 7 6 5 4 3 2 1

Cover Design by Micha Stone and Amy Brokaw
Interior Book Design by Coreen Montagna

Printed in the United States of America

This one is for all my girl friends
who like to laugh, love, and be as naughty as I do
—you know who you are!

Chapter One

Sienna Lloyd eased onto the leather stool behind the shop counter and stared at the official-looking, buff-colored envelope in her hand. Ignoring the sense of foreboding stealing over her shoulders, she drew in a strengthening breath and jabbed her finger under the seal. Tearing out the letter, she darted her gaze over its formal script, her eyes growing with each word.

"No, no, no. An extra three hundred pounds…per month?" She crumpled the edges of the paper, and her throat dried. "How the hell can I afford that? You gutless piece of…you nasty son of a…" She shook her head, her eyes stinging with tears. "You bastard!"

"Darling, please." Her mother strolled in from the back of the shop and tossed the latest copy of *Playgirl* down on the counter, centerfold up. "I'm trying to read here."

"Read? How can you read at a time like this?" Sienna flapped the letter back and forth in front of her mother's face. "You're not going to believe what is in this, this *thing*."

Snatching it from Sienna's hand, her mother snorted. "Must be a marriage proposal to put that look on your face."

"Ha-bloody-ha. My God, what am I going to do?" She pressed her fingers against her closed eyelids.

"What is it?"

"Read it."

A few seconds ticked by before her mother's words bounced from the shop walls. "Bastard. Blood-sucking, business-ruining bastard."

Sienna snatched her hands from her eyes. "I know. What am I going to do?"

Her mother tossed the letter on the counter. "He can't do that, surely? That's daylight robbery."

"Exactly."

"You can't afford to pay that amount of money in rent each month. It'll close you down, finish you off, put you on welfare—"

"Thanks, Mum. I get the picture." Sienna leapt from the stool and marched around the counter. "I know for a fact a landlord cannot just demand an increase in rent out of the blue." Clutching her hair back from her face, she continued, "I mean, an extra three hundred pounds a month for this place? Is he insane? Doesn't he understand what this shop stands for?"

"Of course he doesn't. My God, have you seen your landlord? If that man had any sort of sex life, his face wouldn't constantly look like a slapped ass, would it?"

Sienna looked around the shop that meant everything to her. Sienna's Sexy Solutions held her heart and soul within its four walls.

"I have to do something," she said. "I need this place. Potterford needs it. People who breeze through this town and look in my shop window assume I sell lingerie and women's toys, but it's so much more than that. It means more to me and the women who shop here. It's a…a saving grace, that's what this place is."

Her mother came toward her with arms outstretched. "Come give me a hug."

Tears of frustration pricked Sienna's eyes, and she leaned gratefully into her mother's embrace. She couldn't lose the shop—she'd lost too much already. Her father's image drifted before her mind's eye: the blood seeping through his shirt, the cuts and bruising on his face. Beaten and left for dead. Gone forever in a single twist of fate. Nothing else would be taken from her. Nothing.

Exhaustion and fear settled around Sienna as she took in a shaky inhalation of Chanel N°5 and the L'Oréal moisturizer her mother used. Looking to the front door, she said, "God, no wonder so many other shops on this rank have gone out of business if this is the way things are going to increase from now on. I won't let him do this, Mum."

Her mother sighed. "This place is a catalyst for the well-being of each woman in this town. Simple as that." She gave Sienna a tight squeeze before holding her at arm's length. "We'll fight this, okay?"

The first inkling of Sienna's endless reserves rose up inside her. "Everyone relies on me. Less than half an hour ago I promised Mrs. McGill I'd always be here for her. Now I could be gone by the end of next month."

"Is that when the lease is due for renewal?"

"Yes. I have to do something. Now." Whipping the letter from the countertop, Sienna brushed past her. "I took this place because it's the cheapest I could find. Everywhere else was way over my budget." She snatched up the phone and punched in the number at the top of the page.

"What are you doing?"

"I'm going to give Mr. *Thomas* a call, that's what."

"And tell him what, exactly?"

With confidence burning hot in her stomach, Sienna held up a finger. "Hello, may I speak with Mr. Thomas, please?"

"I'm sorry, but he's in a meeting right now. I'm Mr. Thomas's assistant. Can I help you?"

"Well, is it possible you could ask him to call Sienna Lloyd when he comes back into the office?" She threw her mother a triumphant smile.

"I'm…um, I'm sorry, Miss Lloyd, but Mr. Thomas did tell me to expect your call."

Sienna's smile dissolved. "He did?"

"Yes. Is this about the letter he sent regarding the rent increase?"

"Yes. But—"

"I'm sorry, Miss Lloyd, but the rent increase stands. There is little else you can do but pay or foreclose."

"That's impossible. I—"

"Unfortunately, you signed a contract confirming either payment on the first of every month or a month's notice of any changes made by you or Mr. Thomas. As you will have read in the letter, Mr. Thomas has allowed a generous sixty-day transition period."

Sienna remembered her euphoric attitude at the time she'd signed the contract two years ago, her pure, unadulterated glee at owning her own store at just twenty-six years old. She'd been confident the business would go from strength to strength. Which it had until the recession, one that had no doubt motivated the new and astronomical rent increase.

She gripped the phone. "Surely by law he has to give me more notice. I can't—"

"The contract is here in black and white, Miss Lloyd. If you wish to contest it, I recommend you hire a lawyer. I really don't see what else can be done, or even if you will be successful."

The woman was right. Though Sienna had been advised against it, the need to stay in Potterford with her mother, the need to have something concrete to build on, had overtaken any logical thought when she'd signed that lease.

"I see. Right. Thank you."

"Miss Lloyd, I am so sorry. If there was anything I could—"

Sienna slowly hung up the receiver, desperation creeping up her body from the tips of her toes to her scalp.

"Well?" her mother asked. "What did they say?"

Sienna opened her mouth. Closed it.

"Sienna?"

"What?"

"What did they say?"

She met her mother's soft brown gaze. "It's over." Sienna's body turned numb, but her mind whirled at a hundred and ten miles per hour as the pleasant little bubble she'd lived in the last two years burst with clear and unmistakable cruelty. "I'm going to have to close."

"What? Why? For goodness' sake, will you please at least blink? You're beginning to look like a very weird and very grown up Cabbage Patch Kid."

Blinking, Sienna groaned. "I can't believe this is happening."

"Talk to me, honey."

"He was expecting my call. The bottom line is, if I can't pay the new rent, I move out by the end of next month."

"How can he possibly—"

"I signed the contract, Mum. I never thought…" Her words caught like barbed wire in her throat. "I just thought I'd always be okay to pay. That I could look after my business."

Neither of them spoke for a few seconds, and then her mother sighed. "Look, I know you don't want to consider your dad's money—"

Cutting her off with a raised hand, Sienna said, "No. That money is yours."

"It's ours, and you well know it."

"No. That money is supposed to last you the rest of your life. I'm not letting you use part of it to get me out of this. This is a blip. Nothing more. I'll work something out. I always do."

Her mother lifted her hands in surrender. "Fine. We'll come up with some fail-safe promotions. How about we push the vibrators and play down the chocolate body paint?"

Sienna's shoulders relaxed, and she managed a small smile. "I don't want to push anything on anyone. If I need to, I'll move out of here and find somewhere else. It's okay. It's not the end of the world."

Her mother stepped forward and cupped her hand to Sienna's jaw. "Really? Then why do you look as though it is?"

Sienna closed her eyes. "It's a shock. That's all. It's nothing I can't handle."

"Look at me."

Reluctantly, she did. "What?"

"Have you considered this might be fate? A chance to take your life in an entirely different direction?"

Sienna shook her head. "Don't start that again. I'm not going anywhere. I'm happy here. You know I am."

"I'm not denying that, but things happen for a reason. Maybe this rent increase means it's time for you to get the hell out of Dodge. Start making a life away from your old mum for a while."

"No. I'm not leaving you."

"What about that friend of yours? The one in London with the lingerie chain? He would snap you up in a heartbeat. What's his name?"

"It doesn't matter what his name is. I'm not going."

"Sienna, please at least think about it. You left school at eighteen, started working in retail, and you haven't stopped since. You were named National Salesperson of the Year when you were twenty-one, for crying out loud. Can you imagine what you could do in the city?"

"I'm not leaving you."

Her mother jabbed her finger in the air. "There. You said it. You're not leaving *me*. Do you really think I'm that helpless? That I can't fend for myself? You're my daughter. Where do you think you get your gumption from?"

"Then you know when I say I'm going to do something, I do it. I'm staying. Like it or not, I won't leave Potterford after everything that's happened."

"I see. So, you'll stay here looking after me, living alone for the rest of your life. Good plan, Sienna. Real good." Her mother's cheeks darkened. "You're scared, honey. I get that. In order to grow, you have to face the fear of loss. It's as simple as that."

Sienna's breaths grew harried as her frustration rose. "Did I say my decisions are logical? Did I? Maybe my need to look after you after what happened to Dad is completely irrational, but there it is. I'm staying. Now, can we talk about something else? Like where I'm going to move the shop?"

Her mother sighed. "You're twenty-eight years old, sweetheart. You still have your life ahead of you, but time is running out to make the changes you need *now*."

Her heart twisting at the sight of her mother's tears, Sienna's shoulders slumped. "Mum, I'm sorry. I know you think I need more out of life, but I don't. I'm happy. And time isn't running out." She smiled. "Things happen when we least expect it. Who's to say what will happen a year from now? A month? Right now, I want to stay here with you. Okay?"

"You need to get away from me and start building your life. Dad may be dead, but you're not. Please. Take this opportunity and get out there."

"Mum, stop this." Sienna pulled her into a hug. "You don't want me to leave. You want me to find a man willing to marry my stubborn ass and impregnate me with triplets, that's all."

"Triplets?" her mother exclaimed with a huff. "A boyfriend would be a start."

Sienna laughed. "Been there, done that. Not really sure I miss it all that much either."

"All I'm saying is someone with your brains and looks shouldn't be selling sex toys in a small market town like Potterford. You should be working for some hotshot company in the city by day and sipping cocktails in a fancy wine bar by night."

Sienna pressed a kiss to her mother's furrowed brow. "I love that you care about me, and I love that you think I should be doing more, but I want to stay here. I'm beginning to think I always will." She held her mother at arm's length and squeezed. "Now, come on, we need to start thinking. I'm here to stay. Shop or no shop. Man or no man. You might as well get used to it."

Jack Beaton pulled into the driveway of his new home and turned off the engine. The late June sunshine lit up the house's façade like an illuminated opportunity. The epitome of family contentment, and he hoped to God it would be. Three bedrooms, two bathrooms, a huge back yard, and a small front lawn. Pink rose bushes bloomed along the flagstone walkway to the dark blue front door complete with polished brass knocker. Small-town suburban life. Was it really him?

He swallowed. Maybe not yet, but it would be. For him and his daughters, he had to make this move work. They would be happy there—he felt it.

Jack swiveled around. Holly and Katy slept in the backseat of the car; the journey from the city had been uneventful enough for both of them to nod off over an hour ago. Was he being fair bringing them to a small town like Potterford? The ever-present doubt whether he'd done the right thing poked and prodded at his conscience, and he screwed his eyes shut.

It had been two years since their mother left, and for the last twelve months she hadn't made any contact. That last encounter in court hadn't gone well, and despite Jack trying his best to come to an agreement they'd both be happy with, his ex-wife, Martina, had continued to drink, so he was granted full custody. Now was the right time to start again, so Jack had packed the girls up and moved away.

Of course, if by some miracle Martina did want to see her children, they wouldn't be hard to find. But for now at least, they were free. Peace, stability, and ultimately the children's security—that was Jack's goal from here on out. The bad times were two years in the past, and today he and the girls would build something new.

Opening his eyes, Jack got out of the car and into the embrace of the warm summer sunshine. The house loomed large in front of him, taunting him with its domestic appeal. His smile was slow in coming, but when it did, it stretched to a grin.

Eight weeks earlier, after months considering what to do next and thinking about relocating, Jack had driven farther and farther from the city and stumbled across Potterford. He'd been drawn to the small towns and tiny hamlets nestled in and around southwest England. And when he'd first pulled into Marsden Place, a strange peace had settled over him. This tiny and quiet cul-de-sac was what they needed; its circumference of picture-perfect houses with their whitewashed walls and slate-gray roofs would form a protective circle around him and his children. That was what these houses were built for. Families. Even families without a mother.

The location was perfect. A quiet suburban town would be as attractive to Martina as a garden party to Ozzy Osbourne. She wouldn't come within ten feet of the place.

Jack's scrutiny then settled on the house next door. After making some discreet inquiries about his new neighbor, he'd learned the woman who lived at number sixteen was a young professional with a thriving business in town. The real estate agent hadn't mentioned a husband or children, but even if his neighbor was the "career type," she wouldn't be able to resist falling in love with Holly and Katy. Everyone did.

And if she didn't? Well, that would be too bad because, along with their father, they were here to stay.

"Daddy?"

Jack spun around. Bending down, he peeped his head through the open car window. "Hey, Pud'. Want to get out?"

Katy screwed a fist into her eye and yawned widely enough to display her tonsils before she gave a sleepy nod. "Uh-huh."

Grinning, he opened the back door and lifted her from the car seat. "You sleep okay?"

"Yes." She dropped her head into the crook of his neck, her face directed toward their new home.

Inhaling her warm sleepy smell, Jack pulled her close. "Do you remember this house from when we visited last week?"

"We're going to live here."

"Do you still like it?"

"Uh-huh. It's pretty."

"It is, isn't it?" Relief swept through Jack's chest. "We're going to be happy here, baby. I promise."

"I want to go in."

"We'll wait for Holly to wake up first."

"Daddy? Daddy! Let me out, let me out."

He shifted Katy's weight onto his hip and went around to the other side of the car. "Well, well, well, guess who's awake? It's Miss Bossy Boots herself."

Katy giggled, and Jack opened the door, greeted by Holly's impenetrable glare, her arms steadfastly crossed. "Not funny, Daddy."

He grinned and extracted her from her car seat, lifting her easily onto his other hip. "Sorry, Munchkin. You're still kind of cute, though."

She pouted. "I am not cute. Babies are cute. I'm four."

"Okay, then you're beautiful. How's that?"

Her features softened. A little. "Nice."

Jack bit back a laugh. "Right, Chalk and Cheese, shall we go and check out our new home?"

"Yay!" The girls punched the air with their tiny fists.

With a lion-esque roar, Jack ran toward the house with the twins bouncing up and down, screaming happily. At the front door, he lowered them to the ground, pulled the key from the back pocket of his jeans, and held it aloft.

"Ready?"

"Yay!"

"Are you sure? There won't be any fighting over bedrooms?"

"No, Daddy," promised Katy.

"No, Daddy," said Holly. "Katy will let me have whichever room I want."

He frowned. "Holly…"

"I will, Daddy," interrupted Katy.

"I know, but that's not the point, is it?" Both girls looked at him, confusion etched across their faces. It didn't matter how much Jack tried to teach them to share and share alike; the twins' way of doing things worked perfectly for them. So who was he to interfere? He shrugged. "Forget it. Let's go."

Slipping the key into the lock, Jack swung the door back on its hinges, and like two bullets from a gun, Holly and Katy shot ahead of him and along the hardwood floor of the hallway. Jack stepped over the threshold himself and took a long, slow look around him; he ran his hand over the polished newel post of the staircase and smooth, creamy white walls. The place was spotless. So clean there was still a trace of lemon furniture polish mixed with new paint. A million miles from anything the twins had known before.

Their screams of delight and discovery echoed around him, filling him with satisfaction. Tomorrow they'd move their stuff from the old house and start making a new life.

"Daddy, come see."

Following Holly's call, Jack walked into the sun-filled living room, where she and Katy stood side-by-side holding hands as they peered through the glass patio doors.

"What are you looking at?"

"There's a lady out there," they said in unison.

"Where? In the garden?" He stepped closer and looked over their heads. "Well, look at that."

Jack smiled as his gaze appreciated the toned thighs of the woman crawling across his newly acquired lawn.

Chapter Two

Sienna crawled toward the flower borders in number seventeen's back yard, all the while muttering about landlords, sharp sticks, and the battering of male genitalia. After Mr. Evans from across the street had commandeered her on her way in from work and gleefully informed Sienna her new neighbor would be moving in tomorrow, she realized she'd forgotten to "borrow" a few of the daffodil bulbs from his or her new garden.

Even though there was zero chance of her ever receiving the gardener of the year award, Sienna didn't want her new neighbor overlooking her completely colorless yard next spring while theirs bloomed like a bloody rainbow. So, she would help herself to a few bulbs lurking in the beds waiting to erupt in the New Year. It wasn't as though the new owner would miss what they didn't know they'd had, right?

Having never stolen so much as a piece of candy in her life, she pushed away the guilt hovering around her like a pesky gossamer curtain. After the day she'd had, she was due some sunny pleasure, and nothing was sunnier than daffodils. Brandishing her trowel, she plunged the tip into the soil to catapult the first one out.

BANG, BANG, BANG!

The sound of a fist against glass hurled her back onto her ass. "Holy crap!"

The trowel flew from her hand up into the air, narrowly missing her left ear on its descent. Her blood pumped wildly as her heart beat an out-of-control tattoo. She looked to the patio doors. Two of the most angelic—yet mischievous—faces Sienna had ever seen stared back at her.

Surely those two hadn't the strength to bang on the doors that hard? She frantically scanned the back of the house. Bedroom windows: empty. Kitchen window: empty. Then the back door opened. Scrambling to her feet, Sienna brushed the mud from her knees.

"Oh, Lord. Here goes." She plastered on a smile as embarrassment burned her cheeks.

When the man, presumably the kids' father, emerged into the sunlight, her smile disintegrated and her mouth dropped wide open. *Come to Mama.*

He strode out onto the decking above her. His shoulders were broad, his face handsome in a rugged, careless kind of way. His hair was thick and dark, with bits flopping onto his forehead.

She clamped her mouth shut to lock in a tongue that wanted to loll onto the grass.

"Can I help you?" He walked down the steps toward her.

His voice was deep, husky, and very, very male. Sienna shivered and drew in a shaky breath.

Talk, woman, talk. "Um, hi." She smiled. "Funny story. I was just…"

"Pinching some of my flowers?"

She laughed, the sound far too high-pitched. "I wasn't pinching your flowers. Noooo. I was checking the soil. I've been…um…you know, watering them while the place has been empty."

"Ah, I see."

She bent over to retrieve the trowel. Anything to escape the unrelenting intensity of his gorgeous blue eyes. Lingering for a moment, she cranked her brain into overdrive thinking of something remotely feasible and effective to get her out of there in the minimum amount of time. But her brain remained so unresponsive, she considered the fact she might be dead.

Sienna straightened, but his line of sight remained fixed where her ass had been. Unexpected pleasure swept through her; she couldn't remember a guy of this caliber ever looking at her like that. Unsure what to do or say—but pocketing the silent compliment for another day—Sienna cleared her throat.

His eyes shot to hers, and a flush of color burst from the collar of his shirt to his cheeks. Something hitched inside her chest, and further humiliation flooded her senses at being caught helping herself to his daffodils. God, she had to get out of there. Get out before things got any more mortifying.

She raised her hands. "Look, I'm sorry. I didn't mean…I'm embarrassed you caught me…"

He threw a glance toward the house. A stone dropped into her belly and thawed her heated attraction. The girls. The girls at the window. They were no longer there.

When she faced him again, his mouth drifted into a soft smile; the blush had faded from his face, leaving behind a rich tan. He held out his hand. "Jack Beaton. Nice to meet you."

Feeling more self-assured by his kindness, Sienna took his hand in hers. Smooth, firm, big. "Sienna Lloyd. Nice to meet you too."

After a long moment, he slowly pulled his hand from her grip. "So, I'm guessing if you've been watering my plants, you must be my new neighbor?"

She slid her hands into the front pockets of her shorts, where they couldn't get into mischief. "Yep, number sixteen. There's a gap in our adjoining fence down there. Can you see it? I can get it boarded up in no time." She grimaced as a way of apology. "Seeing as how you found me skulking round in your garden, I will completely understand if you want that done sooner rather than later."

"Daddy?"

At the sound of his daughter's voice, Jack leapt away as though Sienna had lifted her top and flashed her size-D breasts in his face. The two girls who'd been at the window now stood on the decking, side by side like sentries, identical expressions of concern on their faces.

Daddy. Sienna swallowed. She was flirting with their father while Mummy was no doubt inside unpacking boxes. What was the matter with her? Clearly her landlord's letter had sent her over the moral edge. She opened her mouth to make her excuses and get the hell out of there, but Daddy got there first.

"Hey, you two. Come and meet our new neighbor."

Anxiety spread like spilt water through Sienna's veins, turning her blood ice-cold. She didn't know how to talk to kids. She didn't do kids. Was scared of them…and what they meant. Love. Nurture. Eternal dependability. None of those things lasted. Not really. Even these two adorable and incredibly identical twins, struggling down the decking steps as quickly as their four- or five-year-old legs could carry them, wouldn't break her resolve to not get involved.

"I…um…I must get back—"

"Sure, we won't keep you. Let me just introduce you to my kids. You'll love them." Pride rang in his voice like bells at Christmastime.

"You don't understand." She glanced at the twins as they approached at an alarming rate. "I…kids don't tend to like me."

"What?" He raised a brow.

Sienna lifted her shoulders. "I know. Crazy, but there we are. So…"

"Mine will like you." He grinned. "Promise."

Somehow she managed a wobbly smile. What the hell was she supposed to say to that?

The girls reached their Daddy Destination, and each clamped a possessive arm around a thick, muscular thigh.

"Girls, this is Sienna, our new neighbor. Say hi."

Silence.

Sienna widened her frozen smile to a grin and lifted her hand in a halfhearted wave. "Hello, girls."

One of them pointed to her shorts. "You have teeny-tiny shorts like Barbie."

Heat flared in Sienna's face for a second time in the last few minutes, but she laughed. "Barbie? These aren't Barbie shorts, honey. They're just shorts."

The girl's eyes narrowed. "Short shorts."

Feeling more and more like a hooker chatting to a little girl on the sidewalk, Sienna looked to Jack for help. His grin was so wide, it looked glued on. His eyes shone with glee.

"It was lovely to meet your daughters," Sienna said, glaring, "but now I have to get back."

Jack's smile faltered. "Is there a problem?"

"No, I've already explained—"

"Kids don't like you. Right." The tone of his voice had dropped lower.

Sienna cleared her throat. "Right. Well, it was lovely to meet you all. I'm sure I'll see you soon."

She moved to walk away when Jack's voice stopped her. "Their names are Holly and Katy, if you're interested." Sienna pivoted around. "If you want to borrow anything else," he continued, "just ask. We're friendly enough."

"Thanks. I will."

His hands smoothed protectively over his daughters' chocolate brown hair, and Sienna's stomach tightened at the memory of how her dad would do the exact same thing to her.

"I'll…um, see you round," she said. "Say hi to your wife for me."

Jack's face darkened. "My wife?"

"I'm assuming you've got a wife inside to go along with your kids."

Seconds passed before the hardness in Jack's eyes softened. The skin at his neck shifted, and he blinked rapidly a couple times. "I'm divorced."

Sienna watched him warily. Jack Beaton might have looked like he should be served between two slices of puff pastry and covered in squirty cream, but he apparently also came with a side of baggage.

"Okay. Well, I'm sorry to hear that."

With no response, he just looked her over as though searching for God knew what. Shifting from one foot to the other, Sienna glanced at the twins. Had he forgotten they were there? One looked up at him while gnawing her bottom lip; the other stared straight at Sienna with pure venom.

"It was nice to meet you, girls." She smiled widely, in the hope it lifted whatever the hell had frozen their dad to the spot. "I apologize if I get your names mixed up; you look like two peas in a pod." Facing Jack again, she held out her hand. "Welcome to Marsden Place. I hope you'll be happy here."

Finally meeting her eyes, he took her hand in his. He looked so damn vulnerable…yet hugely muscular and demanding. A potentially lethal combination.

Sienna shook her head and laughed to lighten the mood. "And I hope you'll forgive my crawling in your grass uninvited. No hard feelings?"

To her relief, he smiled. "Not at all. We hope to see you again soon, Sienna."

"Indeed, you will. Bye, girls." She looked back at Jack and raised her hand to her head in a salute. "Bye, Daddy."

He laughed and saluted right back. "See you."

Turning, head held high and swinging the trowel nonchalantly back and forth, Sienna hesitated as she neared the fence. Then, after a second's contemplation, she swallowed her pride, dropped to her knees, and crawled as gracefully as possible through the hole to her yard.

She reached her patio doors to a chorus of male laughter mixed with dual-tone giggling. She smiled. For the first time in a long while, the sound of children playing with their father didn't grate on her nerves or stab at her heart. Instead, it was incredibly satisfying. Her impression was that their dad needed to laugh. And seeing as Mrs. Jack wasn't around…

Sienna shook her head. "Nope, the man has issues. Real, bona fide ones. I do not need that right now. At all."

Walking through the kitchen and up the stairs, the problem of her non-existent business premises loomed large, pushing Jack Beaton to the back of her mind. The first thing she needed to do was get some legal advice. Yes. Legal advice was the way forward. This time, no mistakes, no loopholes.

She wandered into the bedroom at the back of her house and peered into the yard next door. Jack and his daughters were running around the grass, playing a rough-and-tumble game of tag. Every time their dad caught them in his arms and lifted them onto his shoulders in a fireman's lift, Holly or Katy screeched with delight.

Sienna crossed her arms over the ache in her chest before snapping the drapes tightly closed. With the world shut out and no one to see her, she slipped to the floor. Once again, her life had taken a downward tumble, and she had to find a new way to start over.

Two days later, Sienna sat across the desk from her lawyer. Tall and slim with a mass of thick black hair nearly reaching her waist, Kelsey Morgan looked more sexy-supermodel than lawyer. She was also Sienna's best friend and a dynamo with the legal ins and outs of the corporate world. Right then, she was worth her weight in designer clothes.

Legalities bored Sienna to tears, but receiving the cursed rent increase hadn't left her any choice but to face them. That made Kelsey her guardian angel…albeit a guardian angel with a penchant for guys in tight leather trousers.

"So?" Sienna asked. "What do you think? Could I legally run the business from Marsden Place?"

"Yes, but why on earth would you want to? It's your home. You don't want sex-crazed pensioners and horny twenty-somethings traipsing in and out at all hours."

Sienna arched an eyebrow. "Pensioners and twenty-somethings? What about thirty-year-old lawyers bringing back what they think is a faulty vibrator at ten o'clock at night, only to discover she's worn out the batteries?"

Kelsey slid on her glasses and glared. "Hey, that was one time."

Sienna laughed. "One I will never let you forget."

"Really? Well, maybe I won't give you the benefit of my advice free of charge, if that's the case. It was me who warned you about the contract for the shop in the first place, if you remember."

Sienna raised her hands. "I'm joking. It's forgotten. I promise never to mention it again."

"Hmm, until next time."

Kelsey's cell phone rang, and she snatched it up. Glancing at the display, her smile dissolved. "Oh, hell. What does he want?"

"Who?"

"Mike Bloody Scott." She jabbed the *talk* button. "What?"

Sienna shook her head and grinned. No matter how much her friend denied it, Mike got under her skin, and if Sienna suspected correctly, a whole lot of other places too.

Kelsey leaned back in her chair. "I didn't promise you anything. I said I'd help if I can…No…Fine, you owe me one. Big time." Her cheeks flushed pink, and she averted Sienna's eyes. "No, not dinner. You owe me a business favor if the occasion should ever arise that I need a vain, conceited family lawyer in my corner."

Sienna bit back her laugh. Was Kelsey aware that she was smiling and doodling hearts on her blotter?

Seconds later, Kelsey snapped the phone shut and cleared her throat. "Asshole."

"God, you are so stubborn."

Kelsey glared. "What?"

"You and Mike," Sienna answered with a grin. "It's burning like a bloody inferno between you. Sooner or later, you'll have to jump into the fire, my friend. Mark my words."

Kelsey gave an inelegant snort. "Yeah, when I'm past desperate and feel as though my vagina's sealed up." She raised her eyebrows. "Which, when you look as good as me, ain't never gonna happen."

"You're so damn modest. I really wish I could be more like you."

They exchanged a smile before Kelsey leaned her elbows on her desk and slipped into lawyer mode. "Right, back to business. You can do this with your shop if you're serious."

Sienna scooted forward on her seat, all thoughts of Mike vanishing. "I am. I'll make sure the peace of Marsden Place isn't disrupted. It helps that my house is at the very end of the cul-de-sac. And I live on the corner of what's already a busier street that people take to cross through town. There's also that bakery just along from me, so my neighbors are used to a little bit of commerce. It makes complete sense for me to do this, Kelse. Think of the money I'll save in overhead."

"True. You'll have to pay business rates and other bits and pieces, but I still think it will work out a hell of a lot cheaper for you. I'm just not sure about you opening your home to the public this way." Kelsey reached across the desk and gestured for Sienna's hand.

"What?"

"Your mum phoned me."

"Do you think I didn't know that? I know my mother like I know myself. She's as worried about this as you are. She wants me to ship out of Potterford and get a career in London."

"Is that such a bad idea?"

Sienna pulled her hand from Kelsey's and rolled her eyes. "Not you as well."

"Come on. I'm worried about you."

"Why? Because I want to stay in my hometown? Does that make me some kind of freak or something?"

"No, it's the reason you're staying here that's the problem."

"What do you mean? Why aren't *you* in London making a fortune? Why are *you* staying here? God, why is the fact I want to stay in the place I grew up such a problem? What's the point in moving to a city where I don't know anyone?" Sienna leapt from her chair and turned her back. The painted landscape on the wall blurred, and she blinked hard in an effort to dispel the threat of tears when Kelsey moved behind her.

"Sienna, look at me."

Sienna counted to five and turned around. "What?"

"Your dad died in the most heroic yet violent way. Something like that has never happened in Potterford before, and I hope to God it never does again. But there was nothing you could have done to protect him, so you cannot put your life on hold to look after everyone else instead. There's your mum, me, every other person in town…who's next? You'll burn out. You need to have some breathing space. Have some fun; go on a date."

Jack Beaton's face appeared in Sienna's mind, and she closed her eyes as if that could shut it out. The wall clock ticked away the seconds as she fought the panic swelling hard and fast behind her ribcage like a balloon nearing explosion. She was better off alone. Isn't that what she'd been telling herself the last two years?

"You're wrong, you know," she said.

"Am I?"

"Yes. This isn't just about Dad."

"Then what? Talk to me."

"I'm scared, okay?"

"Scared of what?"

Sienna opened her eyes. "Scared of all of it. Losing Mum. Losing you. God knows I'd love to get close to someone, but…" Her breath caught.

Kelsey pulled her into her arms. "Okay. Okay, I get it." She sighed. "Fine. You live your life as you want, but shutting down isn't going to change the past. Getting on with it will. Take some time away from here at least. I'll look out for your mum."

Sienna pulled back. "I need to be here, Kelse. Now, are you going to help prevent my business from collapsing after everything I've put into building it or not? Moving it to my place makes absolute sense. This way I'm completely my own boss. Mum can come and go as she pleases—"

"Why, yes, she can, along with me and half the women in town. Coming and going from the privacy of your home so you can continue to fulfill everyone's needs while ignoring your own."

"I thought you understood."

"I do."

"No, Kelse. You don't." Sienna stepped back and whipped her bag from Kelsey's desk. "From a business point of view, it makes sense for me to move the shop home: yes or no?"

"Sienna, sit down. I'm only trying to help you find the escape and self-indulgence you need. Tell me the last time you had a day at the spa or even a cappuccino and wedge of strawberry cheesecake with me? Tell me the last time you let a guy take you out for dinner?"

Sienna opened her mouth to protest, but sexy Blue Eyes came into her mind once more. Damn it. "Look, I'll get the business moved, let all my customers know about it and the date I'll reopen, and then you and I will go away for a couple of nights, okay? We'll have a spa weekend with cheesecake and cappuccino and everything."

Kelsey smiled. "Are you serious?"

Sienna raised her hand as though she was taking an oath. "I promise. Now draw up everything I need to get the ball rolling."

Kelsey wrapped her arms around Sienna in a boa-constrictor-strength hug. "A whole weekend, girlfriend. Pamper by day, predators by night. I'm telling you something right now: use it or lose it. Start living by what you preach, Missy, or your customers will start thinking you're a fake."

They say the truth hurts, and Sienna could only presume the lash that had just struck her chest like a whip had the word *guilty* etched on its tip. She shrugged from Kelsey's embrace. "New premises. New life. We'll go away, and when we get back, I'll think about looking for a new man, too. How's that?"

Kelsey took her elbow and steered her toward the door. "I would so like to believe you, but I don't. You've had men ask you out, but you haven't said yes to one of them in over a year."

"Maybe nobody has sparked my interest for a while." She winked. "Things change when you least expect it."

"What do you mean by that?" Kelsey narrowed her eyes. "Have you met some—"

"See you later." Sienna pressed a kiss to Kelsey's cheek and scooted through the door, slamming it rather succinctly on her friend's question.

Chapter Three

Sienna pulled into her driveway feeling a million times more optimistic than she had before she'd met with Kelsey. She'd only just cut the engine when an ear-splitting scream came from outside the car. Sienna sat bolt upright.

"Bloody hell." She pressed her hand to her racing heart and looked through the windshield.

The sight that greeted her didn't bode well for the quiet night she hankered for.

Yet a traitorous smile tugged at her lips. Why did those twins have to be so cute? Sienna watched Holly and Katy run back and forth across the front yard, and a burst of laughter bubbled in her throat. If her guess was right as to which twin was which, it was Katy who screamed hysterically in one continual stream of terror while Holly chased her with what looked suspiciously like dog poo on the end of a stick.

"You're a little firecracker, my girl," Sienna said, laughing. She then turned to see Blue Eyes was also in the yard, and she groaned. Now that was just cruel.

Clearly, Jack Beaton possessed the same unfathomable gift all parents of young kids seem to have — the innate ability to completely zone out to the chaos erupting all around them and walk about as though they're alone in a silent meadow. But it wasn't the way Jack calmly steered a wheelbarrow around the lawn that made Sienna's heart race, nor the way he stopped and held up a rather raggedy-looking tulip bulb and smelled it, as though checking what it was.

What injected lust into her loins like liquid aphrodisiac would be his half-naked state of undress. His back made a perfect triangle, tapering down to a hard, buff ass encased in what surely had to be tailor-made Levi's. A film of perspiration glinted along the length of his naked, golden spine as muscles rippled beneath the skin in all their sinewy glory.

Sienna sighed. It was pointless to deny he caused sensations in her that hadn't been stirred for a mighty long time. She ran the tip of her tongue over dry lips and squeezed her thighs together to stem the throbbing. Why did a man who looked like that have to move in next door when she had so many problems? Damn, if she hadn't already felt as though her entire existence teetered on a precipice, she might have even tried to get used to the idea of kids for some up-close and personal time with a guy like that.

As if to put Sienna out of her misery, Jack abandoned his gardening, picked up a box from his driveway, and carried it inside the house.

Sienna stepped out of her car and closed its door as quietly as possible. Maybe she could get inside her house before he walked back out for another box and noticed her—God only knew how she'd manage to maintain eye contact with him looking the way he did. She edged to the front door.

But when she glanced toward his yard, she stopped. The driveway looked as though a bomb had exploded in the middle of it. Boxes and crates were strewn all over the place; crockery, pots, and pans spilled from their tops like a multi-colored river of household necessity. A blender, a portable heater, and a million other bits and pieces were scattered everywhere, as well as three or four mobile racks filled with clothes. It was as though a moving van had pulled up outside and just dumped its cargo at the curbside. Jack would be there until nightfall getting everything inside the house, let alone putting it all into some kind of order.

Sienna shook her head. Typical that a man should first turn his mind to gardening, or preferably digging a damn hole, when he didn't have as much as a kettle to boil water in once he got inside. Which, judging by the current state of the yard, would be approximately four hours from now. He had two little girls to feed, bathe, and get to bed as well.

"Damn it." Sienna exhaled, plastered a smile on her face, and sauntered to the picket fence separating their driveways. "Hi, girls."

The twins abandoned their hysterical screaming and ran toward her.

"Is Daddy okay?" Sienna asked. "He looks as though he could use some help."

The one she thought was Katy—because she had less of a laser glare—stared at her with huge blue eyes, wide and sad. She shook her head. "He said we're getting in his way. Daddy never says we get in his way. He's sad."

Sienna glanced toward the house. "Do you know what happened to make him sad?"

Katy opened her mouth to speak, but Holly got there first. She fixed Sienna with eyes that could bend metal. "He's moody with Mummy."

Katy gasped. "Shh, don't say that. He's not thinking about Mummy."

"Yes, he is. He does all the time."

Sienna's mind whirled into overdrive. Thinking about Mummy, huh? The question was, exactly *how* was he thinking about her? Did he still love her? Resent her?

There was only one way to find out.

"Does he miss her?" Sienna kept her voice as quiet as possible without actually whispering. If she whispered, her question could be deemed as snooping. She wasn't snooping. She was just *interested*.

A deep and very male cough made Sienna and the girls simultaneously jump. Sienna guessed her own eyes were as big as theirs and her cheeks equally red. Slapping on a smile that felt wider than the breadth of her face, she turned. Jack stood in the doorway of the house, his arms crossed.

Sienna swallowed. The look on his face wasn't that of the friendly, welcoming neighbor she'd seen two days before. More the face of a mad psycho who had missed the last three months of therapy sessions.

"Hey, Jack." She waved. "I thought you could use a hand."

He strolled toward her, his thumbs hooked into the pockets of his jeans. "That's very kind of you."

The amused shine that had lingered so sexily in his eyes the other day had evaporated, leaving behind nothing but cool detachment. If there were ever any doubt as to the girls' paternity, the need for DNA evidence would have been entirely unnecessary right then. The three pairs of eyes watching Sienna were identical, and more than a little unnerving.

She rolled back and forth on the balls of her feet and stretched out her arms, steadfastly resisting the allure of Jack's naked torso. "It looks like the fall of the Berlin Wall out here. I'll come round, shall I?"

"There's no need. I've got it covered."

"Come on. You've got the twins to sort out, boxes all over the place—"

"You think I can't handle that by myself?"

Sienna dropped her arms. "I was offering to help. That's all."

He stepped closer. His eyes, darkened to almost midnight blue in the evening sun, bore into hers. "Me and the girls can cope just fine. There's no need for you—"

She held up her hands. "Fine, I was just being friendly. There's a cold glass of wine and a hot bubble bath waiting for me inside. I'll leave you to it."

Sienna had moved to walk away when Katy's soft hand reached over the fence and gripped hers. "Please come. I want to show you my new bedroom." She looked to her dad. "Daddy, please?"

Sienna's heart picked up speed, a little trepidation mixing with shock at Jack's coldness. What had happened to this family to make him so defensive and his kids so sad? Couldn't he see they wanted a little fun?

Clearing her throat, she said, "I can give you half an hour. Why don't you take me up on it before I change my mind?"

His eyes narrowed as he stared, and though it made Sienna's bravado seep from her veins to pool into a useless puddle at her feet, she willed herself to stare him down. His gaze wandered languidly over her face, altering as it did so. That shift might have gone unnoticed by someone else, but Sienna ran a shop specializing in sex. She noticed those subtle changes in a person, and she understood what they meant.

She was also aware her nipples had tightened under the thin cotton of her T-shirt. As though attached to them by lengths of string, Jack's eyes dipped to her chest. They widened for an almost imperceptible moment before he looked up.

If she'd thought his intention had been feral before, it was damn near animalistic now.

Dear God, the man had the uncanny knack of making her want to lift her skirt and flash her bits at him in some sort of desperate mating dance. Her heart beating hard, she willed him to help out and say no to her challenge. It would be much safer to flee to her house and bolt the door firmly behind her.

The look vanished, and he faced Holly and Katy. "Half an hour, okay?"

Katy nodded. "Okay. Quick, Sienna."

Damn. Sienna grinned with gritted teeth. "Great."

With her bottom lip trembling with the effort it took to keep smiling, Sienna stepped away from the fence and walked down her driveway and into his at a snail's pace. Why, oh, why had they had to be outside? Why, oh, why did he have the cutest girls known to man? Why, oh, why did she have the urge to slam Jack Beaton down on the lawn and lie on top of him?

Katy ran down the length of the driveway to greet her. She took the hem of Sienna's T-shirt between her thumb and forefinger and pulled her forward to stand face to face with Jack. He held out a box of kids' toys to her, his eyes glinting with satisfaction. Oh no, he wasn't going to get her with those damn eyes and twitching mouth again.

Sienna slid the box from his hands and winked. "Where do you want it, Daddy?"

Jack watched Sienna from the corner of his eye as she unpacked wineglasses from newspaper and carefully lined them up in one of the kitchen cabinets. She intrigued him. The sexual prowess that came off her in near intoxicating waves was enough to make a man set up home in a cold shower. Fortunately, experience had made him wise to a woman with the body to turn men's heads. There was little chance he'd fall victim to Sienna's cocoa-brown stare.

Been there, done that, and look where it had gotten him. Avoiding an ex-wife like the damn proverbial plague.

Yet, it had taken him all of five minutes since meeting Sienna to ascertain she definitely wasn't married. No wedding band, no sparkly engagement ring. Guessing her to be twenty-seven or twenty-eight, he knew a woman who looked like her was single by choice. With her long hair passing thick and lush over pert breasts and a waist a man itched to splay his hands around, she was one good-looking woman by anybody's standards. So if he was so averse to such a package, why the hell was he still staring at her?

Because she was beautiful. He'd be an idiot not to see that, but it was more than that irritating the hell out of him. It was her. The flashes she had of a temptress stalking her next prey reminded him of his ex-wife. Although, the big and noticeable difference with Sienna was how delicate she looked when she thought no one was looking. Almost fragile. When she'd spoken to Holly and Katy over the fence, with her brow furrowed and her cheeks flushed, she'd looked like a woman who could nurture children and make a house a home.

Then again, he'd made the same assumption about Martina. He wouldn't fall into that trap again.

Jack stole a direct glance at Sienna. When she noticed and smiled at him, he snatched his attention back to the blinds he'd been attempting to hang at the window.

The sexual part of Sienna was hazardous enough, the softer side even more so. Stupidly, Jack had thought the "businesswoman" next door would rarely be home and that, when she was, she would be aloof. Sienna was the antithesis of that. Regardless, the impression he'd gotten so far was that, as a young businesswoman, Sienna ranked children far down on her list of priorities. So whatever that softness in her was, it wasn't directed toward family life.

Yet he was unable to resist another look at her. He stared down the length of her body, from her thick chestnut brown hair to the slim waist and firm little butt encased in black denim, down to her bare feet. And when she reached up into one of the higher cabinets, Jack inwardly groaned. The movement had revealed two or three inches of smooth, tanned stomach between her T-shirt and the waistband of her jeans. The temptation to touch her rippled through his fingers.

She caught him staring again, and heat hit his face like an inferno.

"Is this okay?" she asked.

"Hmm?"

"The glasses." She laughed. "I don't know how anal you are with this sort of stuff. If someone arranged glasses in my cupboards, I'd bite their head off."

Blinking his way out of his sexual coma, Jack smiled. "They look great. Whatever you think best."

She placed her hands on her hips. "Wow, you're a real conundrum. Do you know that?"

Her smile was infectious, and he couldn't help laughing. "What?"

"Well, take earlier, for example." She arched an eyebrow. "You were touchy as hell. Now you're happy for me to come into your house and take over the organizing. I'm sorry, Jack Beaton, but you don't add up."

He straightened. "I don't add up? What about you?"

"Hey, I add up." Color seeped into her cheeks.

He shook his head. "Nope. Afraid not."

Still standing on the chair high above him, she lifted her hands from her hips and crossed her arms. Jack didn't think she could look more domesticatedly gorgeous. But, God, he had a feeling she'd shoot him straight in the eye if he said that out loud.

"Let me tell you something, mister," Sienna asserted. "I am who I am. I don't pretend to be something I'm not."

Suppressed laughter vibrated at his diaphragm. "I didn't say you were. Do you think *I'm* pretending?"

She studied him through narrowed eyes. "I think you have *stuff* going on and that's why you've moved here."

Shit. Jack stuck out his bottom lip and nodded a few times. "You're very intuitive."

"Ah-ha." She jabbed her finger in the air, triumphant. "I knew it. So, what I have learned so far is that as long as I don't mention your ex-wife or insinuate you need help in any way, you're a pretty easygoing kind of guy. Am I right?"

Jack's smile wavered. "You're not exactly subtle, are you?"

Shrugging, she said, "I don't see the point in wasting time, that's all. I like you, but you've got a chip on your shoulder the size of

Mount Vesuvius. You let it linger there much longer and the thing is gonna break your back."

He laughed dryly. "Is that so? I think you might have some issues yourself, you know. What's your hang-up with kids? You say they don't like you, but Katy already has you pegged as her new idol. You've knocked Dora the Explorer out of the park."

She frowned. "Who?"

He grinned and shook his head. "Doesn't matter."

"Well, whatever." She looked to the kitchen door as if seeking escape. "The point is, Blue Eyes—"

"Blue Eyes?" He raised his eyebrows.

Her eyes never left his, but Jack didn't miss the shift of her throat nor the two spots of color that darkened her cheeks. There it was again, that vulnerability he'd have to find a way to resist sooner rather than later.

She waved her hand dismissively. "The point is, I may have kid issues, but I don't have any children, do I? You do. That means you need to loosen up if you want those girls of yours to be happy."

Jack set the screwdriver down on the counter and crossed his arms. "How exactly would you know what I should or shouldn't be doing with Holly and Katy if you don't have kids?"

Her eyes softening, Sienna glanced down at her feet. "Doesn't mean I didn't have a daddy, does it?"

"Ah, a daddy's girl, huh?" Jack pushed away from the counter and stepped toward her. "Well, in that case, you must be an expert."

She lifted her head, and her huge eyes widened as he approached. Scrambling off the chair, she reached for another box, opening a chasm of space between them.

"I'm not an expert." She held the box against her like a shield. "I just know they love you and want you to be happy."

"I am happy."

"If you're happy, I'm Father Christmas." Bending down, she put the box on the floor.

"Fine, I'm not entirely happy." He cleared his throat. "Yet. You're right, though, that's why we moved here. I'm planning on making myself and the girls ecstatic."

She straightened. "In Potterford? With little else going on but a stream of gossip and the best sugared donuts in the world at Misty's?"

He smiled. "Absolutely. A nice quiet town away from *Sex and the City*. I want my girls—"

"Sex?" Her normally olive skin grew slightly paler.

Damn it—this isn't the time or place to start spewing out moral standards.

Shaking off his bitter memories, Jack lifted his shoulders. "Yes, sex. I don't want Holly and Katy around anything like that. This small town, as you call it, is perfection as far as I'm concerned."

"Because of the lack of sex?"

"Well, I'm not naïve enough to think people aren't having it. I just don't want it shoved in my daughters' faces every five minutes." He stopped. "Are you all right?"

"Yes, of course. I'm fine." Sienna waved her hand in front of her face. "I feel a little sick, that's all. Hungry. I'm hungry. Right, I'd better go. Are you okay with the rest of the stuff? Yes? Good." She snatched her bag from the counter. "I'll see you then."

Without thinking, Jack slid in front of her and gripped her forearm. "Pizza."

"What?"

"You're hungry. I want to pay you back for your help with pizza. What do you think?"

She glanced toward the door. "I think I need to go. I said half an hour. You've had a lot longer than that already."

He slipped his hand from her arm. Unable to take his eyes from hers, Jack didn't want her to go…despite the dangers of her staying.

"Please stay. The girls would love it. We'll have a picnic in my near-empty living room." Had he lost his freaking mind?

Sienna stared a moment longer before closing her eyes and blowing out a breath. "Look, thanks for the offer, but you're not going to like—"

"Come on, Sienna. We're neighbors. Let's start as we mean to go on. As friends."

"Friends?"

Jack fought the urge to stare at her open mouth. "Friends."

Indecision appeared to be at war in the smoky brown depths of her eyes.

Stay. Please. He bit back the words. It wasn't loneliness making him do this. It was the need to get on with her for the girls…

"Come on," he said, "let's just see what they're up to." He made for the door in the hope Sienna would follow. Hearing her footsteps on the parquet flooring behind him, Jack smiled, and together they peered into the living room. "Ah, maybe having a picnic in here wasn't such a good idea after all."

Katy looked up at the sound of his voice. "Hi, Daddy. Hi, Sienna."

Jack's heart twisted to see the twins looking so happy. While the adults had been busy in the kitchen, it seemed the girls had carried out a hair-band/fairy-outfit/soft-toy massacre. Pink paraphernalia was strewn everywhere, covering every inch of carpet not already taken up by a box, crate, or piece of furniture.

"Just checking you're okay. Pizza sound good for dinner?"

"Yay!" They both clapped.

Smiling, Jack pulled the door closed, and Sienna shook her head with eyes narrowed. "That was a low shot."

"What was?"

"Letting me see them all cute and playing."

"So you'll stay?"

"I must be insane," she said as she dropped her bag onto the floor, then raised her hands in surrender. "Fine. We have pizza, and then I go."

He exhaled. "Great. And wine."

She smiled back and relaxed her shoulders. "Sounds like a plan."

Tipping her a wink, Jack pulled his cell phone from his pocket before Sienna could change her mind.

Early evening had turned into late, and Sienna sat comatose on a patio recliner on Jack's decking. A pale moon appeared wispy and white far away in the twilit sky, and Sienna conveniently chose to ignore the relaxation settling over her shoulders like a much-loved, long-lost blanket. Rather than question her current state of untroubled repose, she surrendered to it. For now. It was interesting the effect Jack Beaton was having on her.

She took a sip of wine. She'd yet to confess what she did for a living. The Sauvignon Blanc slipped down her throat, numbing a little more of her common sense. It would be a hundred times better if she told him her plans right then rather than later.

Kelsey had set the wheels in motion for the shop's move, and Sienna was perfectly in her rights to go ahead and convert the front room of her home. Pride bloomed inside her at the thought of it. A high-brow, classy establishment, Sienna's Sexy Solutions helped women achieve sexual unity with their partners…or alone. It wasn't a backstreet porn shop, and Jack wouldn't make her feel any differently about a business that had made a cool forty-thousand pound profit last year. More than that, the shop was the only thing she had left to hang her damn hat on.

The smells of lavender and a neighbor's newly mowed lawn wafted over Sienna on an idyllic, barely-there breeze. She inhaled and looked at Katy asleep beside her.

Thump-thump. There it was again. That lurch in her chest. She darted her gaze back to the horizon, though she had to admit it: as kids went, Jack's seemed better than most. Yet she wouldn't fall for their identical faces and opposite personalities. It was nothing more than a scam. Kids played games…they learned from adults.

Beside her, Katy looked gorgeous in her peaceful slumber, and Holly, despite her evident dislike of Sienna, had somehow managed to fall asleep curled up at Sienna's feet. It felt weird but kind of nice.

"Hey, you're not smiling at them, are you?"

Snapping her head up, Sienna saw a soft smile playing at Jack's lips. She'd been so absorbed in her thoughts, she hadn't heard him rise from the recliner on her other side.

"So?" She shrugged. "They're cute…when they're asleep."

"Ha-ha. Right. It's time I got them to bed. Want a refill?"

She sat bolt upright. It was one thing flirting with him knowing there were two four-year-old bodyguards between them, but alone? Um…no. Time for a sharp exit. She placed her glass on the low table between them.

"No, thanks. That's my cue. But thanks for a great evening."

When she stood, his mouth hovered only inches from her forehead.

Kiss me.

The thought had catapulted into her head from nowhere, and she stumbled backward. His hand thrust out quicker than she could catch her breath, and he gripped her wrist.

"Got you." He grinned, his eyes shining. Happy. He looked happy.

"I like seeing you smile, Jack Beaton." The tremor Sienna felt in her stomach as she said it was surely due to eating cold pizza washed down with half a bottle of wine. "It suits you."

"Thanks."

The soft, masculine timbre of his voice skittered over her skin, making the hairs on her arms stand to attention. With his fingers still grasping her wrist, surely he felt her pulse rapidly beating against them. He continued to stare, his smile slipping, his eyes darkening and dropping to her lips. *Oh, God.* No. He couldn't. They couldn't. They'd barely met…

He then stepped back so quickly the back of his legs hit the recliner, and he wobbled precariously. After a comedy-sketch struggle, arms flailing, Jack managed to regain his balance, and Sienna giggled, trying to think of something witty to say. Something, anything to fill the God-awful silence rising between them like an invisible boulder and making her want to lunge forward and mash her mouth to his.

Thankfully, he got there first. With words. "Um…maybe you should go, after all. It's getting late."

"Absolutely. That half-an-hour sure stretched on." Sienna brushed past him, away from his dark, gorgeous eyes saying one thing and his lips another. But when she heard one of the girls stir behind her, she turned. It was Holly, who then sighed and folded herself tighter into the fetal position. Sienna released her held breath. "I'll leave you to it, then."

"Okay, once I wake this one up." He nodded toward Holly and winked. Sienna's stomach wound in a soft knot as he leaned down to lift Katy from the recliner and into his arms. He looked at Holly's curled body again. "Holly? Come on, stand up. I know you're listening to everything we're saying."

Silence.

His laugh was a low, love-filled rumble from deep within his chest.

Sienna looked on, intrigued and impressed. This girl had some nerve.

Jack coughed. "Holly, I'm warning you…"

After another couple of seconds, Holly sat up, and her inherent scowl slipped into place like a favorite mask at Halloween. "No, I wasn't."

"Yes, young lady, you were. Come on, up you get. Say good night to Sienna."

Sienna struggled to keep her smile under wraps when Holly faced her. After a long and ruthless appraisal of Sienna's entire face and upper body, Holly thrust out her hand.

"Good night."

Somehow, Sienna managed to keep a straight face and solemnly took Holly's offered hand. "Good night, Holly."

Holly honored her with a curt nod before stomping past Jack and toward the back door.

"Good job," Jack said, and followed his feisty daughter inside.

Sienna stared after them. Now what was she supposed to do? Creep through the house and make her escape through the front door? She considered the fence separating their yards; the hole still wasn't patched. No. That would be insane.

She needed to leave, wanted to leave. For all her bravado, all her knowledge of what worked and didn't work as far as foreplay, sex, and general hanky-panky were concerned, Sienna had never felt more like an inexperienced seller of all things sexual in her life as when Jack had stood just inches away from her. She was overwhelmed with the horrible feeling of being the awkward, shy, bespectacled virgin she'd been at eighteen.

No, she'd wait for him to come back and then say her goodbyes.

But not before telling him the nature of the business that would soon be setting up shop next door. That would cool the sexual tension between them like a vibrator dropped in water. He was a great guy. A great, good-looking guy, and as much as it pained her to admit it, his daughters were cute too. And they clearly meant the world to him, so there was no way he'd approve of what she did.

Walking to the balustrade surrounding the decking, Sienna curled her fingers around the smooth wooden railing and sucked in a sharp breath as pressure bore down and hot tears sprang into her eyes. She knew the man had come to Potterford looking for something lacking in the city, but she had no other income — and women needed the shop open. She had to tell him.

Although, *sex shop* wouldn't be the best phrase to use under the circumstances. Sienna tilted her head in thought. Maybe *female temptation palace? Sensual delight store?* She shook her head. He'd see through either of those like he would a pair of lace panties.

"When I look at that sunset, I know I made the right decision to move here."

At the sound of his voice, Sienna turned and saw Jack staring at the horizon.

"Will you just look at that?" he continued. "It's amazing."

She followed the direction of his outstretched hand. "It *is* beautiful."

"It's more than that. It's a new start for me and the twins."

It's now or never. "Jack, there's something I need to tell you."

"Sounds serious."

"It is."

He swiveled around and leaned his backside against the balustrade. "Okay. Tell me."

How was she supposed to handle this? They'd flirted pretty much the entire time they'd known each other. It was fun watching him leap from Dad to Hunk and back again—but nothing about her business moving home was amusing.

"Okay, here goes. You need to know what I do for a living—"

"You run a store in town."

She flinched. "You know?"

He took a drink. "Sure. So what sort of place is it? A floral shop? Shoe shop?"

Oh, crap. "Not exactly."

"What, then?"

"It's…" She moved back by the recliners, her heart thumping in her ears. Closing her eyes, she counted to three, opened them, then picked up Jack's half-full glass of wine. "Here. Drink this."

He chuckled. "I need to drink before I can hear this?"

"Uh-huh."

Shaking his head, he accepted the glass and sipped from it, his eyes meeting hers over the rim.

In one seamless rush, the words flew from her mouth: "It's a sex shop, and I'm moving it next door."

The wine that burst from his mouth projected directly into her eye, warm and entirely unwelcome.

"What?" His eyes grew to the size of a bush-baby's.

Sienna swiped her hand over her face. "My God, just how big is your mouth to hold that much wine?" She laughed in a futile attempt to lessen the tension shooting through her body at a hundred miles an hour.

"You run a sex shop." He'd said it as a statement rather than a question.

She tugged her wet T-shirt away from her breasts, thinking that now might not be the best time to enhance her assets. "Yes. Well, it's more sensuous than sexual."

"And you're moving it next door." He stared at her for a long moment before blinking and putting his glass on the table. Sienna didn't miss how his hand trembled. "This is insane." He scored his fingers into his hair and held his head. "I can't believe…how can I…" He squeezed his eyes shut. "Just…stay there. I'll get you a towel. You need a towel."

He wandered back inside enveloped in a stunned stupor. Walking on rubber legs herself, Sienna sank back onto a recliner. She'd done the right thing by telling him. Honesty was the key to success. Honesty meant the two of them could live side by side just fine from here on. Therefore if they could maintain honest communication and equal compromise, there was no reason why she and Jack couldn't still get along.

Picking up his glass, she drained the rest of it and glanced toward the door. She'd given some sharp, honest communication all right, and now all Jack had to do was surrender to a teeny bit of compromise—and agree to the shop opening next door to where his four-year-old twins played. Yep, they were good to go.

She sighed. "God, that doesn't even sound moral to me, let alone him."

"Does talking to yourself help?"

His voice made her jump, and she grimaced. "Kind of."

His stubbled jaw was set in a hard line of granite. Sienna bit down on her bottom lip, thinking it best she said no more until he'd had his turn. Jack sat as he handed her a towel, and their knees hovered millimeters apart.

"Are you serious about the shop?" he asked.

Oh, God. He's hoping I'm kidding. She screwed the towel in a ball and forced herself to maintain eye contact. "Yes."

Jack tipped his head back. Sienna stared at the soft hump of his Adam's apple as guilt pressed down on her. She'd clearly taken a huge fat needle and plunged it into his happiness. His girls' happiness.

"But why would you do that? Why would you run a sex shop from your home?" He exhaled and met her eyes.

"It's not by choice, believe me." Mr. Thomas and his damn eviction notice burned like a ball of fire inside her. "The landlord has raised the rent sky-high, leaving no choice but for me to move the shop here. It won't be all bells and whistles, Jack. It will be low key, running from the front of my house."

"And the landlord is raising the rent, why?"

She shrugged. "I don't know. His prerogative, I guess. The point is—"

"You can't." His eyes had turned cold. "I won't let you."

"Jack—"

"It's not fair. Not after everything I did to move us here."

She instinctively wanted to reach for his hand but clamped hers together instead. "This is not the end of the world."

"You don't understand."

"I do. You're upset—"

He huffed out a breath. "Upset? God, I'm way past upset."

"It's not as bad as it sounds. Just hear me out."

"No."

Sienna recoiled. The way he looked at her then was a million miles away from the look that had made her feel like the prettiest woman in the world. Her hands grew clammy. What was happening to her? Usually she stood up to this type of confrontation like a tower of immovable strength. She was a strong, independent woman whom her father had raised with love and support, belief and guidance.

Now she wanted to take that horrible desperation from Jack's eyes and make it all better. But she only pursed her lips together, trapping her confused emotions inside.

Seconds ticked by. This was insane.

"Enough," she finally said. "Quit staring at me as though I've grown a second head. I don't deserve it. I know this is not the best situation with children living here, but I promise—"

"What do you promise? That my kids are going to feel secure and comfortable around sex toys and perverts walking in and out of your house?"

"Excuse me?"

The tone of his voice had chilled her to the bone. He was livid, something Sienna didn't have the best level of experience dealing with. Although used to sexual frustration from her clients and maternal frustration from her mother—and even friendly frustration from Kelsey—this was entirely new territory.

Sienna pushed to her feet, the recliner scraping across the decking. Jack followed suit. They stood toe to toe.

"Do you know what?" she said. "I'll talk to you about this when you've calmed down."

"I am calm."

"The hell you are." She took a few steps away then stopped. Whirling around, she fisted her shaking hands on her hips. "Tell me something, Jack. You have sex, right?"

"What?"

"Which is it? Yes or no?" She had to get the upper hand on the conversation before Ol' Blue Eyes and his angry stare could weaken her resolve. He was six-foot-three and built like a male model. The guy had sex. He had to have sex. If he didn't, it was a crime against the entire female population.

He continued to stare, a nerve leaping in his jaw. He said nothing.

Fine, she'd fill the silence. "My point is, I run a sex shop. Big deal. People have sex, and people love my shop. I provide a service that makes my clients happy and, in turn, makes me happy. I'm not hurting anyone. In fact, I like to think I bring people closer."

"You like to think you bring people closer," he echoed and tilted his head to the side as though she'd spoken in a foreign language. "Are we talking black leather, whips, the whole nine yards?"

"What?"

He shrugged. "It's a simple enough question."

"Give me strength."

"Pardon me?"

"Why do men always think of sex in such a completely different way than women?"

"You're not answering the question."

"No, Jack. I don't sell what's needed for a full-on bondage session. That stuff is licensed, okay? For God's sake, if that's the first thing that went through your mind, I understand your reaction." No wonder the guy had looked as though he might keel over. Whips?

Sienna looked out across the yard. Night had fallen, and the heavy darkness surrounded them. As his smell drifted softly beneath her nostrils, she sensed him behind her. Close behind her.

"Sienna?"

She slowly exhaled. "Yes."

"Look, maybe I shouldn't have overreacted…I'm sorry. Can we start again?"

She turned, and he smiled in a soft, boyish kind of way. "You're sorry?"

"I shouldn't have jumped to conclusions."

"No, you shouldn't have." She looked to the floor before she could drown in his two blue pools of loveliness. "You can relax, honestly. I just sell good old-fashioned lingerie. You know, baby-dolls, suspenders, that sort of thing. Then there are the toys, of course."

"Toys?"

She looked up and waved her hand dismissively. "Dildos, vibrators, handcuffs, butt plugs—"

"Butt…" He didn't finish. His throat gulped as though he'd swallowed the "plug."

Sienna pretended to duck a punch and raised her hands. "Whoa there, sport. I'm joking. There are no butt plugs, but everything else."

Jack coughed a few times, and Sienna laughed. She needed to leave and give the poor guy time to absorb what she'd told him. Maybe he'd be in a better frame of mind in the morning.

"Right. Well, thanks for the wine and pizza," she said. "I'm out of here."

"You're going?"

God, he looked so cute, all lost and…edible. She winked. "Don't worry, Jack. No doubt you'll see me again soon. Now go make yourself a cup of tea. Lots of sugar."

"Why?"

"They say it's good for shock."

Sienna patted him on the shoulder before turning and walking back through the house and out the front door.

Jack stared at his computer screen: *Sienna's Sexy Solutions.*

Thank God for the genius of the Internet. Jack leaned closer as he clicked on a page allowing him access to the inside of Sienna's shop, thus saving him from the totally terrifying prospect of visiting it in person. That was the last thing he wanted to do. He'd spent a sleepless night wrestling with the dilemma of whether to march next door and tell Sienna in no uncertain terms there was hell's chance of the shop moving there or satisfy his need to know the turnover such a shop made in a place masquerading as a "quaint market town," as per the real estate brochure.

It was an outrage. False bloody advertising.

Jack frowned, conveniently slamming the door on the voice in his head reminding him of the other nocturnal dreams that had filled his mind the last night. Dreams that involved an awfully large amount of time with Sienna dressed in a basque, suspenders, and four-inch stilettos…

He cleared his throat and shifted in his chair. Damn woman. It had been four days since he'd seen her. Their last encounter had been when they'd both left their houses at the same time and met halfway down the driveway. The fence had acted as a shield between them.

She'd smiled. He'd smiled. Then they'd both ducked into their cars like a pair of fugitives facing an arresting cop. It was ridiculous, but necessary. They'd waged a silent war — he knew it and she knew it. And if she didn't, she would tonight.

Jack did realize, however, that he shouldn't have lost his temper the way he had that night on his patio. He couldn't ignore the fact Sienna hadn't lied to him. Despite her intention to bring his worst nightmare next door, she had been nothing but honest and upfront.

That simple fact managed to tie a knot of guilt deep inside him. But as image after image flashed onto his laptop screen, anger simmered once more.

He was afraid of what exposure to the shop — a blatant invitation for any sexual female predator in the land to come knocking — would do to the twins. Okay, so maybe he was being irrational, but he was the twins' father. It was his job to protect them.

They'd already watched their mother diminish in front of their eyes until she'd reeked of nothing more than cheap perfume and alcohol, wearing nothing more than short skirts, tight tops, and see-through underwear. Witnessing Martina walking around the house like that, half-dressed and drunk, talking to God knew who on the phone, or dumping them with yet another babysitter so she could go and sleep with someone other than their father could have scarred their daughters in ways Jack couldn't see on the surface. He couldn't have that stuff around them. Not again.

He glared at the screen. Sienna had claimed the shop wasn't sordid but something that did good in the town. Well, he wouldn't be taken for a fool again. What was the word she'd used? *Sensuous.* That was it. Sensuous!

From the things he saw on her website, the woman might be honest, but she was also deluded. As far as he was concerned, when a place sold products called Champagne Lick and a Rabbit vibrator that had four ears rather than the customary two, she sold sex. Period.

Jack cursed, logged off, and snapped down the laptop lid, determined to sit there and fume a while.

He looked around the open-plan office of his new workplace. *The Potterford Post* ran out of a converted barn on the outskirts of town. Just a small team of eight men and seven women produced this quality weekly read for the town's residents. And it had been only a little over a month ago that, after an interview and perusal of Jack's credentials, the editor had offered him the job without hesitation.

It was nearing the end of his first week working there, and already Jack's job as a local reporter suited his new life well. Gone were the risks and late-night stakeouts of life as an investigative reporter. Although proud of the international company frauds he'd uncovered, the drug and pedophile rings he'd obliterated, Jack now had a schedule Holly and Katy could rely on. How would he have known, then, that the first danger to threaten their new lifestyle wouldn't be a grudge-carrying felon from his past but a five-foot-seven inch package of temptation who went by the name of Sienna Lloyd?

Maybe his investigative days weren't over after all. She'd said the move was the result of a sudden rent increase. Who did that to loyal tenants in a recession? It made bad business sense to force people out when there was little chance of someone else taking over. There had to be more to it — and if there was, Jack would find out.

But how could he confront Sienna again if the woman already felt backed into a corner? He wasn't a bully.

Jack glanced at his watch. Three o'clock. That gave him an hour to go into town and ask a few questions, do a little more research on his new neighborhood and neighbor before it was time to collect the girls from daycare.

He stood and locked his desk. Sliding his laptop into its carrier, his pulse beat at his temple.

"You off somewhere, Jack?"

Jack shot his attention across two meters of desk space to his newest friend at the paper. As a father and avid soccer fan, Jack had already found common ground in both respects with Steve and didn't want to jeopardize their burgeoning friendship by hurrying through the door without talking to him.

Forcing the scowl from his face, Jack smiled. "Yep, I've…um…got a lead on something. I need to pop into town and ask a few questions."

Steve tapped his pen on the desk. "Anything I can help with? Lived here close on twenty years. I feel like the Potterford oracle most the time."

Jack shrugged. "It's something and nothing. I noticed there's quite a turnover of businesses on Canterdown Road and Bourton Way. Something in my gut is telling me that's due to more than just the recession."

Steve arched an eyebrow. "I know one or two closed down on Bourton Way last month, but apart from that, I don't see how one more makes a newsworthy story. Come on, Jack, level with me. What's this about? We know you were a hotshot reporter in the city before you came here. We want to learn from you."

Knowing full well the "one more" Steve had referred to was Sienna's business, Jack relaxed his tense shoulders and smiled. "That's all behind me now. I'm just interested in the local stuff. Anyway, you know more than me right now. Who owns the latest one to go under?"

"Sienna Lloyd." He shook his head. "To be honest, I find the rumors she's shutting the place hard to believe."

"Oh?"

Still young enough to consider himself the "boy around town," Steve grinned and looked left and right over his shoulders before wriggling his eyebrows. "She owns the…what shall we say? The 'palace of pleasure' down on Canterdown."

Jack raised an eyebrow. "The what?"

"It's a woman's place. You know, all sexy lingerie, lotions and potions…toys."

In the name of male camaraderie, Jack slowly smiled. "Toys? I'm liking the sound of the place more and more."

"I'm telling you, mate, if Sienna closed up shop, there would be a hell of a lot of disappointed husbands and boyfriends in Potterford."

"Don't you mean disappointed women?"

Steve chortled. "Nope. It's the men who'd have hell to pay. She's a phenomenal lady, Sienna. She makes our ladies feel like goddesses, and that, in turn, is good for us." He winked. "If you know what I mean."

"I think anyone would know what you mean by the glint in your eye." Jack laughed. "What about the lady herself? Is she…?"

"She's hot. Real hot."

A stab of something Jack didn't want to contemplate assaulted his gut. It twisted and burned and felt strangely like jealousy to hear Steve talk about Sienna that way. He tapped the side of his nose. "Good to know, my friend. Good to know."

"So, I'm guessing you're going to drive there even faster now, huh? Check it out for yourself."

Jack nodded. "Abso-bloody-lutely."

"Yep, she is one hell of a girl." Steve faced his computer monitor. "One hell of a girl who hasn't been seen out with the same bloke more than once since her dad passed away. None of them seem to be what she's looking for. She's one in a million. But, man, what a waste."

"What happened to her dad?"

Steve met his eyes. "He was a cop. High up the ranks."

"He was killed on duty?"

Steve sighed. "No. That would've been easier for Sienna and her mum to deal with. He was walking past a house on Steller Way and interrupted a group of kids breaking and entering. Four of them beat the poor bloke with bats. Left him for dead. He died at hospital."

Jack's blood turned cold as Sienna's beautiful cocoa eyes filled his vision. "Were they caught?"

"Yep. None of them will see the light of day for a while, I can tell you that much."

"How long ago did this happen?"

"Five years. The two of them were pretty inseparable. He thought Sienna was the most precious thing to ever grace the earth, and he was her shining light. It was a beautiful thing to see them together, but when he died…"

Jack stared. "What?"

"She changed, mate. Sienna went from a girl who everyone assumed would go to London and make a fortune selling whatever the hell she put her mind to, to settling in this tiny town in a tiny shop. Took the wind out of her completely."

"What do you mean, sell whatever she wanted to? She's always been a salesperson of some sort?"

"And then some. Started young and worked her way up the ranks to become the highest-selling lingerie consultant in the southwest by the time others her age first completed university. That girl could convince Jabba the Hutt he'd look good in a thong."

Jack didn't laugh. What was he supposed to make of that? Wasn't it just possible she put her sales skills to use manipulating people into believing they were something they weren't?

But this wasn't about whether or not Sienna was a good person, whether her life had been as crappy as his. This was about his children, and Sienna's place would only remind them of what Jack strived so hard for them to forget. She was the enemy—even if everyone else seemed to love her. He had no choice but to pursue this.

"Jack?"

He jumped. "What?"

"What are you thinking, mate? You look like you could punch someone out."

"Nothing. Look, I've got to go. I'll see you in the morning."

Steve raised his hand in a wave, his attention already back on the computer.

Leaving him to it, Jack walked to the door and outside, where gunmetal clouds covered the sun that had been shining an hour before. He slid into the front seat of his black Ford Focus, and turning the ignition, he pulled on his seatbelt and slammed the car into first.

Twenty minutes later, he pulled into a parking lot situated just behind the rank of shops running along Canterdown Road. Sienna's place was slap-bang in the middle. The gathering clouds had since burst wide open, sending shoppers scattering left and right for cover. Jack smiled. Perfect—the shops would be overrun with customers, thus providing him the opportunity to have a subtle word with some of them.

Crossing the street, he studied the façade of Sienna's Sexy Solutions. Though he hadn't noted its name at the time, he did now recall passing by the shop before moving to Potterford. But not once had he thought a lingerie shop in town would affect him out among private residences. Come to think of it, Sienna hadn't exactly looked thrilled with the prospect herself.

Jack contemplated the property. Had to admit it looked classy. There was nothing cheap or degrading about the gossamer curtains draped on either side of the huge picture window or the way the lingerie was laid out across pink satin-wrapped gift boxes. The absence of cheap plastic mannequins and posters of the usual near-emaciated, half-naked models told the whole world what Sienna's business was about: women. Not men.

It was sexy, alluring, and totally inoffensive. Goddammit. He could hardly deny the woman knew what she was doing, whether or not the place was closing down.

In case Sienna was inside, he quickly moved along the street and tried to figure out what to do next. Seeing the grocers next to him,

Jack smiled. He was bound to find some disapproving busybodies in there. Some elderly lady who'd be more than happy to see Sienna's shop close, even before he let slip she intended to reopen in a residential street. That little nugget of information he'd keep to himself until the perfect opportunity came to unleash it.

Mentally high-fiving the devil sitting on his shoulder and urging him on, Jack strode forward. Picking up a basket from the stack outside, he walked under the blue-and-white-striped awning and into the grocers. He scowled when the various fruit and vegetables taunted him with their suddenly explicit sexual shapes and sizes. Narrowing his eyes, he studied the clientele.

There was a pair of women who looked in their late fifties standing by the bananas. He approached them and stood staring at the produce.

After a moment, he cleared his throat. "Excuse me."

They turned.

Ignoring the particularly scary glint in the eyes of one, Jack turned to the other. "This is kind of an embarrassing question…"

She smiled. "About fruit? How embarrassing can it be? Go ahead."

"Um, well, it's not about fruit. It's about the shop across the street."

"The shop…oh, you mean Sienna's." She winked. "You looking to buy something for your girlfriend, honey?"

Jack laughed. "Yes, but she's…um, how do I say this? Bigger. How I like my women to be."

Her gaze traveled up and down the length of him. "I like you more and more."

Jack grinned. "Well, the thing is, half those types of shops don't cater for curves, do they, and—"

"Hey, there's no need to worry about that, honey. That's why we love Sienna so much. She won't have any of those stupid size twos and fours in there. She caters to us. To real women."

Another pang of failure shot him in the eye. Goddammit, couldn't the woman make one mistake around here? "Great, then that's all I need to know. Thanks."

He moved to walk away when the other woman grabbed his arm. "If your girlfriend doesn't like what you fancy, you can always come back here and find me."

Both ladies erupted into giggles, and Jack moved away before the saucy one could pounce on him and tackle him to the floor. Who next? The young woman at the register caught his attention. Smiling and happy, probably only two or three years younger than Sienna, she would surely shop at Sienna's place. In fact, Jack would bet fifty pounds she knew what else was behind that painted door, apart from the fairly safe underwear on display in the window.

Tossing a couple of red peppers, some onions, tomatoes, and a bag of potatoes into his basket, Jack approached his target. He placed his basket by the cash register and smiled.

"Hi."

She looked up from her notepad, a flush spreading across her cheeks. "Hi."

"Just these, please."

She smiled and started ringing up his purchases. He let a second or two pass in silence before he spoke again. "Must be kind of interesting working here with that place across the way."

"Pardon?" Her eyes met his. Suspicion appeared to replace the previously flattering admiration. Maybe she'd already heard him asking the other women about the place and now thought he was some sort of pervert.

He grimaced. "That was awful. Can I start again?"

After a long moment, she exhaled a breathy tinkle of laughter. "Sure."

"Not the best way to open a conversation with a pretty girl when you're new in town, is it?"

Her blush deepened. "No, but you're forgiven."

"I moved to Potterford just over a week ago, so I'm still finding my bearings."

"I'm guessing you didn't expect a shop like Sienna's to be sitting dead-center of town."

If only you knew. "Exactly."

"It's not some sort of illegal brothel, you know." She laughed. "It's absolutely lovely inside. As is everything Sienna sells."

He arched an eyebrow. "You've been in there? Wow."

She looked at him from beneath lowered lashes. "Yes. Lots of us have. It's…a necessity sometimes, don't you think?"

Feeling like an absolute fraud, Jack quickly slipped this situation into the "Investigative Journalism" file of his conscience. "What is? Sexy lingerie?"

"Maybe. Plus other stuff. That's seven pounds, twenty-nine pence, please."

"Sure." He pulled his wallet from his trouser pocket and passed her a ten-pound note. "Do you know the owner?"

She typed the sale into the cash register, and the drawer sprang open with a *ping*. "Yep, and she's amazing."

"Amazing?"

She handed him in his change. "Yep, amazing. Trust me, if you meet her, you'll fall in love. She's gorgeous, funny, and has a figure I'd die for."

Jack might not have wanted Sienna's business next door or needed a love life right then, but even he had to concede the girl's summary of her was spot on.

"I see."

The cashier sighed and looked toward the shop's open front doors. "Yes, she's fabulous, and I'm going to miss her so much when she closes up at the end of the month."

Here goes nothing. "She's closing?"

"Unfortunately."

"Why would she do that when the place is so popular?"

She lifted her shoulders. "There's rumors it's something to do with the rent, but I don't know. I can't see that it can be anything else. She's always busy, but who knows?"

Jack swallowed. So Sienna really *wasn't* closing by choice. Bloody hell. Now he couldn't even pin a bullheaded, selfish determination on her to make her less attractive. "What will she do, do you know?"

The cashier opened her mouth to answer, but then her focus diverted to something behind him. The blush that had revealed itself once or twice during their short conversation was nothing compared to the inferno coloring the girl's face right now. He turned around. *Oh, shit.*

"Sienna."

"Hi, Jack." She smiled, her eyes flashing in the most ridiculously sexy, knowing way.

His penis twitched. God, she was so beautiful even when just wearing jeans and a tank top; her hair was pulled back in a ponytail with little bits hanging down the side of her face.

Swallowing the ball in his throat, he at last replied, "Hi."

Sienna lifted her basket onto a space beside his and turned to the cashier. "Hi, Emma. How you doing?"

"I'm fine…thanks." Emma quickly snatched a bunch of bananas from Sienna's basket and rang up the sale.

Jack waited for the other foot to fall. Sienna wouldn't let this go easily.

After what felt like an eternity, she lifted her head and met his eyes. "You asking people about my business?" The tip of her tongue poked out to wet her bottom lip.

He followed the movement with his eyes. "Something like that."

She grinned, revealing her beautiful white teeth. "Well, I tell you what. Why don't you talk to the organ grinder and come join me for dinner tonight?"

He stiffened. "What?"

She leaned closer. "Dinner, Jack. Six thirty, my place. Bring the girls if you like. It'll probably be safer."

Jack silently cursed. He hated the sudden need to breathe in the scent of flowers and fresh air emanating from her. He willed his brain to function as a journalist rather than a seventeen-year-old boy being asked out on a date by a centerfold model. "What do you mean 'safer'?"

"I've got a TV and a sofa. We can eat, they can play, watch TV, and crash out when they've had enough. I'm not asking you, by the way. I'm telling you." She passed Emma some money and winked. "Thanks, sweetheart. See you later, Jack."

He watched the sway of her ass as she walked from the shop.

And he couldn't help wondering if she intended to cook his gonads and feed them to him for dessert…

Chapter Six

Sienna grabbed the steaming pan of cheese sauce from her kitchen stove and shook her head. "What the hell was I thinking, acting like some sort of femme fatale at the bloody grocers?" She poured the sauce over the pasta. "God, I wish you'd been there to kick me in the shins. Hard."

Kelsey laughed. "Tell me again what you said."

Turning to her, Sienna reenacted her line: "'I'm not asking you, by the way. I'm telling you.' I mean, where the bloody hell did that come from? I sounded like some big-busted chick spinning a line from a seventies porn movie."

"What did Emma say?"

"Nothing. Absolutely nothing. Jack would've been perfectly in his rights to laugh in my face and walk out of there, leaving me looking like an idiot in front of her." Sienna winced and returned the pan to the stove. "She's no doubt sitting in the pub right now, regaling her friends with a rerun of Sienna Lloyd's attempt at being a woman in control."

With shaking hands, she grated cheese over the top of the lasagna with gusto, heaping more and more on until confident it was as sinful as possible.

Kelsey laughed again. "What's the plan now? Death by lasagna?"

"If I can't get him eating out of my hand with this, I'm done for." Sienna bent down to slide the earthenware dish into the oven and slammed the door. "Can you believe he was in town asking questions about my shop? Of all the sneaky, rude, snide things—"

"You really like this guy, don't you?"

Sienna met her friend's eyes, her heart picking up speed. "What?"

Kelsey grinned. "I said, you really like him."

Cursing the psychic connection she usually cherished sharing with her friend, Sienna glared. "I don't like him. How can I like someone who's determined to ruin my life?"

Kelsey drained her wineglass and placed it on the drainer by the sink. "He's not out to ruin your life. He's doing what he thinks is right for his kids. The problem here is you…and that stubborn head of yours. You like this guy."

Goddammit. Do I have an "I want Jack Beaton in My Bed" sticker stuck to my left boob?

"I do not like this guy. He doesn't care what's happened to make me move the shop here. Why would anyone move their business to their home address unless they had to, huh?"

Kelsey shrugged.

"Exactly." Sienna waved her hand. "He doesn't care. That's the bottom line. This is about what he wants and flicking the bird to everyone else. Well, sorry, but he's the new one in town, not me. He needs to fit into my life, not the other way round." She snatched up her glass of wine from the counter and took a hefty mouthful.

"He needs to fit into your life?" Kelsey grinned. "Geez, this is bad."

Sienna narrowed her eyes above the rim of her glass. "Haven't you got somewhere you need to be?"

"Look…" Kelsey leaned back against the counter, clearly not finished. "So he was asking questions. It doesn't change what's going to happen. The shop can move here whenever you're ready. Everything is sorted, and the ball is rolling. It doesn't matter what this Jack whatever-his-name says about it. You're doing nothing illegal, but—"

"Ah, how did I know there would be a 'but'?"

"I kind of like the guy for protecting his kids. It's like something your dad would've done."

The point hit Sienna's face like a slap. She'd said the exact same thing to herself over and over again since arriving home that night. Her father would've had a fit if he'd known a shop selling women's toys was moving next door to his precious four-year-old daughter.

She shoved her guilt into submission. "Well, what the hell am I supposed to do? I have merchandise. I have customers. I have a business I built from scratch. It's not my fault the landlord stuck such an astronomical rent increase on me. I'll talk to Jack, make him see sense."

"Or strike him down via his taste buds."

Sienna lifted her shoulders. "Whatever it takes. He started this dirty game, not me. I'm not moving the business anywhere else, so he needs to deal with it."

"Why not? You should be able to find somewhere cheaper. Away from Potterford."

"Don't start. This is just another blip. I'll sort it out. Plus, there's nothing cheaper. We both know that."

"Is he good-looking?"

Heat immediately warmed Sienna's face, and her body tingled. "He's all right."

Silence. She struggled not to squirm under Kelsey's careful study. Comprehension lit her friend's eyes like they were damn aqua-colored stadium lamps.

"He's the guy." Clapping her hands, Kelsey leapt away from the counter. "He's the guy you've met."

"No, he's not. I haven't met—"

The chime of the doorbell halted Sienna's words. She looked to the kitchen doorway. "Oh, my God. What time is it?"

Kelsey looked at her watch, and her mouth stretched into a wide smile. "Six thirty. Right on time."

Panic clawed up from Sienna's small intestine, threatening to strangle her. "Go out the back door."

"What?"

"Go. You can climb the fence."

"Sienna, I am not climbing any fence." She hitched her bag onto her shoulder and smoothed her manicured hands over her sleek black pencil skirt. "I'll just say hi at the door and leave, okay?"

"Really? Then why the hell are you laughing?"

The doorbell rang again. Sienna groaned as she whipped her "Beats Burning Your Nipples" apron over her head.

"Let's just get this over with." Leaving Kelsey to follow her, she hurried from the kitchen, pausing at the hallway mirror to fluff her hair and smack her lips together. "No chattering. Just say hello and go."

"We'll see." Kelsey wiggled her eyebrows in the mirror's reflection.

Cursing, Sienna strode forward and planted on a grin before yanking open the door.

"Jack, you're here." Her voice sounded far too high to be natural. What was she? Twelve?

"We certainly are." His gorgeous blue eyes lingered bright and intense on hers for far too long before moving to Kelsey standing beside her. "Hi."

Silence.

Sienna snapped her head around. Kelsey was staring at Jack, her eyes wide, her mouth open. Closing her hand around her friend's elbow, Sienna steered her out the door. "This is Kelsey. My friend, a lawyer, believe it or not. She doesn't say a lot." She nudged her down the top step. "Bye, Kelse. I'll ring you tomorrow."

Kelsey waved, her eyes not leaving Jack's face. She slowly turned and walked down the path.

Sienna clapped her hands. "Well, you're right on time."

His eyes danced with amusement. What? Did she have tomato sauce on her face? She lifted her hand to her cheek. "What's wrong?"

"Nothing. You look…nice."

Nice? She was wearing jeans with a white slash-neck top and had flip-flops on her feet. Okay, her underwear was top-notch, but he couldn't see that. Could he? She quickly looked down at her breasts. No, it was fine. Everything was fine. He was just being nice. Jack was nice. Kind of.

He was nice when he wanted to be. Other times, the man was unnerving—and, considering the incident in the grocers, sneaky.

Holly and Katy stood on either side of him. Pressing her hand to her chest, Sienna smiled. "Wow, don't you guys look cute in your pajamas with your stuffed toys tucked under your arms."

Her observation earned her a glare from Holly and a shy smile from Katy. When neither of them spoke, she stood back from the door and held out her arm, gesturing them inside. "Why don't you go into the living room? I've rented all sorts of DVDs from the store. I wasn't sure what you liked to watch."

They both looked at their dad, silently asking for permission and most likely a big dollop of reassurance judging by the way their wide-eyed gazes flitted over Jack's face. He smiled and gave a wink that knotted Sienna's stomach.

"Go on. Go see if Sienna has any Dora."

The twins sprinted past her. "I forgot about this Dora person, whoever she is. They're not going to find her in there."

He laughed and whipped a bottle of white wine and a bunch of daffodils from behind his back. "For you. I know how much you like them."

She feigned annoyance, even as traitorous warmth stole through her. "You're a funny guy, Jack Beaton."

He stepped inside. But instead of continuing down the hall as she hoped he would, he stopped. Right in front of her. So close, she had to tip her head back to meet his eyes. Her heart picked up speed as his gaze wandered over her face, coming to a stop at her lips. His eyes darkened to a midnight blue that curled her toes.

She cleared her throat. "Why don't we go through to the kitchen?"

"I'm sorry about what happened at the grocers. I shouldn't have been snooping around asking questions like that."

She'd expected this conversation at some point in the evening. That was why she'd asked him to dinner in the first place; it was inevitable a battle of wills would ensue after the second glass of wine. But an apology before she'd served her tomato and basil bruschetta appetizer? Before she'd even shut the front door? Any response lodged in her throat.

Say something.

Why did he have to take the wind out of her sails by acting the damn gentleman? Worse, why did he have to wear that aftershave he seemed so bloody keen on? Or the white shirt, opened at the neck and showing a smattering of dark hair to torment her…

She didn't want a gentleman living next door. She wanted an asshole she could take pleasure in pissing off by moving her business into her front room. Jack being "nice" made things a whole lot harder to settle in her continually nagging conscience.

"Sienna?"

She jumped. "What?"

"I said I'm sorry."

She sniffed. "Yes, well."

"So, what do you say?" His lips twitched. "Apology accepted?"

She drank in every handsome feature of his sun-kissed face, and the shallow well of her resistance popped its cork, the bubbles trickling onto the carpet.

"Fine. Apology accepted." She pushed a finger into his chest—it was harder than brick—and nudged him back so she could breathe easier. "But you're not getting away that easily. I still want an explanation."

He raised his hands in mock surrender. "I expected nothing less."

"Good." She shut the front door. "Go through to the kitchen. I'll see if the girls are okay."

Silence. Damn it. Why didn't he ever do as he was told?

He raised an eyebrow, his eyes deliciously teasing. "Sure you're okay being alone with them?"

She glowered and thrust the daffodils toward him. "I like daffodils, Beaton, but not enough I wouldn't shove these up your ass. Go. Now."

Laughing, he headed into the kitchen.

His behind was sculpted and pretty damn bitable in jeans that fit just right. He disappeared out of view, and Sienna took a moment to gather her wits. This was about her business. Her life. She couldn't allow a man to deter her from what she needed to do. That was the bottom line.

The sound of the television blasting into action shook her from her trance, and she hurried into the living room.

Holly and Katy stood side by side in front of the TV. Their faces were barely inches from the screen, their heads moving side to side. Sienna looked at the TV and froze. The busty female chef, who was near bursting out of her low-cut wrap top, sashayed from fridge to stove to counter and back again while eyeing the camera like it was about to stick its lens in her knickers. When she popped a spoon in her mouth and started licking the chocolate sauce off it in a way that had even Sienna's cheeks bursting into flame, Sienna rushed forward and took a hand of each twin.

She propelled them toward the sofa. "Hey, girls. Why don't you sit there, and I'll turn that silly lady off and put on some *Winnie the Pooh* instead, eh?"

The light that lit in Holly's eyes sent a shiver up Sienna's spine. "You look like that lady when you look at Daddy."

The furnace burning Sienna's face turned up a notch. She laughed. "Oh, you."

She tweaked her nose and focused back on the TV, fumbling and dropping the DVD several times before managing to get it in the damn machine and pressing *play*. Only when the Disney emblem appeared in all its Technicolor glory did Sienna release her held breath.

"There. That's better."

Katy smiled, her eyes soft with what could only be described as affection. "You're funny."

Sienna's shoulders dropped down from around her earlobes as something tugged deep in her chest. "You're cute."

"Daddy told us to be good because you're scared of us."

Sienna snapped her head to the left and met Holly's demonically gleaming stare. "Is that so? Do I look scared right now?"

Holly was a hurt little girl. The pain shone in her eyes as clearly as Sienna's did every time she looked in the mirror and thought of her father. Sienna would have reacted no differently had her parents divorced when she was only four years old, so Holly's confusion, fear, and protectiveness for the hunk of love waiting in the kitchen was totally understandable.

But the kid wouldn't rule the roost while she was under Sienna's roof.

"Holly?"

Holly glared, an angry red flush staining her cheeks, and her mouth pulled tightly together. Katy nudged her in the ribs. "Don't, Holly. I want to watch the movie."

"Everything okay in here?" Jack's husky, should-be-deemed-illegal voice broke through the atmosphere, slicing it in half and transforming Holly's expression into that of a cherub.

"Yes, Daddy," she said. "We're going to watch *Winnie the Pooh*."

Sienna bit back a smile. The kid was fabulous. Pushing to her feet, Sienna looked at Jack. "Yep, we'll get these two monkeys some drinks and pizza, and they'll be good to go."

"Great." He held out his hand. "Shall we?"

Her stomach tightened. *What is he doing?* Handholding was far too dangerous at any stage in the evening, let alone within ten minutes of him stepping through the front door. Had he forgotten what she'd told him a week ago? Was this some strategy on his part? To lure her into a false sense of security? Well, he was way off the mark if he thought she was some kind of schmuck.

Ignoring his outstretched hand, she brushed past him and out the door. "Let's grab a glass of wine."

She marched to the kitchen with her head held high, all too aware of his soft footsteps behind her. Heading straight for the refrigerator, Sienna yanked open the door and pulled out a chilled bottle of white wine. Closing her eyes, she silently counted to three and waited for the lingering scent of the man's aftershave to abate. The smell of him messed with her goddamn mind. Autumn mixed with musk, tinged with fresh pine leaves…she inhaled.

The scrape of a chair against tile told her Jack had made himself comfortable at the kitchen table. She opened her eyes and pulled her smile into place.

"Pinot Grigio okay?"

"Sounds great." He nodded toward the stove. "Whatever you've got cooking in there smells fantastic."

Snatching the corkscrew from the counter, Sienna moved to the table. "Thanks. Lasagna with lots of garlic, served with homemade garlic bread. So don't even think about kissing anyone but me tonight, you hear?" *What the hell?*

If a grown man could pass out on the spot, that's what Jack wanted to do, judging by the paling of his usually olive skin. Her momentary despair dissolved. Yes! He looked terrified. One point to her. Clearly, the getting-up-in-her-face and smoldering looks he'd been firing out like bullets since he'd stepped inside the house were nothing more than a smokescreen. The man still had the same reservations about her and her shop that he'd had when she'd delivered him her bad news that night on his decking.

Satisfaction welled within her. A worthy opponent was nothing to be sniffed at, and she gave a bark of laughter. "Look at your face, Blue Eyes. Here." She poured some wine into a glass on the table and prayed to God the trembling bottle wasn't as obvious to him as it was her. "Drink this before you self-combust. I'm not going to jump you, so you can relax."

He raised the glass to his lips and took a mouthful while watching her over its rim like she was a cobra ready to strike. The longer he observed her, the more her smugness became embarrassment. She reached for the second glass and filled it to the brim.

"Shall we start again?" She took a drink. "I'm nervous. You're nervous."

"Why are you nervous? Because of me asking questions?"

"No, because I'm moving my business here whether you like it or not, and I've got a horrible feeling you're going to be nothing but a royal pain in the ass about it."

Chapter Seven

With a scathing retort burning his tongue, Jack drummed his fingers on the kitchen tabletop while his leg bounced the fandango beneath it. He snapped his mouth shut. What would be the use in making Sienna any madder than she already was? He needed to bide his time.

Sienna whirled around and headed for the stove. Her long brown hair was caught up in a bronze clip that glinted under the soft overhead lights. Tendrils teased her long neck, curling down to meet shoulders revealed by the wide neck of her top that had slipped over the smooth curve of one shoulder, showing a pale pink bra strap. A slash of pink nougat against caramel. Jack picked up his wine.

The feminine top teamed with blue denim jeans and white flip-flops revealing scarlet-painted toenails should have been nothing out of the ordinary, but she oozed sexual confidence. How could a woman like that not make a lingerie business successful? She was a walking advertisement for what *sexy* meant.

Yet for all her good looks and perfectly curved figure, the thing messing with Jack's mission against the shop moving there was Sienna's undeniable kindness and popularity. Even the few people he'd managed to talk to in town all knew and loved Sienna, and if he had met her somewhere else, under different circumstances, Jack couldn't deny he would have been pretty bowled over too. But these weren't different circumstances, and his girls lived right next door. A flesh-and-blood reminder of what he needed to get done.

He put his glass back on the table, the impending confrontation lingering like a smoldering rock behind his ribcage. He didn't like doing this, but it had to be done. New life, new terms. That meant no pandering to other people or letting anyone or anything upset his children.

"Right. One margherita pizza and one bowl of chips ready for delivery."

Sienna's voice had cut through his study of her, and Jack sat up a little higher in his seat. "They'll love that."

Her brow creased. "Are you sure? Is it okay for them to share? As I've said before, I'm not…used to kids. Is that what you'd give them? Will they like it?"

The rush of questions gave away her nerves, and Jack's gut clenched as he smiled. "Pizza and chips are always a winner. Don't worry about it."

Carrying two plastic plates to the table, she held them out in front of him for inspection. He had a sneaky feeling she'd bought them after their meeting at the grocers — he couldn't imagine for one minute that Sienna Lloyd kept Tom & Jerry crockery as a matter of course in her cupboards.

He met her worried expression. "That's perfect. You'll be their new best friend."

"Will I?"

"Sure. I try to play the good-dad role and shove vegetables down them as much as I can. They're gonna love you for this."

Two spots of pink colored her cheeks as she smiled. "I'm fine doing the bad-unhealthy-neighbor thing. I don't mind."

He laughed and pushed to his feet. "Shall I follow you in with the drinks?"

"Sure. There are some cups by the sink. I have Coke, lemonade — "

"Water will be fine. Give them a fizzy drink and they'll be bouncing off your lovely white walls within thirty minutes." He arched an eyebrow. "Believe me. I've learned the hard way."

"Water it is, then." Her flip-flops slapped toward the door until the hallway carpet silenced them.

Jack picked up the two matching Tom & Jerry cups from the counter, and following Sienna's lead, mustered the strength to go through with what he needed to say. The prospect of arguing with her was otherwise growing less and less appealing with every passing second.

Ten minutes later, he eased his butt back onto his vacated chair in the kitchen, having left Holly and Katy to enjoy a mini-party in the living room. He took another sip of his wine as Sienna carried two plates from the stove and placed one in front of him.

"We're eating simple but good. Anything you don't like or want, I'll keep for tomorrow, so don't worry about offending me. I don't cook two days in a row for anyone. Including myself."

"It looks great." He met her smile as the rich fragrance of basil hit his nostrils.

"Tomato and basil bruschetta to start, and then we move on to my homemade lasagna. Hope you're hungry." She sat down in the seat opposite him. "My best friend claims she adds forty pounds to her hips every time she eats it. A fact I'm proud of." Meeting his eyes over the rim of her wineglass, she added, "What Kelsey fails to realize is most people only have one portion. I tend to cut her off at three."

Jack laughed. "I'll consider myself warned."

Their eyes locked, and the ticking of the wall clock suddenly reverberated in the room. Even the sound of Rabbit having a meltdown over his carrots on the living room TV did nothing to lessen the atmosphere. A palpable undercurrent of what hadn't been said whispered between them, filling the air with an injection of tension like a hovering hammer waiting to fall.

"So." Sienna's voice was higher in its pitch. "Tuck in."

The first course passed in stilted conversation and frequent sips of wine. The crunch of bread and the clatter of cutlery against crockery filled the bouts of strained silence, and as soon as their glasses were empty, Sienna refilled them. Jack noticed the bottle tremble ever so slightly as she poured. Then, after too short a time, she scraped her chair back to clear their half-finished bruschetta. Had stomach somersaults ruined her appetite too?

"I'll go check on the girls," Jack said, and headed out the door.

It was cowardice rather than fatherly concern that made him leave the kitchen. He needed time to think. Time away from the distraction of her perfume, her eyes, her smile. The subject of the shop still hadn't been raised, and Jack was well aware the initiation sat on his shoulders. The reason they were there, feigning interest in a meal when a whole other issue lingered like a boulder between them, was his fault not hers. *She* had no problem moving the shop — *he* did, and he owed her an explanation why. Which meant it was his responsibility to take up the baton.

He whispered a curse. If he could only find the words — without saying too much.

Like a floating raft in the middle of a turbulent sea, Jack absorbed the calming sight of his daughters on entering the living room. The urge to scoop them into his arms and draw strength from their unending love burst through him. They sat side by side watching TV, identical grins on their faces, slices of pizzas in their hands. They were happy, content. Just how he wanted them to be every day for the rest of their lives. Walking forward, he ruffled their hair one after the other and then laughed when they ducked and dodged around him to see the TV. *Tossed aside in favor of Tigger.*

He walked back into the kitchen. The lasagna sat in the center of the table, plumes of silver-gray steam escaping around the edges of its terracotta dish. Next to it, sliced garlic bread lay on a rustic chopping board, and two white china plates set at their places. Sienna stood beside the table, her eyes carefully watching Jack while she wielded a lethal-looking knife in one hand and a spatula in the other.

She cleared her throat. "I'll serve, you talk."

Slumping his shoulders, Jack sat down. His throat was drier than the Sahara. He hated doing this to her, hated spoiling anyone's plans. He used his journalism to make people's lives better, not destroy dreams and livelihoods. Why couldn't Sienna run a bookstore? A cake shop?

He drew in a breath. "Okay. The last thing I want is to have us become enemies. None of this is about some vendetta or me throwing my weight around as soon as I move to a new town."

He paused, waiting for a response. She said nothing, just continued filling their plates, her eyes obscured from view as she concentrated on the task at hand. Jack pushed on.

"I have to think of Holly and Katy. Things have happened that I want deleted from their memories, and unfortunately, your business will only bring them straight back."

Sienna remained focused on the lasagna as she cut and served his portion and then hers. "You're going to have to give me more than that, Blue Eyes."

Jack scowled. "Will you stop calling me that?"

"No," she replied with a wink.

"This is serious, Sienna. There's too much history built on sex in my life…and theirs. I can't handle it."

"Ah, that's more like it."

"What?"

"*You* can't handle it. I suspected as much from your very first outburst." She sat and nodded toward his plate. "Eat."

"Don't dismiss me like I'm an overreacting idiot."

Her smile waned. "I'm not. I'm listening to you, but you're not telling me anything. We'll talk, but let's at least eat while we're doing it."

Jack battled the insecurity simmering at the base of his throat while his pulse beat hard in his neck. His gaze focused on Sienna's wine, and Martina's cold face rose up in front of him, her makeup smudged and gray under her eyes, the smell of alcohol tainting his skin as she spat vicious words at him like tiny darts of venom. He squeezed his eyes shut against the memory. He wouldn't go there. He couldn't compare an innocent glass of wine or two over a meal with Martina's drinking. This wasn't about that. It was about the sense of failure that remained a fire-hot brand inside him because of the part he'd played in the disintegration of their marriage.

He looked across the table at Sienna studying the lasagna on her plate. Her jaw slowly moved as she chewed, her face redder than it had been a few minutes before. She didn't deserve this bitterness that poured from him, spreading across the tablecloth toward her.

The silence stretched.

"Sienna?"

"What?" Though humor had filled her words just a second before, now angry accusation burned in her eyes. And yet she wasn't saying no to him. Wasn't haranguing him. She was damn well listening.

The right words floundered outside the periphery of Jack's intelligence, tapping at his conscience. "I know this is hard for you to accept. Having your shop next door sets all sorts of things in motion that I can't tell you about."

She put down her knife and fork. "Fine. Even if I understood that—which I don't—what am I supposed to do? Abandon my plans for some guy who moved in next door less than a fortnight ago? That's not really fair, Jack, and you know it."

What could he say to that? His mind darted all over the place. "I suppose it's too much to expect you to just accept what I'm saying?"

For a long time, Sienna said nothing. With brow furrowed, she slowly put her glass down and picked up her fork. She stabbed it into the lasagna. "This is all about you, right? It has nothing to do with the fact that some lingerie or the occasional maid's outfit might send Katy and Holly hurtling into therapy?" she asked.

Jack tightened his grip around his knife and fork. "No, but giggling, screaming women coming back and forth up the driveway next door might."

The fiery confrontation in her eyes hitched up a notch. So this was Sienna the businesswoman. Paternal protectiveness unfurled in Jack's gut.

"Look," he said, mimicking her violent assault on the lasagna, "all I'm saying is I don't want the twins exposed to something they shouldn't be."

"Do you really think I'm the type of person who runs a place for cheap thrills and dirty magazines? It's a respected establishment. I wouldn't want those girls upset any more than you…What's wrong?"

Jack had taken his first mouthful of lasagna and all thought momentarily froze. Holy mother of God. It tasted like Italy. Smooth pasta, rich sauce, thick chunks of braised mince steak…When he looked back at Sienna, anger had given way to triumph in her eyes. Her mouth twitched at the corner.

"Good?" she asked.

He swallowed. "Nice try."

Though her smile would knock a lesser man off his stride, Jack stabbed his fork in for a second bite. So what if she could cook the best damn lasagna he'd ever tasted? It didn't mean she was an Italian chef. And it didn't mean she could open her shop next to his girls' home. Nothing would weaken his resolve…until he took another bite. Goddamn.

Sienna interrupted his internal battle. "I'm giving a service my customers want and love. Just because you're wound tighter than a thong strap around a dildo does not give you the right—"

Jack coughed against the food sliding down his throat. "See? I cannot believe you just said that. The girls could walk in here any minute."

She glanced toward the door and back again. "And what? Do you think they even know what either of those things are? Just stop stalling and tell me what this is really about. Otherwise, we have nothing else to discuss. I need my business. It's not just about the money. It's part of who I am. Your turn."

She might as well have thrown a gauntlet down between them. Putting down his utensils, Jack picked up some garlic bread and tore it in half.

"Fine. My ex-wife shoved as much bare skin, fun, and frolics of that kind down my daughters' throats to last them a lifetime. They don't need any more."

"Then I promise not to add any more to their misfortune."

He narrowed his eyes. "How can you say that? That's what your business is all about."

"The fact is, you haven't told me anything to change my mind, but I'll make sure nothing happens outside these four walls. If any of my clients are filled with the urge to wear a negligee home on the number forty-nine bus or wave their tasseled nipples around as they walk down the driveway, I'll ban them. How's that?"

Jack's heart beat hard. She deserved more explanation, but he couldn't give it to her. Not yet. Not the gut-splitting regret he harbored, not the raw anger that lingered deep inside.

"Look, I need a guarantee from you that nothing is going to happen that could cause concern for the welfare of my kids."

"Are you serious? Their welfare, Jack? It's a shop, not a brothel."

He took a voracious bite of his garlic bread and ground it between his teeth, stalling. This was madness. He had to give her something.

Swallowing his pride with his bread, he at last admitted, "I loved their mother once."

Sienna stopped chewing as the teasing in her eyes slipped to something like empathy. No, interest.

"I can't imagine anything less from you, Jack Beaton. You strike me as a man who'd only makes babies with a woman he loves."

Jack pushed the lasagna around as nerves leapt in his gut. "We were happy. We did a lot of things together. Met when we were young and fit like two pieces of a puzzle."

"So, what happened?"

"I worked. A lot."

"Doing what?"

He looked up. "I'm a journalist."

"A journalist? Here in Potterford?" She visibly paled.

"Is that a problem?"

"That depends on you."

"What do you mean?"

"I mean, are you going to use your job to cause me trouble?"

Shame crept through Jack's veins. The idea to write something disparaging about Sienna's shop had occurred to him the night she'd told him about it—but then promptly disappeared once she'd caught him asking questions behind her back.

He shook his head. "No. I won't do that."

"Do I have your word?"

Who could blame her for not trusting him? He nodded. "I'm a respected journalist, not a tabloid vulture. I won't use the paper as a way of scoring points."

She dropped her shoulders and popped another forkful of lasagna into her mouth. Jack fixated on the way she chewed, the way it moved the skin at her throat and all the way down to her collarbones…

"You're staring, Jack," Sienna said without even looking up.

He glared at the board of garlic bread and tore off another chunk.

"Anyway," he continued, "to cut a long story short with regard to my marriage, the expanding cracks split wide open when the twins were born. I was barely home, and Martina grew discontent with her new stay-at-home role. She resented me and undoubtedly the girls by their first birthday." He lifted his glass and took a drink of wine, his mouth too desert-dry to eat bread without it. "Her first… *indiscretion* woke me up. Number two was the falling ax."

"She had affairs?"

"One-night stands. Not affairs. Martina doesn't do 'domestic or emotion or responsibility.' Her words, not mine."

Sienna looked to her plate and murmured, "Slut." After a second, she met his eyes and smiled sheepishly. "Sorry."

Only the sound of the TV broke the silence that fell around them, yet Jack smiled back in reassurance. "I might be a lot of things, but I'm not a mug. If Martina thought I'd hang around while she made up her mind whether she wanted to be a wife and mother, she was wrong."

"So you filed for divorce?"

He nodded. "After I found her in bed with some faceless stranger while Holly and Katy slept in the next room."

Another silence.

Jack exhaled a shaky breath. "That's not even the half of what finally drove us to move here, but…well, anyway, *now* do you understand why I'm concerned about your shop next door? Why I want that sort of stuff as far away from my kids as possible?"

Sienna placed her knife and fork on her plate, side by side with perfect regimented precision before lifting her wineglass. Holding it with both hands, she carefully watched him. "No, actually, I don't."

Jack's head thumped with the start of a headache. He'd just told her some, though not all, aspects of his failed marriage, yet it hadn't done him a damn bit of good. Fine. Then she could bring on the battle, because he wasn't willing to tell her any more.

Sienna drank and stared straight into his eyes. "I get why you'd want to be rid of a woman like that," she continued when he didn't speak, "but not why the business, which you clearly don't understand at all, frightens the hell out of you."

"I told you. My girls—"

"Jack?"

"What?"

"This is not about your girls."

Frustration churned in his stomach. Hot and sticky. Clinging to his insides and coating them with self-defense or the safer option to get the hell out of her house and just walk away. He pushed to his feet, the chair legs scraping sharply against the tiled floor.

"I think I'd better go."

"Sit down."

"No. I'm sorry to walk out after your feeding us and everything, but you can't do this, Sienna. You can't sit there mocking me when my ex-wife messed up our entire lives. You can't—"

"She didn't."

His heart pounded. Her face was pinched red, but her eyes were alight with what looked so much like understanding that Jack didn't know where to look. He tipped his head back. The ceiling showed white and empty. No answer up there either.

"I don't know how you can say that," he said.

"Jack, look at me."

Clenching his jaw, he dropped his chin.

"She gave you an opportunity. She gave you a reason to move here. To this beautiful English market town where the girls can grow up without their lungs being blocked with London smog. She made you slow down, move away, spend more time with Holly and Katy. Can't you see that? Can't you see what is right in front of your face?"

His heart beat with the partial truth of what she'd said, but what did she know about it? What did she know about marriage? Children?

"Sounds nice."

She frowned. "What does?"

"Your idea of life. The whole naïve notion things are sent to try us. That we should grab opportunities as they present themselves. That's what you're saying, right?"

"Don't mock me. I know what I'm talking about. You haven't the monopoly on wanting to protect people, you know. The trouble is, you have no idea what your kids need protecting from."

"Is that so?"

"Yes, because if you did, you'd know there's no way in hell I would ever hurt another person, let alone Holly and Katy." Her shoulders stiffened. "Do you know what? If you feel like that, you can turn around and leave."

"I didn't want it to come to this."

"No? Well, you could've fooled me."

Staring at her bent head as she looked at her plate, Jack fought the overwhelming need to go to her, to apologize, to say…something.

"Goddammit." He whirled around and left the kitchen. Holly and Katy never said a word as he took their hands and led them from the house.

Chapter Eight

Sienna let herself into the shop at eight a.m. the next day, her eyes itchy and her mood tetchy after a restless night's sleep. Jack had left her house under a storm cloud, Holly and Katy jogging along either side of him, trying to keep up with his long strides as he'd marched down the driveway. Sienna had let him go without even saying goodbye.

There was no getting through to the man. That much was clear. He was fooling himself that his issue over the shop was about his kids, and as far as Sienna was now concerned, that was fine. He could get on with it. She had enough on her plate without dealing with someone who didn't have a legal leg to stand on. She'd called and double-checked with Kelsey about the legalities of switching shop locations, and all had been confirmed: there was nothing Jack could do. So that part was simple.

But the damn threat of legal action wasn't the reason she'd watched the changing light pass over her bedroom ceiling until three o'clock that morning…

It was how Jack already affected her, within only two weeks of knowing him. The innate need she had to make him smile. How the breadth of that smile took her damn breath away.

And the look she'd recognized in those ridiculously blue eyes of his that made her feel like crap.

Fear.

That's what had kept her tossing and turning all night. But it had been during the slowly passing hours of the night, when her thoughts of Jack had turned from disdain to pornographic, that Sienna had leapt out of bed and gotten busy. Jack was the enemy. She refused to spend any more time thinking about his eyes, his damn hair, or his stupid three-foot-wide shoulders.

Yet what really burrowed deep through her concrete walls of resistance was the way he constantly touched Holly and Katy's hair or picked them up and hugged them close. Continual, unconscious, yet sincere gestures that knocked at her heart. His concern for his children was way past what she'd seen in other parents; he seemed to walk around under a perpetual cloud of guilt.

And she wanted to know why.

Sienna's hands shook, and she clamped them together. She liked Jack. A lot. He had the potential to distract her from her mother, her friends, the people who relied on her. Something nobody had done since her father had been killed. He made her want to be with him—constantly. But if she got involved and anything was to happen to him…

Life was not kind, no matter how much other people tried to convince her otherwise. Bad things happened to good people. And the fear of loving and losing someone again resided like a slumbering animal inside her. Jack had woken that animal, and it now paced back and forth, contemplating the half-open gate and whether it should step out into the wilderness.

God, she didn't want to feel this way.

"And I won't. Whatever it is I'm feeling isn't real. No, it isn't. No, it isn't."

She walked farther into the shop, switching on lights and making the glossy black floorboards gleam. When the red-and-white-striped walls flickered into bright and forthright flamboyance, Sienna frowned. The decoration didn't appear as cheeky, sexy, and fun as it had the previous two years. It looked garish and cheap. No prizes for guessing who'd made it feel that way.

Walking behind the counter, she took a large notebook out of her bag and tried to focus on things other than Jack Bloody Beaton. Which shouldn't have been a problem because she wasn't getting involved with him. Eventually, the pain in his eyes would leave her memory — she hoped.

She opened the notebook. Today she had plans. Lots and lots of plans. Adrenaline and excitement pulsed through her as she looked at the next job on her to-do list:

LAUNCH PARTY

Sienna grinned at the words printed in big bold letters at the top of the page. How would Mr. Misery cope with that? A party for women. Real women with real needs and desires despite whatever a sex-phobe might think. She tapped each job in turn:

~Pack up and move stock from shop to house.

~Clear front room and put up shelving and displays.

~Send out invitations.

~Put ad in local paper.

~Rearrange and put out stock.

~Buy wine and nibbles.

She bit the end of the pen as she thought and then scribbled down the final task:

~Organize games.

Adding the period with gusto, she slapped the notebook shut. There was plenty to be getting on with while she left Jack to his ideas of shutting her down that would never come to fruition.

She switched on the stereo, and Luther Vandross's dulcet tones filled the shop. Sienna jigged her way into the storeroom. First job was emptying the shop shelves and packing up the stock. She might officially have weeks before she needed to be out of there, but every day that she lingered just pulled the noose of apprehension tighter around her neck. Getting out and announcing to the world she intended to set up shop at Marsden Place would make it real. If nothing else, Sienna was used to dealing with reality.

She grabbed some packing crates stacked at the back of the room and carried them out into the shop. As she busied herself with the "summer sizzler" display, the next hour passed in a frenzy of bras, thongs, and baby-doll negligees, her fingers nimbly extracting garments from hangers and shell-pink cases to pack them in boxes.

Each time the merchandise blurred in her vision, Sienna swiped at her tears and pushed on. The closing of the shop would feel good… eventually. It was the closing of one chapter and opening of another. Wasn't that what her dad had taught her? Move on, adapt.

By the time ten o'clock rolled around, a six-by-six-foot space at the front of the shop stood empty. Sienna sighed. Everything would be all right. Jack was a good man and would see sense sooner or later. She would stay in Potterford, and her business would carry on as always.

Lifting her arms above her head, she stretched out the kinks in her back and neck, just as the first customer of the day strolled into the shop. Sienna dropped her arms.

"Hi, Mrs. McGill." She wiped her hands on the cloth hanging from the waistband of her skirt. "Is it warming up out there?"

"Is it true?" Mrs. McGill hurried toward her and froze when she saw the empty shelves. "Oh, my dear Lord. It's true. I saw the note in the window. You're moving? The shop here is closing?"

Sienna stepped over a crate and took the woman's elbow. It trembled in her grasp, and she tightened her grip. "It's going to be all right. We're just relocating."

"How will I get there? I have no car. No money for buses. I'm scared of trains and planes and bikes—"

"The shop will be at my house," Sienna assured her and couldn't help but smile. The woman was apparently oblivious to her priority for lingerie over transport.

Mrs. McGill gaped. "Your house?"

"Yes."

The older woman slapped her hand to her throat. "You can't do that. I can't have people watching me enter your home and leave with a little red bag under my arm."

Sienna laughed. "How is that different than when you leave the shop? Surely it's better than walking out onto the street here?"

Mrs. McGill's face dropped. "There is nothing funny about this." She pulled her arm from Sienna's grasp and clamped her hands to either side of Sienna's face. "I need you. We all need you. You're a relationship angel sent down from heaven to spread good sex around like a magic dust."

"That won't change—"

"No, now you listen to me because you need to understand. You are to our lives what cream is to chocolate. What Colin Firth is to *Pride and Prejudice*." Releasing Sienna's face, Mrs. McGill stretched her arms heavenward. "My God, you are what my nether regions have been waiting for their entire life."

Sienna moved her jaw from side to side, checking it still worked.

Mrs. McGill clutched her arm. "Did you hear what I said, honey? Do you get it? Do you *really* understand what I'm saying?"

"Yes. Everything is going to be all right. The shop will open again in a few weeks, and I'm going to make everything perfect. Just you wait and see."

"A few weeks?"

"Yes."

"I'll need more than my usual amount of you-know-what if I'm to keep Roger happy for that long."

Gently extracting Mrs. McGill's hand from her arm, Sienna walked over to the shelf holding the chocolate body paint and nipple tassels. She picked up a party-size tub of chocolate.

"Here." She held it out to her. "On the house."

Mrs. McGill grinned, her eyes lighting up. "Really?"

"Really. All I ask for in return is you spread the word that I'll be opening the shop at Marsden Place. But first, I'm going to say farewell to the shop by holding a party in my new room at the house. I want you and everyone else to come along and enjoy yourselves. If everyone supports me and embraces the move, not only will you save me from financial ruin, we'll also show my landlord that Sienna Lloyd won't be outdone by anyone. Rent increase or no rent increase."

Mrs. McGill inhaled a long breath through flared nostrils. "I'm on the case. You leave everything to me. I'll rally round the girls and allay their worries. Sienna Lloyd isn't abandoning us. She's keeping us. She'll deliver us from frustration and continue to spread the sexual light."

Okay. Shoot me now. "Absolutely. Now go on. Get out of here before you make me cry."

"Of course. Of course." She smacked a wet kiss to both of Sienna's cheeks and dabbed at her eyes with a lace-edged handkerchief before turning toward the door.

Sienna bit down on her bottom lip to stem her smile as Mrs. McGill waddled away, her huge behind shifting from side to side beneath the tent of her floral skirt. When the door closed, Sienna covered her face with her hands.

Now she'd done it. The word would be out about the move in no time. If Jack didn't want to string her up by her lace panties before, he certainly would now.

Across town, Jack thought about Sienna as regret for past mistakes furled into a hard ball at the back of his throat. Mistakes he wouldn't repeat. He had to start as he meant to go on — no more burrowing himself in work or other people's lives when he had problems of his own.

They'd only been in Potterford two weeks, and already things weren't going as planned. And he feared they'd soon get worse. After the row with Sienna, his nerves were stretched to breaking point. He wasn't the type of man who fought with women in their homes. He knew that. But Sienna didn't. He hoped to God he hadn't scared her.

As if anything could scare her. Her anger rang in his ears once more: *"Can't you see what is right in front of your face?"*

Part of him denied her words meant anything, and he stood by what he'd said — what could she possibly know, not being a mother? Yet the sincerity in her voice lingered, a clear belief and faith that there had to be more with each twist and turn life threw at you. The torment…the challenge in her tone was undeniable, and instead of facing her, he'd walked out.

Jack swallowed. He'd acted like an asshole and scapegoated her for a concern irrelevant to her shop. The concern Martina could show up one day and wreak havoc on their peaceful new lives would never lessen for him until he dealt with it. What if she found them and got to the girls before he did? Would she hurt them? Run away with them? Just as a reason to hurt *him?* The notion was irrational and unfounded, but fear of losing his children ran deep, and Sienna's words haunted him.

The ringing of telephones and non-stop whirring of printers inside the busy newspaper office faded into the background as Jack stared at the cell phone on his desk. He needed to take action, and he needed to take it today.

Saving his work, he snatched up his phone and walked outside. He continued away from the office and out into the parking lot, hoping for some undisturbed privacy. He leaned against the hood of his car and tapped his phone against his bottom lip. If he called Martina's mother, would it put his mind at rest or stir up more unnecessary worry? Dark gray clouds gathered in the distance, and Jack shivered. Paranoia. It was all just paranoia.

He punched in his ex-mother-in-law's number.

"Sylvia? It's Jack."

"Jack! Oh, how lovely to hear from you. How are you? How are the girls?"

"They're fine. I'm fine. Look, I can't talk for long. I just wanted to ring to see if you've heard from Martina lately." Silence hovered like a phantom menace, and Jack tightened his grip on the phone. "Sylvia?"

"I haven't seen her for weeks. I have no idea where she is. She calls me every few days or so, never saying where she is."

"Does she sound okay?"

"She hasn't called me drunk for months, if that's what you mean."

Jack stared ahead. "Has she mentioned me or the girls?"

"No."

He released his held breath and looked to the pavement. "Well, that's something, I suppose."

"You could at least tell *me* where you are. I'd love to come visit."

"No. I can't do that. I explained everything when I left London. I can't run the risk of Martina turning up here. Surely you understand that after the last time she came to supposedly see the girls?"

"That was over a year ago. You can't hold on to that forever."

"She threatened to hurt them, Sylvia. Really hurt them. Our three-year-old babies." The memory of that fateful day came alive behind his closed lids. Of Martina showing up months after she'd walked out and snatching Katy up from the floor, violently shaking her, and Jack ripping his baby girl screaming from her mother's arms. "I failed them by letting her into our house that day. It won't happen again. I won't let any more damage be done to the twins."

"What damage? Those girls are perfectly fine."

Jack squeezed the phone. "They are not fine. All I can hope for is their nightmares aren't as bad as the ones that haunt me."

"You made mistakes too, Jack. We all did."

Jack closed his eyes. "I did my best, Sylvia. How was I supposed to keep the girls around Martina when she was so volatile?"

"You know what you should've done. You reacted to Martina breaking down by giving up. You should've tried harder, worked at it."

Jack opened his eyes. There was no way she was laying Martina's breakdown entirely on him. Yes, he was guilty of certain things — but, damn, Martina was too. And Jack *had* worked at it; he'd spent a good six months trying to fix their marriage. He'd lessened his work hours, tried to get Martina help. Nothing had worked. For any of them. "I didn't want to walk away. I loved her. She had affairs that damn near ripped my heart out, yet even then I believed maybe there was a small chance. But it was over when it became a problem around the kids."

Silence.

"I tried my best, Sylvia. I tried to help her even after she left. She didn't want to listen or even know me."

"Well, unfortunately, you don't get to decide whether she can see them. The judge does. Is that why you chose now to move away? Because it's been a year and she can now contest your sole custody?"

Jack swiped his hand over his face. No matter how many times he'd told himself otherwise, that was exactly what he'd done. Yet all he said in response was, "She still hasn't earned her right to see the girls yet."

"She's their mother, Jack."

"She's not. Not yet. A mother doesn't have sex with a stranger with her girls asleep in the next room. A mother doesn't drink half a bottle of vodka and then send toddlers outside to play in the damn street. A mother doesn't slap her children, and a mother certainly doesn't walk out on them."

"Jack, please. Don't shout at me."

Jack blew out a breath and said, more calmly, "This is as hard for me as it is for you. I know you're an innocent party in all this, but I'm trying to move on here. I want the girls to be happy."

"And I'm desperate to see my grandchildren."

Indecision battled with his conscience. By law, he was supposed to tell Martina where he was. He hoped to avoid that for as long as possible yet couldn't afford not to play by the book.

"Look, if I let you know where I am, you have to promise you won't give Martina the address yet. I'm not ready for her to know where we are. Not by a long shot."

"She's come a long way in the last twelve months, you know. She's stopped drinking, and I'll even go as far as to say she's working again. I can't be sure, but her lack of contact makes me think she's getting herself straightened out and earning her own money again. I can't remember the last time she called asking for a handout."

"I'm glad if that's the case, but it doesn't mean I'm ready for her to see the twins."

"It's not fair to keep punishing her."

Dread sped Jack's heart as he considered the very real possibility of a judge ruling in Martina's favor if she'd stopped drinking as well as managed to get a job. Didn't the courts always want children with their mother unless the circumstances made it impossible?

"It's too soon, Sylvia. A year is not enough for me to be convinced she won't relapse. I won't expose the girls to that risk."

Her exhalation rasped down the line. "So you won't tell me where you are? Is that what you're saying?"

In the back of his mind, it was inevitable Sylvia would tell Martina, but the pressure of going against the court order ate at him. If he passed on their new address, his part would be above the law.

"Jack, please," she continued. "I promise I won't give it to her. What she did to Holly and Katy…" Jack could hear her stifle a sob. "What she did ended her contact with them back then. I understand that. I only want it so I can write to them. And, in time, maybe you'll let Frank and me come visit. Surely they miss Grandpa's piggybacks?"

A smile pulled at his lips, and Jack dropped his hand from his hair, his shoulders slumping in defeat. "They do. Of course they do. In time, okay? Just promise me you'll say nothing to Martina until I say so."

"Absolutely. You have my word. Those girls are everything to me. You know that."

"Okay. Well, have you got a pen?"

"Yes. Right here."

"We are at seventeen Marsden Place, Potterford. It's in Wiltshire."

"Wiltshire? That's in the country." She said it as though he'd moved to Skid Row.

He rolled his eyes. "That's a good thing, right?"

She let out a tinkle of laughter. "Of course it is. I didn't mean anything."

"Good." He glanced toward the office. "Look, I have to go. If Martina turns up or says she wants to see the girls, promise you'll ring to let me know."

"Of course I will. Pass on my love to Holly and Katy. You look after yourself and them for me, okay?"

"I will. Bye." Pressing the *end call* button, Jack marched back inside the office. He sank into his seat and dropped his head into his hands.

"Jack?"

He looked up to see Steve.

"You okay?" his coworker asked.

"I'm fine." Jack sighed. "Just some personal stuff, that's all."

"Anything I can do?"

"Nah. It'll sort itself out."

"Well, I might have something to distract you from whatever it is making you look like you could punch out a wall."

Jack relaxed his shoulders down from his earlobes. "Yeah?"

Smiling, Steve picked up a scrap of paper from his desk and shook it. "How did you get on with that lead you had about the shops closing down on Canterdown Road yesterday?"

Jack eyed the paper. "Why? You found something?"

"No, but I thought you might be interested to know how our local people deal with threats of rent increase or intimidation. Or, more specifically, how Sienna Lloyd deals with it."

Jack sat up straighter and contained himself from leaping over the desk and snatching the paper from Steve's hand. "Oh, yeah? What's that, then?"

"Here." He tossed Jack the paper. "Sienna's having a closing-down party. She'll be setting up the shop at her house sometime over the next few weeks. Fair play to the woman. It'll take a hurricane to keep that girl down." Pride rang in his voice. "Nothing will stop her. Not anymore."

On the paper scrap was a scribbled note asking for advertising space in Friday's issue of the paper.

A closing-down PARTY?

"Suppose not," Jack replied, trying to keep his voice blasé. "Wow, wonder how many people will turn up to this thing."

"Lots, I expect. Sienna's clientele are loyal." He winked. "Why don't you get yourself an invite and see what goes on? Sienna's shop is fantastic. I, for one, am right behind her. Tell Ed it's a local interest story. You'll be good to go."

"Hmm, would you be right behind her if she was moving the shop next door to your house?"

Steve frowned. "What?"

Jack tossed the paper onto his desk and stood. "I'm her new neighbor, Steve, and there is hell's chance of that shop opening or this goddamn party happening."

"You're her neighbor?"

"Yep." Jack whipped his jacket from the back of the chair and shrugged it on. "What's more, she knows I work here. She knows I'm a journalist, and she knows I've got four-year-old twin girls. She's taking the piss out of me."

Steve raised his hands. "Jack, calm down, mate. If Sienna thinks—"

"She doesn't think. That's the problem. From what I know of the woman, she acts first, thinks later. There's no way that attitude is going to mess up my girls' future."

Grabbing his laptop, Jack stormed outside.

Chapter Nine

Sienna hauled her box of inventory from the back of her car and strode up the driveway to her front door. Entering the house, she kicked her leg out to close the door when it hit something solid before it could shut. She turned and promptly dropped the box onto the hallway floor, causing "display" vibrators of varying sizes and colors to roll every which way across the floorboards—a multi-colored river of female satisfaction.

"Jack! What do you think you're doing?"

"I'm coming in to talk to you, that's what." He strode over the threshold and slammed the door.

Sienna stepped back even as irritation pinched hot at her cheeks. Who the hell did he think he was, coming into her house uninvited?

She raised her chin and gestured toward the floor. "Now look what you've done."

"You're having a party. A *party*, for crying out loud."

Ah. "And? Does that give you the right to storm into my house like the Incredible Hulk? What's next? A bit of shirt-shredding?" Actually, she wouldn't have minded that…

He opened his mouth and then snapped it shut as he glowered at the glorious obstacles at their feet. "God, it never ends, does it?"

"No, it doesn't. So why don't you help me pick these up before you end up slipping on one and taking me to court for breaking your back on top of everything else."

He sneered with evident distaste. "I don't think so."

"Grow up, Jack. You're being ridiculous."

Their glares locked. He might have looked as though he should be lying on his back in her bed while she rode him like a bucking bronco, but God, the guy lacked a sense of humor.

"Well?" she demanded.

"You really don't care, do you?"

"Insult me if it makes you feel better, but if you can say that, it means you haven't learned a damn thing about me since we met. Now, are we going to stand here all day or go into the kitchen and have a civilized conversation? I assume you want this straightened out before it's time for you to pick up the girls from pre-school? Isn't that why you're battering your way into my house at eleven o'clock in the morning?"

"Where were you last night?" His gaze searched her face and hair.

Ignoring the flush of heat that tingled over her skin from such a blatant appraisal, Sienna lifted her eyebrows. "Excuse me?"

"I waited for you."

"You waited—"

"I must have looked out my living room window forty times waiting to see your car in the driveway. Where were you?"

She huffed out a laugh and bent down. "None of your business." She reached for the nearest vibrator.

"I needed to talk to you."

She snatched up an electric-blue intermediate dildo and straightened, pointing it in his face and stabbing out each word. "Like. I. Said. None. Of. Your. Business."

He stepped back, and a smile pulled at her lips. Scared of a dildo. What next? Crying over spilt vaginal lube?

"Help me pick these up and then we'll talk." She cocked her head. "Please."

"You're unbelievable."

Her smile expanded. "Thanks."

Scowling, he bent down to help her.

A couple minutes passed in silence as they picked up the vibrators. Sienna fought her laughter as she glanced time and again at Jack. This was killing him, judging by the expression on his face as he tossed the devices one by one into the box. When they were done, she stood.

"Come on, then." She walked into the front room of the house, Jack following. She put the box on the floor and threw out her arms to encapsulate the room. "Welcome to my new shop. Or at least it will be in a few weeks."

His eyebrows shot to his hairline. "In here? You want to set up shop in here?"

She dropped her hands to her hips. "Not want. I am."

"Over my dead—"

"Coffee? Come on, I need coffee."

Leaving him standing there, Sienna walked into the kitchen. Seconds later, his footsteps sounded on the tile floor. She moved to fill the electric kettle at the sink, then returned it to the countertop and switched it on, willing her courage to not falter. None of Jack's hostility was about the shop, and by the time he left, Sienna was determined they would take some steps toward resolution.

"Black or white?" She grabbed two mugs hanging from hooks.

"I don't want coffee. I want you to tell me what the hell we're going to do about this situation."

Sienna silently counted to five as she spooned coffee into the mugs. She needed to think of the right words to say. Despite her nonchalance, Jack's antagonism swirled around her in a heavy mist; his apparent bullheadedness in opposing the shop's move tightened a vice around her heart that felt far too much like panic. No one had challenged her about anything for so long, it was unnerving. She made people happy, not angry.

She turned around to find him looking at her with the same no-way, no-how expression her dad had worn when, at age thirteen, she'd wanted to go to a party lasting until midnight. That had been the last time someone had told her off, and defensiveness now raised her hackles again, making the hairs at the back of her neck prickle. *Back off, Dad. This is between him and me.*

As for Jack, he wasn't her father. And he'd soon know it.

Sienna crossed her arms as the kettle cranked and wheezed to boiling behind her. "I'm not doing this to piss you off. Why can't you understand that?"

Jack pulled out a seat at the kitchen table and sat down. Leaning his bare forearms on the table, he met her eyes. "Believe it or not, I don't want to fight with you about this either."

Sensing some of the ire leaving him, Sienna's heart settled to a more regular beat. "Then we need to come up with a solution to fit us both. I'm thinking the first step is to tell me what this is really about, and then maybe we can do something about it. I don't want us to end up enemies over this…I kind of quite like you."

His lips curved into an incredibly slow, sexy smile. "You're not too bad yourself."

Sienna grinned. "See? Better, much better." She cleared her throat. "The point is, if I had any other choice, do you really think I'd bring the business here? Into my home? I took that shop because it was the cheapest in town. It was a bargain deal I cut with the landlord. How was I to know he'd whack things up once the going got tough?"

"I sympathize, but I can't handle it being around my girls."

"We're in a recession, Jack. We all have to make allowances."

"I never said any of this was fair. Me moving my kids here for a fresh start only to have a sex shop open next door isn't fair. You're doing what you have to, and I'm doing the same. The problem is, one of us is going to lose." He paused, a muscle jumping in his jaw. "I hate to say it, but it won't be me."

"You are one cocky bastard when you want to be, Beaton."

They appraised each other before Sienna whirled back around to the kettle. Damn him. He clearly thought himself her match. So why wasn't it annoying the hell out of her? Why did she feel something far too close to respect for him?

"Black or white?" she asked once more as she poured water over the coffee.

"Black, no sugar."

Sienna rolled her eyes. A man's coffee. Adding milk and one sugar to hers, she carried the mugs to the table and put one down in front of him.

"Thanks." He closed his hands around it.

Sienna watched his knuckles turn white as she took a seat opposite him. "My shop is a place for the women of Potterford to come and talk, laugh, and have fun. They feel safe there. I make it safe." Despite the tension throughout the rest of his body, Jack's eyes appeared open and interested as he listened. She struggled to concentrate on them and not his mouth. "When my dad was killed, it sent shockwaves through the community like nobody had seen before. People were scared. My mother spiraled into depression…"

To her distress, tears filled her eyes. Jack slid his hand across the table and took hers. She stared at their interlinked fingers.

"Your dad died in the worst way possible."

She snapped her head up. "You know what happened? Who told you? They had no right. It was my place to tell you, nobody else's."

He remained silent, and pain gripped her chest. Of course he knew. Who couldn't resist telling him he'd moved next door to the daughter of the town's hero. A hero who had died and left a great gaping hole in her heart and the responsibility of her mother in her hands?

"Who told you, Jack? I want to know."

"A colleague at the paper mentioned it. I don't want to upset you more than you already are, but—"

"You're going to anyway?"

His eyes grew soft. "From what I've been told, your dad sounds like one hell of a guy."

"He was. One hell of a guy I miss every day."

"Sienna—"

"I'm okay."

Silent seconds passed. What she wouldn't give to stand up and plonk down in his lap, wrap her arms around his neck…

"The day we buried him, I made a vow to stay in Potterford, to look after my mum and do my part in making this a good place to live. I don't want to leave. I don't want some hotshot career in the city. This is my home. My shop is a place for women to chat, rant, rave, or whatever the hell they want to do. I won't close it, no matter how hard you push me."

He looked at their joined hands. "This whole situation stinks. I don't want to be the one up in your face." He lifted his head. "The mess with the twins' mother? Not entirely her fault. I want to make things right."

"And forcing my business out of here will do that?"

His hand slipped slowly from hers as he shook his head. "No."

Relief quivered in her belly. Maybe they could resolve this after all. "Good. Then the next job is to work out what will."

He nodded, and an invisible thread wove between them. She was aware of every part of her face, her body, her entire self as he studied her. When his appraisal glided down to her chest and back again, Sienna's heart raced. She wasn't a virgin; she knew how these things worked. And she sensed he wanted to kiss her. Worse, she wanted him to. It felt appropriate, a way of sealing the deal.

But nothing could happen between them. He'd only get inside her and tear away her resolve; his potential to leave her open to his desires had been tangible just from the feel of his hand around hers. She was nowhere near ready for a relationship. Relationships took compromise and time. Her makeup wasn't prone to either, hadn't been for a while.

The tension stretched taut between them. Sienna opened her mouth to say something, anything, when he pushed to his feet, the chair scraping along the tile and hitching her nerves higher. Their coffees steamed, abandoned on the table.

Taking her hands, Jack slowly pulled Sienna to her feet as well.

No. Stay back, she thought, but the words lodged in her throat. They now stood so close, she saw flecks of silver in his midnight-blue eyes.

"Jack…"

Like a giant handling a porcelain doll, he gently smoothed his thumbs over the backs of her hands. She shivered as tiny darts of electricity shot up her arms.

"You're beautiful, do you know that?"

He'd spoken so quietly, Sienna wasn't sure she'd heard him right. "What?"

He raised one of her hands to his mouth, and her heart stopped. His lips brushed on a whisper against her knuckles. "I said you're beautiful. And kind."

"Jack…" Why did she keep saying his name like some swooning heroine from a Charlotte Brontë novel? She cleared her throat. "Jack." *Yeah, great, Sienna. Much better.*

He leaned closer, and her eyelids grew heavy. She couldn't fight him if she wanted to. He brushed his mouth softly, tentatively against hers. Asking permission. She nodded.

His tongue touched hers, and easing her hands from his, Sienna lifted them to grip his muscular biceps. She groaned, and the pressure of his kiss increased as his hands gripped her waist. A feverish heat whirled around them on a palpable wave until Sienna teetered back on her heels. Jack touched her neck, then plunged his fingers into her hair and held firm.

No sound but their breathing, no sound but the joining of their lips.

Until, after a moment, they separated. Jack's eyes were wide with shock, undoubtedly mirroring hers. Words battled on Sienna's tongue, but her brain was mush. She blinked and, with it, regained the ability to speak.

"Well, that's gone and done it."

Sienna Lloyd, you should write a freaking novel.

What the hell had he done? Jack ran his hand through his hair. His chest was a pool of nothing, like Sienna had reached in and ripped his heart right out.

Her cheeks were flushed, her eyes dark. Melted chocolate under the rays of golden sunlight. Jack considered running through the door.

Coward.

"I don't know what to say." He lifted his shoulders and walked to the table to sit down. "I shouldn't have…I don't know what just happened."

She took the seat opposite him. "We kissed."

Jack laughed. "You're too damn hard to resist, I guess."

The quick comeback he expected from her didn't come. It was still his turn. She'd been honest with him about the effect of her father's death and what the shop meant to her, so he owed her the same courtesy. His lingering concern about Martina wasn't Sienna's fault, after all. God, it wasn't either of their faults, and the fact was, each time he looked into Sienna's beautiful eyes, concern about his ex-wife slowly dissipated.

He'd kissed a woman whom he really liked. He'd opened up a chance of something maybe happening between them. Why ruin that? Why let an *if, but,* or *maybe* prevent a different future for him and the twins? Did he really want to be that guy who never let go of the past? He had to find a way to fix this, and as far as he was concerned, it started with her landlord.

"Do you have your landlord's details?"

"What?"

It was a cold thing to say after sharing such a passionate kiss, but surely they could both use the diversion? The awkwardness in the room was palpable.

"I want to find out who this guy is."

"Why?"

He shrugged. "It a hunch, but I think there's possibly more to this rent increase than what we're seeing. It's not just you who's been forced to shut down in a short amount a time, and I think it's worth investigating."

She studied him for a moment as if weighing his words. "And what are you hoping to find?"

"I don't know yet."

"I'm not stupid, Jack. I've had my lawyer-friend, Kelsey, who you briefly met the other night, look over the contract, and the guy is perfectly in his rights to kick me out if I don't agree to the rent. Simple."

"But why do it? Why slam on an increase that leaves the shop empty. Does he own the others who've shut down?"

Interest sparked in her eyes. "He could."

Jack smiled as the familiar excitement of a story clutched inside him. "Then let me do some digging. It might help."

After a moment, Sienna pushed to her feet and walked over to a stack of papers on the counter. She rifled through them, and drawing out an envelope, she tossed it onto the table in front of him. "I must be mad to trust you after you've looked at me like I'm some sort of rabid dog more times than I can count. But it's all there. That's where he works and how much he wants from me and when."

Without looking at it, Jack slipped the envelope into his shirt pocket. "I'll let you know what I find out."

She seemed to inspect his face for sincerity before giving a curt nod. "Okay."

They both took a sip of their coffee. Putting hers down first, Sienna asked, "So what else?"

Jack coughed. "Else?"

"Come on, Jack, you have to give me something."

"What do you mean?"

"You owe me an explanation." She winked. "Not for the kiss. That was kind of consensual."

Her eyes were dangerous. Jack picked up his coffee and drank until the dryness in his throat eased enough that his words could flow. His mug clinked against the tabletop. "You were right. None of this is about the girls and your potential to turn them to the dark side."

Sienna smiled. "I didn't think so."

"It's my ex."

Her smile dissolved. "Ah."

"Two years ago, before we officially divorced, she left us. Just up and went. It was no big deal at first. Our marriage was over the minute she had slept with someone else and left my girls to fend for themselves. The trouble came when she started ringing me up, out of her head on God knew what, demanding money and threatening to take my babies away."

"And she's still calling now? Is she still threatening you?"

"No. I've heard nothing from her in a year. She rings her mother every now and then, though, as do I." He took a breath. "To be honest, I spoke to her mother recently, and there's a chance Martina is finally straightening herself out."

"Which is a good thing, right?"

"Of course. No matter how much I, her parents, or our friends did to help her back then, nothing worked. Clearly she wasn't ready for it, but she is now." He straightened, relaxing against the back of the chair. "I wish her all the luck in the world, but it doesn't mean I'm prepared for her to see the twins."

"I understand that," Sienna said, nodding. "You need more time."

"I moved Holly and Katy here in the hope she won't find them. I'm not proud of it, but I've done what I feel is right considering everything she put them through. Legally, they're mine. I can take them where I want. The problem is, by law, I should be letting Martina know where I am. But I can't. Not until I'm sure she's one-hundred-percent on the road to recovery."

Sienna's hand covered his. "She isn't likely to find them here. Potterford's tiny."

Jack drew in a long breath. "I told her mother where we are. I had to. The legal implications binding me to that far outweigh the odds she'll actually turn up here." He exhaled. "But now her mother knows…I don't know. She promised she won't tell Martina where we are, but I'm not ashamed to admit I'm concerned she'll slip. Until I know for myself Martina can be trusted around the girls…" Jack tightened his jaw.

"Wouldn't it be a good idea to find out sooner rather than later? This not knowing is eating you up from the inside out as far as I can tell."

She had a point. Jack was a fool to think he could run and hide. Sooner or later he had to face Martina, but…"Not yet. I don't…like the man she turns me into."

Sienna pulled her hand from his, and Jack looked into the depths of his coffee mug, knowing he'd probably just sealed the deal of his first and last kiss with her. Her father had been killed with violence, and now she lived next door to a man capable of it for all she knew. He pulled his hands into his lap.

"She's the twins' mother, but I'm their father. I should've been there, and I wasn't. I neglected them, too, back then. I should've seen what was happening sooner, and I'll never forget that. I failed as their father, big time. But I won't again." He looked at her, willing her to understand his motives weren't entirely insane. The compassion he perceived in return ignited a new realization. "Maybe it's time I moved on. What will be, will be."

She gave a soft smile. "Sounds like a plan."

"Sienna—"

"How about we call a truce, Jack? How about we just get along and forget your ex-wife for now? I need to move my shop here, and you need to be there for the twins. We can both do that without anyone getting hurt. Can't we?"

Chapter Ten

Sienna glanced at her watch. Time to call it a day. She'd been working on decorating the front room all morning and afternoon, and things were finally shaping up. The walls shimmered as they dried to a soft cotton-candy pink. The ceiling glistened with a fresh coat of paint. The floorboards were sanded and stained walnut.

She stretched out the kinks in her back. If nothing else, she'd given her front room the makeover of its life.

Everything would be dry by morning, and she could start erecting shelving and putting out stock. All would work out just fine. She and Jack were talking, and there would be at least twenty people coming to the closing-down party in less than a week's time. Most importantly, her heart was still firmly in its place. Kind of.

She leaned against the doorjamb. With her and Jack having called a truce, things felt better in her mind and soul, but his kiss still lingered. She licked her lips and immediately regretted it. It was as though the taste of him was branded there, tormenting her. It had only been a simple kiss; she'd kissed plenty of men over the years, and it had never been something to get her all hot and bothered and sleepless over. Yet, with Jack, her entire body had come alive from that soft, erotic interlude that had allowed her a tiny peek into the potentially explosive and sexy pairing the two of them could be. Sienna shivered. How good could he make her feel if she ever got beneath the surface of the man?

Whether he realized it or not, he'd spoken to her through that kiss; she had sensed how much he hurt. His ex-wife wouldn't come anywhere near Jack and his children if Sienna had anything to do with it, but that wasn't even the problem. Jack was defending the twins against something that hadn't happened, and though it told Sienna a million things about him that made her like him more and more, he shouldn't be living a life that uncertain.

Yet wasn't she doing the same thing, albeit in a different way? Fighting against the past becoming the present?

Jack fought to protect his girls; she fought to protect her heart.

Pushing away from the doorjamb, Sienna wiped the worst of the paint from her hands on a rag as she walked into the kitchen. Night was falling, and the room sat in semi-darkness. She shook off her stupid melancholy and focused on the evening ahead. Wine, bath, bed.

After trying and failing to switch on the overhead light with her elbow, she made her way to the sink in the moonlit kitchen. Humming softly, she attacked the paint on her fingers with vigor. Yet as Jack filled her thoughts once more, her vision blurred, and she scrubbed away more than paint—hopeless wanting stripped away from her skin and swirled down the drain.

She couldn't consider the possibility of him becoming a part of her life, no matter how attracted she was to him. It wasn't just Jack either; it was Holly and Katy. They were a package, a unit. An amazing unit. For so long, she'd given every effort to encourage people to embrace the moment and live it. Effort she knew was poorly lacking in her own psyche, but hey, she was working on it…and Jack and the girls were nudging that work into overdrive.

The flicker of a flashlight across the window snapped Sienna from her thoughts. She froze. "What the hell was that?" Her voice sounded loud in the empty room.

As she turned off the faucet, her shock converted into adrenaline and infused her with the need to defend her home. Yanking a carving knife from the wooden block on her counter, Sienna made for the back door. She snatched it open and stood at the threshold, her body shaking and blood pumping.

"Get the hell out of here, whoever you are. You come near my property again, and I'll stick a damn knife in you. Do you hear me?"

Silence.

She strained her ears for the sound of footsteps, breathing, anything. The whimper when it came was so pathetic, Sienna wondered if she'd imagined the light and it had merely been the passing shadow of a cat crossing her window.

"Hello?" Nothing. Feeling like a foolish old woman with a cat obsession, she bent at the waist, her eyes scanning the area. "Here, kitty, kitty."

Nothing.

Shrugging, she moved to go back inside when a flashlight rolled along her decking from behind a huge potted plant in the far corner. Her heart picked up speed, and she raised the knife once more.

"Come out of there. Show yourself, you damn yellow-belly son of a—Katy?"

Katy came out with her hands raised as though expecting Sienna to turn a gun on her. She hastily dropped the knife and rushed toward her as the child's tears shone in silver trails under the porch lights.

"Katy, what on earth are you…?" Sienna was about to embrace her when she dropped her arms. She didn't cuddle children. She never cuddled children. It must have been the shock reverberating through her entire body that had made her yearn to.

But when Katy met her eyes, the complete sad and desperate plea there stole Sienna's final shred of resistance; it snapped and pinged across the garden. Sliding her hands gently under the little girl's arms, Sienna lifted her onto her hip and guided Katy's head to her shoulder. She swayed back and forth, smoothing her free hand over the back of the child's head. The soft scent of Katy's curls crawled into Sienna's nostrils and all the way into her heart.

"What are you doing here, sweetheart?" she murmured, walking slowly into the house, leaving the knife where it was. "Does Daddy know you're here?"

Damn stupid question. Like hell he did. If Jack knew she was there after dark, he'd burst a blood vessel.

Katy's hair brushed Sienna's jaw. "No, but I needed to come and get you. He won't go to bed."

Sienna frowned and stopped inside the kitchen. "Won't go to bed? That's okay. It's not late for a grownup, sweetie. Only four-year-old little girls should be in bed."

"He's upset." Panic showed in the glassy shine of Katy's eyes. "Please come."

With trepidation, Sienna proposed, "I'll take you home, but—"

"Can you stay with him until he goes to bed? Daddy needs to sleep too."

Jack in bed…Sienna blinked and forced a smile. "Sure. Come on. Let's get you home. If Daddy knew you were here in the dark, he'd have a meltdown."

"A what?"

Sienna laughed. "Don't worry. Come on."

Lifting her keys from the rack in the hallway, Sienna shut the front door behind them and walked next door. She took a deep breath and rang the bell. Katy stiffened in her arms, and Sienna held her tighter. Whatever was going on with Ol' Blue Eyes right then, it was enough to scare at least one of his daughters into coming out in the dark dressed in pajamas.

She rang again.

The door yanked back on his hinges, and the Grinch—or Jack—stood there with his teeth clenched, his eyes ablaze, and his hair spiked all over the place.

"Hi, there." Sienna smiled and waited for the explosion.

His gaze darted from her to his daughter's. "Katy? Oh, my God."

He gently pulled her from Sienna's arms and covered Katy's face in about a hundred kisses before closing his eyes and pressing his cheek to hers. Sienna moved to walk away while she still could.

"Sienna, wait," he said. "Where are you going?"

Damn it. She rotated back around. "Just returning what's yours. And now I'm going for a bath."

"What? You can't leave. She clearly wanted to see you. Why else would she—" He looked at Katy. "Why did you go and see Sienna?"

Sienna's heart twisted like a damn tornado as father and daughter stared at each other. The mutual love beamed from them like a beacon calling back *The Waltons*.

"I wanted her to make you go to bed and stop being mad."

He looked from Katy to Sienna, embarrassment showing in the way he jammed his free hand into his hair and held it there. Thus explaining the spiky, dragged-through-a-hedge-backwards look.

"I was…I was talking to someone on the phone," he offered, widening his eyes in silent insinuation. "Katy's nanna."

Nodding, she said, "I see. Is everything all right now?"

"I'm not sure." He opened his mouth, shut it, and opened it again. "Why don't you come in for a cup of coffee? I'll put Katy to bed, and we can have a chat." He turned to Katy. "Would you go straight to bed if Sienna comes in and sits with me for a while?"

The little girl flashed Sienna such a huge smile that protesting Jack's offer was futile. She raised her hands in surrender. "I guess I'm coming in for coffee."

Jack kissed Katy's brow and tucked her sheet closer around her shoulders. His heart still rocketed around in his chest thinking about what could have happened to her on her visit to Sienna's. More and more macabre notions tiptoed into his brain — notions he knew would continue haunting him when he turned out his bedroom light.

But for now, Katy evidently wasn't giving her nocturnal escapade another thought as she closed her eyes and drifted into peaceful sleep. She whispered a soft sigh as she pulled her teddy bear closer. When a smile curved her lips, Jack managed a small one too.

Straightening, he walked to the door and pulled it closed behind him, letting a dart of light from the landing spill across the carpet the way Katy liked it. Making his way downstairs, he hesitated at the kitchen door. What would Sienna think of him now? Not only had one of the girls he'd banged on about protecting managed to creep next door, but Katy had also told Sienna he'd been mad.

Taking a deep breath, he walked into the kitchen. "Hi."

Sienna was seated at the kitchen table. "Hi."

Jack rubbed his hand over his face. "I'm not sure what I'm supposed to say. Doesn't make me a prospect for the father of the year award, does it?"

She lifted her shoulders. "I don't know. The girl obviously adores you."

"Maybe."

"There's no 'maybe' about it. She must've gone through the back door and crawled through the hole in the fence. I've no idea where she got the idea it was okay to do that." She gave a wink.

"Well, I'm just glad she came to you and didn't decide to just run out into the street. If anything would've—"

"Hey, it didn't."

Their eyes locked, and the urge to repeat the kiss of three nights before heated Jack's blood. He quickly moved to the counter and flicked on the kettle.

"Her mum's told Martina where we are." He gripped the counter. "Martina's been ringing me tonight for the first time in over twelve months. But I haven't been able to answer, and she doesn't leave any messages. It's probably just a matter of time now before she shows up. I couldn't help ringing my ex-mother-in-law and telling her how upset I am she did that." His chin fell to his chest, and he looked to the floor.

"Hey, are you going to look at me? You've got a damn fine back and ass, but right now, I want to see your face."

He smiled as he obliged. "How is it you can make me smile even when I should be punching something?"

She grinned, and Jack's heart turned over. Jesus, he was in seriously deep shit. He wanted to touch her, feel her body against his. For want of comfort or sexual need, he couldn't be sure. He pushed away from the counter and took a step toward her.

"Sienna—"

"Do you know this is the second time you've messed up my plans for a glass of wine and a bubble bath? What is that, Jack? Is this going to be a regular occurrence from now on?"

Forgetting the coffee, he leaned one hand on the back of her chair and the other on the table in front of her. She smelled like paint. Was it crazy it did nothing to curb the desire to drop his face to the curve of her neck?

"Thank you for bringing her back and not judging me."

Her cheeks flushed, and when she lifted her chin, her pulse visibly beat in the hollow at the base of her throat. His stance made her uncomfortable. It was written all over her face. Yet instead of moving back, Jack relished it. It meant she felt it too — whatever hummed between them like an electric field. It had been a long time since a woman made him so aware of his masculinity.

With her gaze trained on his mouth, she cleared her throat. "I never judge anyone…well, maybe I'm judging your ex-wife a little right now."

Jack straightened and slid onto the chair beside her. Allowing his brain time to overpower his penis, he silently counted to three and concentrated on the Formica tabletop. He had to get a grip on his attraction. One of his girls hadn't thought twice about letting herself out of the house after dark, and he didn't feel as though he could trust anyone anymore. Especially himself. "Things are not going as I imagined."

Sienna exhaled. "Then let's straighten them out so they are."

"You don't need to get involved in my problems. I'm trying my best to keep you out of them."

"I don't need protecting. Now, your kids are a different matter, so why don't you tell me what Martina's mum had to say? Who knows? I might be able to help."

"I don't want your help. I don't want her or Martina to know you exist." He seethed at the thought of Martina coming within ten feet of Sienna and tainting her goodness. "You have no idea what she's like. She's a manipulator."

"I'd like to see her try to manipulate me."

"I can't risk letting the girls…and you down."

"You haven't let me — "

"This is nothing I don't deserve."

She stared into his eyes. "No one deserves this endless punishment you're putting on yourself. We all make mistakes, Jack. It's what we learn from them that matters."

Jack waved his hand, dismissing her sympathy. "I just want to make Holly and Katy happy, not fight the woman who gave birth to them like she's enemy number one."

"So don't." Sienna rose from her chair and stood in front of him. There was hesitation on her face before she closed her hand around his bicep. "If she wants to take you on, let her come to Potterford. In fact, you should actively encourage it. That way, you'll have more control. Let her come. Once we know want she wants, what her intentions are, we can deal with it."

"No. No 'we.' I'll deal with it."

"You're already trying to help me by finding out what my landlord's up to, so won't you at least let me try to help you in return?"

"I appreciate that, but I can't. The last thing I wanted by moving here was to bring trouble to a stranger's door. You have nothing to do with this."

A flash of affront passed over her eyes. "Hey, I'm not a stranger."

His fingers itched to pull her close. "No, you're not. Of course you're not. Jesus, see what she turns me into? I didn't mean to dismiss you. I'm sorry. This whole situation with Martina and me just makes me so damn mad. It wasn't supposed to be this way."

Jack tried and failed to look away from her. The intensity, the intimacy of the kiss they'd shared burned, and he longed for another.

As if reading his thoughts, Sienna stepped back, her hand leaving his arm and gripping the back of her neck. "Potterford is a nice place, a good place. Yes, things happen…" Her voice cracked. "They happen everywhere. But the twins will be happy here…so will you."

She's thinking of her dad. His gaze meandered from her face down to the neck he wanted to taste like it was his only hope for survival. "If you really want to help me —"

"I do."

"Then don't open your shop. Don't have a party."

"What?" She pulled her hand from her neck, her face once more the mask of determination he was getting to know so well. "The shop has nothing to do with it. You're bigger than this, Jack. Why can't you see that?"

"Because this *isn't* all just about her. I don't want that stuff around the kids."

"Why not? What harm will it do, really?"

"It just reminds me too much —"

"You, Jack? *You.* Not them." She crossed her arms. "This is becoming a broken record. Don't you want to move on and have a life again? Whatever your ex did or didn't do, a pair of lace knickers is not going to threaten your kids' future. So why the hell are you letting it threaten yours?"

His mind was blank as she glared at him.

Throwing her hands out, she asserted, "Well, I'll tell you something right now. If that's the way you feel, I recommend you sort out some babysitting for next Saturday."

He tightened his jaw. "The party."

"Yep. Unless you do want Holly and Katy to see sixty-year-old women coming down the driveway dressed in thongs with their bare breasts smeared with chocolate body paint. Mrs. McGill is so excited, there's no telling what she'll be like after a few glasses of wine. So keep your diary free, Blue Eyes. You're going to be busy these next few days — either preventing or helping me get ready for a party that will light up your life like never before."

Chapter Eleven

Sienna's eyes blurred as she scanned her newly painted "shop" room at the house, the late morning sun showing off the feminine pink walls. Was she doing the right thing? Jack's reaction to it continued to niggle at her conscience even if she did suspect the shop only symbolized what he deemed was doing "the right thing" by his girls this time around. Even if it was entirely misplaced.

She groaned aloud. "This is my life too, Jack."

The silence of the room wrapped around the chaos along with a dank, dark thought things would never get better. Her new beginning felt laden with hesitation, guilt, and more than a little doubt. Two days ago, she'd tried to convince Jack they could fight the bad people in life, but what if she was wrong? What if life was meant to be this way? Who said God owed anyone an easy journey?

She slid to the floor and rammed her knuckles against her teeth to contain the scream rising in her throat. Self-control was everything. She had to be strong. Her feet kicked up against some packed boxes she'd brought home from the shop. They would be emptied, and she would start again.

Kelsey's words echoed in her head: "*You cannot put your life on hold to look after everyone else. There's your mum, me, every other person in town…who's next?*"

Jack. Holly. Katy. Martina. Their names leapt in her mind again, along with her father's and mother's faces. Sienna's frustration accelerated as warm tears escaped under her eyelids. All she wanted was to be able to have a civilized drink with Jack, a meal…*maybe* even some sex. She just wanted to take a risk and be happy, but life was again proving fruitless. Maybe she wouldn't be able to save the shop or even herself; then all Sienna could do, perhaps, was try to ensure her mother suffered no further pain, no further heartache.

She pressed a hand to her quivering stomach. The more adamantly Jack insisted the shop could cause a problem, the more thoughts of her friend in London hovered in her mind. Sienna didn't want to be anyone's problem. If she didn't have her mother to think of, maybe now *would* be the time to explore something new. Yet, when she also considered the possibility of being with Jack, it made her want to stay and fight for him.

Sienna drew in a shaky breath. "Help me, Dad. Tell me what to do." Her words whispered from the walls and engrained themselves deep into her heart. "I like him. I want him."

Her phone vibrated in her pocket. She pulled it out and looked at the display. "Hi, Mum." She rolled her eyes heavenward. *Thanks, Dad.*

"Don't you 'Hi, Mum' me. I've just had Edith McGill on the phone. Do you really think one of your aunt's closest friends wouldn't tell me about a party? A party my daughter has planned and has yet to tell me about?"

Sienna rubbed her hand over her face. "Nothing was certain until today. I've been thinking about it but only just decided I definitely want to do it. I only mentioned it to Mrs. McGill a few days ago because she happened to drop by the shop and got upset about the move."

"'Nothing was certain,' she says."

Sienna sat back on her haunches. When her mother spoke to an invisible person, it meant one thing: she was worried about her daughter, and her husband's death once again tormented her heart and soul.

"What's going on, Mum?"

"Nothing. I'm just hurt I had to hear about this secondhand from Edith, that's all."

"Are you sure?"

Silence.

"Mum?"

"That and the fact I haven't heard from you. I was worried. Worried that with the prospect of the shop closing…you might be depressed. You might do something stupid."

Sienna snapped her eyes open. "Mum, you must never think like that. I would never do that to you. I'll always be here for you. Always." The idea of London vanished.

"Oh, I'm sorry. I just hate you being alone. It's not right."

"There's nothing for you to worry about. I'm fine." Sienna forced some cheer into her voice. "I'm more than fine, especially now we have a party to look forward to. I've got games planned—"

"Games?"

Sienna grinned. Lord, her mother loved a game of anything that anyone over the age of twenty-five had no business playing.

Her mother giggled. "Have you let the police know we're having a party?"

"No…"

"Remember Kelsey's party a couple years ago? They were all over her house like dung beetles on a cow pat when the neighbors complained about the noise."

Sienna laughed. And people wondered where she got her sense of humor. "Hmm…maybe I'd better warn them." *Especially with Jack living next door.*

"Maybe I could come round now? Help you plan. Have you got any more of that glittery booby paint in? Edith will love it."

"Umm…"

"Right, I'm coming round. You kids don't know what a real party takes to organize."

Sienna's smile faded. Once her mother was in a party-planning mood, even professional event planners ran for cover. "Mum, no. I—" Childish laughter tinkled somewhere outside the window, and Sienna froze.

"Hello? Sienna?"

Children. At her house. Sienna's stomach knotted. "Mum, you can't. I've got company." Sienna scrambled to her feet. Rushing for the shop room door, she slipped through it and yanked it closed behind her.

When she then opened the front door, Jack's hand fell away from the doorbell, and he smiled. "Hi."

Sienna held up a finger, giving him an apologetic smile and refocusing on the job of getting her mother off the phone. "They're here right now." She stepped back and gestured for Jack and the twins to come in.

Her mother snorted down the line. "Ha, I'll believe that when I see it. I'm coming round."

Shaking her head, her eyes locked with Jack's. "No, Mum. I mean it."

"Why should I listen to you when—"

"I have to go."

"Sienna Ann Lloyd, don't you dare—"

She snapped the phone shut. "Hey, you two." She forced a wide smile and kept her eyes on the girls rather than Jack. If she looked at him, she'd splinter. "What are you doing here?"

Katy held up a bag, the name of the local market emblazoned in green across its front. "We brought party balloons."

Tears burned behind Sienna's eyes like red-hot pokers. "Daddy told you I was having a party?"

She nodded. "Uh-huh, for grownups."

"That's right. Grownups." Sienna turned to Holly, who stood beside Katy. "Have you come to help too?"

Holly scowled. "No. I'm going to play in the garden."

Sienna fought the urge to laugh hysterically. As long as Holly never changed, maybe things wouldn't be so bad after all. "Ah. Okay, well, you know the way. Why don't you both go through the kitchen and out into the back garden? I'll bring out some drinks in just a minute."

As expected, they looked to Jack for permission. Sienna willed herself to face him. Insight lit his eyes to a vivid blue, and concern seemed to set his jaw. Sienna swallowed the lump that lodged in her throat like a boulder and turned to shut the front door.

Don't ask me if I'm okay. Don't make me cry and fall apart. What are we doing here, Jack?

"Sienna?"

Forcing a smile, she faced him. "Yes?"

"Is everything all right? You said to come over whenever we were ready, right?"

"Uh-huh."

He stared for a moment longer before reaching down and taking the bag from Katy. "Go on, both of you, go in the garden. We'll be right out."

Katy moved toward the kitchen and the back door leading to Sienna's back yard. Holly looked at them each in turn before huffing and following her sister. Sienna shifted from one foot to the other.

"What's going on?" Jack's gaze traveled over her face, then cut to the shop door and back again. "Is everything all right?"

The fleeting thought to lie, to spare him the weight of her indecision rose up inside her. The man's life already teetered on the edge of a very wobbly precipice thanks to his ex-wife.

"Sienna?"

Her resistance to tell him the truth dissolved as she drowned in the care shining from his eyes. She relaxed her shoulders and said, "Bad day."

"What's happened?"

"I've been decorating." She tilted her head toward the shop room. "In there."

"And?"

"And it got me thinking. I don't want to cause you more hassle, but I have to do this. For me."

"And that's why you're standing there looking at me like I'm about to have some sort of breakdown?"

"I feel guilty, okay?" She brushed past him and strode to the shop door. Opening it, she said, "Why don't you see for yourself?"

He quirked an eyebrow, a smile pulling at his lips. "Is it that bad?"

Sienna met his smile and expelled a heavy breath in relief. "No." She stared at his profile as he strolled around the space.

"It's looking good." He faced her. "It looks great."

"Wow. Then I'm hazarding a guess from this reaction, and the balloons, you've had a change of heart?"

He walked slowly toward her, and when Sienna saw the predatory look in his gaze, her stomach flipped.

Taking her hands, he said, "I've had enough worrying about what will or won't happen. Why don't we just see what happens with the shop and…us? If you want *us*, of course."

His voice was a soft caress, and his breath warmed her lashes. As the smell of him drifted toward her and threatened to take her under, he brushed his lips against hers.

Sienna couldn't move as his mouth covered hers, only stared at his closed eyes. What the hell had happened to him?

After a second, he pulled away. Her heart raced, her mind whirled. *Oh, God.* Having him look at her the way he was now was worse than having him mad at her.

"The twins," she squeaked out. "Let's go and check on the twins."

She turned and rushed toward the kitchen. She needed air. Lots of air. Yanking on the back door, Sienna stepped out into the yard. She swallowed hard, steadfastly watching Holly and Katy play a game of tag. Half of her wanted them to leave. The other half desperately wanted them to stay.

As Jack's footsteps sounded behind her, an odd loneliness crept over her shoulders and lay there heavy and uncomfortable. She should ring Kelsey. That's whom she relied on…not Jack.

How could they start something? He lived next door. He was a *father…*

He came up beside her and leaned his forearms on the balustrade. "Sorry."

Sienna swallowed against the dryness in her throat. "Don't be."

"I shouldn't have kissed you. Shouldn't have asked you about us. I…you were standing there looking like you didn't know whether to laugh or cry. I didn't mean to —"

"I liked the kiss, Jack. I liked it just as much as the first time."

"Good," he said, smiling, and pulled her into his arms.

At first she resisted, then surrendered. She laid her cheek against his chest. His heart beat against her ear, matching the rapid thump of her own.

He tightened his arms around her. "I'm going to start taking control and do what I want with my life. I can't keep blaming myself for Martina's demise. And if she *was* coming here, she'd want me to know. She'd come to Potterford and knock on my door. Enjoy watching me squirm. But if she wants to see the girls, I'll deal with it."

Sienna breathed in the scent of him. Pine, fresh air, and solidarity flowed into her lungs and through her blood, making her want to stay that way forever.

Yet she pulled away, forcing herself to withdraw. He didn't need another crackpot woman in his life when he hurt so much already. She was meant to be his strength, not the other way around.

"Then from now on," she said, "we take everything — including us — one small step at a time. Agreed?"

"Agreed."

Sienna wrapped her arms around herself in an effort to gain the same sense of peace she'd found in Jack's. She wiped the tears from her cheeks and looked across the yard. Side by side, the twins' faces were etched in identical expressions of concern and shock. Well, kind of identical. Holly's eyes were narrowed whereas Katy's were wide.

"We've got an audience." She pulled back her shoulders and plunged her hands into the front pockets of her jeans. "You'd better go."

Right then, Jack's phone rang. He looked at the display and pressed *talk*. "Hi, Mum. I'm just next door. I'll be right there. Yep. Okay. I'll be two minutes." He snapped the phone shut. "My mum's here. She's taking the kids out for a burger or something and then having them overnight."

Sienna stared dumbfounded. No kids for the night. Jack. Her. Alone…

She cleared her throat. "Right. Great. They'll love that."

He winked. "So will I."

What does that mean? She gave a nervous laugh.

"So I'll see you in half an hour or so?"

"But — " She tipped her head back to look at his profile as he pulled on a smile and waved at the twins.

"Girls, come on!" he called. "Grandma's next door."

Sienna's breath left her lungs in a rush. "Jack, you really don't have to come back here, you know. Go out, have some fun. I'll be fine."

"I know you will, and I'd rather have my fun with you than anyone else right now."

"Oh."

Sienna's nipples tightened as attraction tugged hard at her insides. Fear of losing control pushed her usual flirtation shield back into place—it clanked in her head. Coward.

The girls trundled onto the decking and stood beside them. Jack took their hands.

"I'll see you in a while," he said.

Sienna put finishing touches on the window and door trim, tossed the angled brush into a tray, and tucked the hair sticking to her face back into her ponytail. Now that she took a step back and studied her shop room, optimism lingered around the periphery of her mind. Her worries about making things harder on the girls and Jack had been unfounded—the touch of Jack's lips against hers had told her he was going to try. Whatever *try* meant.

Did it mean with her? The shop? Their friendship?

She shivered as her smile broke. The heat between them was bordering on combustion. They were adults. They both knew what was inevitable.

That's if she wasn't just a nymphomaniac and he a good stand-up kind of guy, of course.

The front doorbell rang, and Sienna stood paralyzed. He'd come back.

Excitement skittering over her skin, she smoothed her hair back and walked—forcibly quashing the desire to run—to the door. She took a breath and pulled it open.

"Hi, Jack—" Her breath caught. "Holy mother…"

He quirked his eyebrow. "Told you I'd be back."

Sienna smiled as she relished the bare expanse of Jack's bronzed chest before meeting his eyes, shining like two blue crystals in the fading sun. She prayed her tingling nipples weren't visible through her cotton T-shirt. "You did."

Jack held up a screwdriver and small tool box. "And I'm at your service."

"Then you'd better come in."

He moved past her, his chest flat and strong, almost touching her breasts. Sienna stared wide-eyed at his denim-clad butt before it disappeared into the shop room. She shut the door and stumbled back against it.

"Oh, Lord, am I in trouble."

When she entered the shop room, Jack's hands were splayed on his hips, further expanding pectorals that screamed for a smothering of Champagne Lick.

Her turn to arch an eyebrow. "Is it hot out there or something?"

His grin added to the light that flickered on behind his baby blues and did little to dampen the rush of arousal warming Sienna's blood.

"You could join me if you like." He wiggled his brow.

"What?"

He nodded toward her chest. "Get rid of the T-shirt."

Heat flared at her cheeks. What the hell had gotten into the man? One minute he thought of nothing except the safety of his girls. Now there was such a huge glint in his eyes, it was clear those girls were the very *last* thing on his mind. Her center twitched. May the devil punish her, but God, it felt good to have him look at her that way.

She grinned. "Who are you? What have you done with Jack Beaton? You know, the stuck-up pain in the ass who lives next door?"

He laughed and held up his hands. "Hey, I'm just making a suggestion. That's all."

"I'm serious. What happened in between you leaving the house less than an hour ago and now?" She panned her sight one more time over his phenomenal pecs and washboard stomach. The man was built. "Not that I'm complaining. Just concerned."

He put the tool box and screwdriver down and took a step toward her. "Like I said before, I've come to a decision to take control of my life, and that includes not letting it plow over yours. You don't deserve my worries becoming yours, and you don't deserve me banging on about the twins like you're going to strip their innocence the minute my back's turned."

Her entire body yearned with the need to touch him, to feel the weight of that rock-hard body against her. The look in his gaze was unmistakable. Dangerous. A look Sienna was pretty sure reflected in her own.

"Wow, I'm liking the new Jack."

He looked around the room. "I want to help. For as long as you want me. I'm going to do everything I can to make it up to you for being an idiot." He turned to her. "I like you, Sienna. A lot. I don't want to throw more problems into your life."

As he brushed some hair from her face, Sienna tried not to shiver — or even cry. Jack cared. She saw it in his eyes, felt it in his fingers.

"You make me laugh," he continued with a warm smile. "You make me look at things differently. You make things better."

The words stuck. She didn't know what to say. In that moment, she knew Jack was a man with the potential to sweep her up and have her beg for mercy. That notion terrified the hell out of her, yet her body screamed for him. She opened her mouth to respond, searching her deadened brain for a witty comeback, a smart reply to get him to step back and open the space sizzling like a frying pan between them.

"At last, no words." He winked. "I guess I've finally left you speechless."

Sienna tried and failed to drag out a single syllable as Jack walked across the room. He glanced at the shelving on the floor and then surveyed the walls. Where the hell was he going? If he thought he could wind her up, making her all hot and ready, only to walk away…

"Are you going to just stand there?" he threw over his shoulder. "The sooner we get started, the sooner we can get to the good stuff." He opened his tool box and picked up a level and a carpenter's pencil. "You ready to mark the walls for the shelves? We work together and we'll be done in no time."

She gawked at his tanned, broad, and ridiculously muscular back before licking her lips. Her body vibrated.

And for the first time in a long time, Sienna did what she was told. She handed him a layout of the room she'd drawn, showing where she wanted the shelves to be, as her father's told-you-so laughter rang inside her head. Sienna grinned. Jack Beaton wouldn't know what hit him when she found her legs again.

Chapter Twelve

Jack straightened and surveyed his handiwork. Two walls of shelving were complete and ready for merchandise. He looked at Sienna, and his body instantly responded. She'd twisted her ponytail up into a messy knot at the back of her head, revealing her slim neck and its perfect curve to her shoulders.

Despite the drop in temperature and the breeze coming through the windows, she'd lifted her T-shirt and knotted it beneath her full breasts. The sheen of perspiration glistening on her skin added to her sexiness. The blatant challenge made his jeans feel tight. Damn, she was good.

He smiled. Hadn't he started this particular game? Maybe—and he'd make damn sure he finished the winner too.

"Ready to call it a day?" He kept his eyes on her as she lifted her head; the knife she used to cut open boxes glinted in her hand.

"Sure. I feel like I've gone ten rounds with a heavyweight boxer." She rubbed her free hand over the back of her neck.

"Then it's time to close the door on this lot and start again tomorrow. We'll have everything done and ready for your party in no time."

She put the knife on top of a stack of boxes and came to stand beside him. When she placed her hand on the small of his back, Jack tensed. And when she smoothed it in a soft circular motion over and over, he nearly exploded. *Electric.* That was the word that popped into his mind as his skin burst with goose bumps and his cock pulsed.

He dipped his chin to her, and she stared up at him, her deep brown eyes shining. "You're a good man," she said. "Thank you."

Jack swallowed against the dryness in his throat. "You're welcome."

He tried to look away, tried to refrain from touching his finger to her jaw, tried not to draw an invisible line from there to the curve of her neck down to her collarbones — but did it anyway. She shivered.

"Let's go through to the back garden." She tossed him a flirtatious glance from beneath lowered lashes before hurrying out of the door and into the hallway like she had power flames on her shoes.

Jack grinned. There was something entirely wrong but so damn right about spooking her. And she *was* spooked — no matter how hard she tried to hide it under her façade of self-control. He was a journalist. He'd seen through more practiced masks than hers.

With his heart beating hard and his libido working overtime, Jack gathered his tools and put them by the front door. Then he picked up the dirty paintbrush and tray and walked out of the room. When he reached the kitchen, it was empty. Heading for the sink, he ran the water and cleaned off as much paint as he could in case more touch-ups were needed in the morning.

The sink colored with diluted paint, and he watched it spiral down the drain, his mind filled with Sienna, his girls, and the whole new turn his life was taking. A bang on the window made him jump and look up.

Sienna held up a glass of white wine outside the window and pulled her face into a goofy expression.

Jack laughed. "What?"

"Get your butt out here," she shouted. "I've plenty of brushes we can use in the garage. Leave that one to ruin. I don't care. Come on. It's a gorgeous evening."

He didn't need telling twice. Especially seeing she'd not pulled that damn T-shirt out of its knot yet. Tossing everything into the sink, Jack filled it with warm water and rushed outside like a prepubescent teenager about to cop his first feel of a breast.

She offered him the wine. "Dusk is falling, Blue Eyes. Why don't we sit on the swing and watch the sun go down? After that, I might think about buying you takeout to say thanks for all your hard work."

Jack clinked his glass to hers. "Sounds like a plan."

They walked to a long three-seater swing, and Jack lowered into it beside her; the swing moved softly backwards. He stared ahead at the horizon. "Wow."

The sky bled into the shades of pink and purple that now covered Sienna's shop walls, blurring the line where the sky ended and the sheep-dotted hills began.

"And my mother wonders why I won't leave," Sienna whispered.

Jack took a sip of wine, controlling the need to take her hand, which lay so tantalizingly close to his. She appeared so delicate but was a damn firecracker inside. The combination was irresistible. He liked her, admired her, and feared her in equal measure. Her eyes told him she felt the same way, but there was a barrage of reasons for them not to overstep this silent mark of friendship. It was as though Martina, the girls, his mother-in-law, even Sienna's dead father all stood between them, telling them to behave, to maintain control, to not touch each other or sit together in the twilight as they were.

Was that fair? Was it what she wanted? What he wanted?

"Sienna—"

"Jack—"

They laughed as their spoken names blended into one in the soft silence.

Jack nodded. "You go first."

She exhaled. "I just wanted to say I'm happy you're here. I'm even happier you've decided to trust me and not quarrel about the shop anymore. I won't let you down. I never let anyone down if I can help it."

"I believe you."

She smiled. "Good. I know I said I don't do kids, but your two…" She shook her head. "Your two are kind of special."

"They are, huh?" As he grinned, a faint blush colored her cheeks.

"Yep, somehow the pair of them have snuck under my armor. I'm not happy about it, but there you are."

"Well, if it's any conciliation, they like you, too. A lot." He took a sip of wine as the panic of the other night flashed through his heart. "I have never known Katy to do anything like leave the house on her own. Not even when things were bad with Martina."

Sienna frowned. "But wouldn't the girls have only been two by the time she walked out? Katy couldn't have left the house at that age even if she'd wanted to."

"You don't know kids, do you?"

Her cheeks grew redder. "What does that mean?"

Touching her forearm, he said, "Hey, it's not an attack. Just before we split up, I came home from work one night to find Martina slumped on the settee, half-drunk. The front door was wide open. Either one of the girls would've wandered out of there eventually without thinking twice."

"God, Jack." She cupped her hand to his jaw. "I'm so sorry you had to go through that kind of worry."

The air all around them fell silent. Jack's heart pounded in his ears as he studied Sienna's beautiful face. Before he could stop himself, he put his drink down on the low table in front of them and slid his hand across the length of thigh revealed beneath her short skirt. Her breath caught, but he kissed her anyway. Every nuance of tension left his body and drained away, leaving him unable to think or care about anything but Sienna.

He gripped her soft skin, increased the pressure of his kiss. She seemed to tense up with hesitation, but Jack kissed her deeper. After another beat of his heart, her body slumped against him as though defeated, and the tip of her tongue found his. Jack poured his entire being into that kiss, let her know he meant it, that she mattered.

Who knew if this would happen again? If, when they drew away, she'd tell him he'd lost his mind and he'd tell her the same.

The clink of her glass on the table and the feel of her hand coming up to grip the back of his neck spoke volumes. Her fingers scored up his nape and into his hair, fanning the flames of desire ripping through his body. He'd forgotten about this…need, desire, rush of want. Sobriety wasn't going to come any time soon, and he hoped the hangover wouldn't be too harsh to handle.

Kissing her deeper, he took more of what he wanted. Her thigh was hot beneath his hand as he inched it over the curve, moving between her legs. Her lips left his on a gasp.

Her eyes were closed as she tipped her head back, revealing that damn sexy neck as his for the taking. He leaned forward to discover and taste the barely-there scent of perfume she must have sprayed on naked and alone that morning. That notion sent his senses soaring, his need rushing. He caressed the soft silken skin inside her leg.

His cock ached under its tightened restraint of denim as Sienna trembled. Jack hesitated. He wanted to go further, discover more of this amazing woman who lived next door, but he wouldn't unless…

"Touch me, Jack," she sighed.

He lifted his head from her neck. Her huge brown eyes were glazed with lust but totally aware and beautiful.

"This is crazy," he said, the need for her winding tightly inside his gut.

"That's why I'm not going to think. We can think anytime. Not now."

So he plunged his tongue into her mouth, and she welcomed it. Her lips were soft like silk but firm. Jack held her tighter as she kissed him back with a ferocity that seemed to demand more. Keen to oblige, he slid his fingers inside her panties, felt the smooth slick of moisture and lost his mind. She groaned, and he moved back, wanting to see her, needing to see if she wanted him as much as he did her.

Her eyes were closed to his scrutiny, but she clutched one of her breasts in her hand, her mouth open. Jack couldn't remember seeing a woman so confident in her sexuality. So open, bare, raw. She trusted him — in that moment, it was as clear as if she'd said the words. They were alone, and whatever happened, this would be their memory.

Returning to feast on her neck, Jack massaged her hardened nub, and she writhed against him, inviting him inside. Squeezing his eyes shut, the urge to satisfy her, to have her call out his name in the quiet semi-darkness rose up inside him. His erection actually hurt; he couldn't remember wanting a woman so much or feeling such urgency of a woman wanting him.

With one hand gripping her neck, he plunged two fingers deep inside her. Her heavy lids opened and her mouth dropped wide. Her harried breathing was like an airborne aphrodisiac coursing through the pores of Jack's skin and into his blood. He was in over his head, and he gritted his teeth to control his own desire to come right then and there.

She was his for the taking. He rubbed and pushed, massaged and teased. Her excitement slipped between his fingers, and Jack's need to have Sienna pummeled through him at a hundred miles an hour — this woman could make him live again.

"Jack, I'm going to come."

Pride surged through him. "Do it. Let yourself, Sienna. I want you to."

She reached for his zipper, but he trapped her hand there. "No, this is about you. I want you to take it all. There will be other times. God, let there be other times." The breath left his lungs.

"Oh, God."

Her hand dropped from her breast to grip the cushion beside her. Her other hand clutched his bicep as her muscles tightened around his fingers. Jack kissed her, silently telling her he was so very, very afraid but so damn loath to ever leave her alone again. The shudder of her orgasm was all the permission he needed to stay. Right there. With her.

Sienna sat back in Jack's arms as the night closed in around them. Their half-empty takeout dishes lay strewn across the table by their knees, their plates wiped clean, and their bellies full. She couldn't remember feeling so scared yet liberated. The fact she'd shimmied back into Jack's arms so carelessly and he'd drawn his legs over hers as though they did this every night was neither lost on her nor taken for granted.

Were they together now? A couple?

She wrinkled her nose. God, he'd just brought her to orgasm, and now she debated whether they were together or not. What sort of woman was she? He might have had his arms around her body, his warm, soft lips nibbling her ear at the moment…but tomorrow? Tomorrow was going to be damn awkward when the twins came home and fatherhood slammed Ol' Blue Eyes back to reality.

"I know what you're thinking, you know." His breath whispered along her earlobe.

Sienna shivered involuntarily and smiled. "What are you? A mind reader now?"

"No, but I feel as though I've known you for three years rather than three weeks."

Three weeks? She'd let a guy massage her to orgasm, in the open air of her back porch, and she'd only known him three weeks?

"Please, don't say that out loud." Covering her face, she groaned into her hands. "That makes me sound like such a cheap—"

"Sexy. Gloriously sexy woman." Jack kissed the sensitized skin just beneath her earlobe and continued lower. "It makes you a woman who coerced a guy out of his blackened, doomed, and pessimistic world. Nothing more. Nothing less."

Sienna's nipples leapt to attention when he teased his teeth and tongue over her shoulder. His hand gently caressed her breast through her T-shirt.

"Jack, stop."

He froze, his hand still at her breast, his lips still on her shoulder. She hadn't meant to sound so abrupt, so cold, but it had come out into the night air like a warning. His hand slowly slipped away, and he sat back yet pulled her with him, his hand smoothing up and down her upper arm instead.

"I know what this looks like, Sienna, but I'm not the kind of man who…gets physical with a woman and then tosses her aside. I promise."

She offered a coy smirk. "I'm not the kind of woman who goes around letting men do what you just did either."

Pressing a kiss to her hair, he said, "Good."

"But this…thing between us is moving at the rate of a freight train, and I need to catch my breath, okay?"

Silence. Doubt over what she meant to him—and fear of what he could come to mean to her—beat like a drum inside Sienna's chest. Jack's children set the pace even higher.

"You're right," he eventually replied. His fingers gripped her arms, and he gently eased her forward so he could swing his legs around and sit up. "I haven't a clue what we're supposed to do next either. I didn't expect this to happen. Not at all. At the same time, now it's happening, I feel as though we need to ride with it."

Sienna turned to sit beside him, and they stared into the darkness. "I'm not saying no, but…I don't know if I'll be any good at this. I don't know if I can let you in and certainly don't know if I can let Holly and Katy in. I have…stuff going on."

He huffed out a laugh. "You say that like I don't."

Sienna looked at him. "I know about your stuff. You don't know about mine."

"Are you talking about your dad?"

Sienna lifted her shoulders. "Partly…maybe. When he died, I changed. I loved him more than life itself, so the fear of losing Mum as well, of not being there for her, kind of took over. Now I can't *not* be there for her. I know it doesn't make sense, but if we get into this and I lose you…"

Jack took her hand and raised it to his lips, kissing her knuckles. "Hey, like you said. One step at a time. Neither of us has to make any promises right now. I just…like being with you. Why don't we go with that for now?"

She smiled, her shoulders relaxing. "How did you get to be so sensitive? Aren't guys supposed to be blind-dumb about this sort of thing?"

"I'm not your usual kind of guy."

"You got that right." Sienna bit her lip as the red-hot memory of her orgasm thundered straight back to her nether regions. She looked away and mentally fanned herself. "So you have your stuff. I have mine. I think the best thing to do is say we'll take this as it comes. Deal?"

"Deal."

She leaned against him. "What a duo of tortured souls we are, huh?"

He touched his finger to her chin. "Tortured and honest. As long as we're honest, no one gets hurt."

Her body responded to just that feel of his finger at her chin, and she examined his handsome face. "I'll never lie to you, Jack."

His finger slipped from her chin. "I know that. This is my problem. Trust. Trusting myself. Trusting others. I was an idiot to not be there for my family when I knew Martina was struggling. I don't want to make that mistake with anyone ever again."

"You won't."

He released a tremulous breath and drained his glass. "I've spent the past two years thinking it would just be the twins and me, but you've changed that. I want a life past my ex-wife and the mistakes I've made. If I'm ever going to move on…let my kids move on, I have to take a risk."

"Same here."

For a long moment, neither of them said anything. He studied her face in a way that made Sienna feel as though she was the single most beautiful woman in the world. If she could bottle that look, she swore she could sell it in the shop for a hefty profit. He lifted her hand from his leg and pressed a lingering kiss to her palm.

"When I saw you crawling along the garden that first day, it was like someone punched me straight in the gut. I thought…" He smiled, his eyes lighting with amusement. "I thought…wow. Then we started talking, and I struggled to think at all."

Her heart melted.

"But I was right to do what I did," he continued. "To back off. To try to fight my attraction to you given all that's happened in my life and what could still be at stake. Now I'm sitting here with you in the dark, wondering when I can kiss you again."

Sienna smiled. "Right now if you want."

He leaned forward, and his delicious mouth covered hers. The frantic need that had rushed her senses when he'd touched her before now gave way to something softer, deeper; it was as though they were silently vowing a pact. The hair at Sienna's nape and across her arms prickled.

But then she felt her father. Felt the violence of his death, saw his open casket at the funeral, and worse, the anguish on her mother's face when she'd dropped to the kitchen floor and mewed like a wounded animal once she'd heard he was dead.

Sienna pulled back, but Jack smiled at her before they both watched the moon disappear behind the clouds. On a long inhale, she asked herself again: Could she really start something with Jack? A man who had so much baggage she needed a shopping trolley to help him carry it?

She had to. She couldn't stop this with him even if she wanted to.

Chapter Thirteen

The following morning, Jack stood outside Sienna's house and looked up at the drawn curtains of what he assumed was her bedroom.

He'd left the night before with his lips swollen from kissing her. After such an explosive start, they hadn't progressed past lip and tongue action again. That's not to say their sexual restraint hadn't lingered like a lit stick of dynamite between them, crackling and sparking hotter and hotter. Yet the confessions of their mutual fears had slowed things down, and now, as Jack knocked on her door for a second time, he couldn't wait to start today's slow burn.

No answer.

He glanced at the car. Holly and Katy watched him through the window, both sitting forward in their car seats, expectancy on their faces. He waved. Katy waved back, but Holly gestured for him to come back to the car. He raised his finger, indicating he'd be one more minute. Stepping back from the door, Jack cupped his hands around his mouth.

"Sienna!" he yelled. "Wakey-wakey!"

Two seconds later, the curtains snapped back, and Sienna stood scowling, her glare trained on his face. Pushing open the window, she leaned out. "If someone ignores knocking at their door, it means go away."

"You were ignoring me?"

"Yes. What's the matter with you, banging on my door like a damn caveman at this time in the morning?"

With her beautiful face devoid of makeup and her hair all mussed and sexy, she looked gorgeous. Grinning, Jack swallowed at the sight of her nipples jutting through her thin cotton tank top. Hot damn.

Wishing he could take the girls back to his mum's so he could pound up Sienna's staircase, two steps at a time, Jack cleared his throat. "You're running late. Get dressed."

She frowned. "Running late for what? It's Saturday, and I'm planning on spending the whole day face-down on my pillow."

"You're not going to break your promise, are you?" He lifted an eyebrow. "Not after I promised the girls."

Her gaze flicked behind him and hovered for a moment before she ducked away from the window out of sight.

Smiling, Jack called after her, "Sienna!"

A few seconds passed before she reappeared at the window wearing a pink robe. She pulled it tight with no idea her breasts were now round and inviting through satin. Jack pursed his lips together. What was the use in telling her? She'd be embarrassed, and the view was fantastic.

She leaned her hands on the windowsill. "What promise?"

"Don't you remember?"

Her eyes narrowed. "No, I don't remember making you any promises. Least of all one that involves you shouting on my front lawn at eleven o'clock in the morning while your kids stare at me through the car window like I've grown an extra head."

"Go and get changed," he said, laughing. "Trousers are probably better than a skirt."

"What?"

"In fact, jeans."

"Where are we going? I mean, *if* I decide to give in to this obvious, child-induced blackmail."

"Lodge Park."

Her eyes stretched to manic proportions, and she flung her hands out, waving them back and forth, the robe forgotten. It gaped wide open.

"No, no, no. There's no way you're getting me inside any theme park. Not now. Not ever."

He grinned. "Ten minutes." Jack headed back to the car. When he glanced back at her window, she was gone.

Smiling, he slid into the driver's seat. "Sienna's just getting changed, girls. She won't be long."

"Is she really coming with us?" Katy asked. "Really?"

"Yep."

"She needs to put something on her boobies."

Struggling not to laugh out loud, Jack spun around in his seat. "Holly, that's enough."

Katy giggled while her sister scowled and crossed her arms. "I could see them."

"Enough." Jack faced the windshield, his smile wide.

Fifteen minutes later, the girls had devoured a bag of chips, but finally Sienna's front door opened. Jack let out a low whistle through his teeth at the sight of her. Dressed in illegally tight white jeans, a dark blue silky shirt, and ballet pumps, she looked carelessly phenomenal. Her long brown hair was tied back with a blue and white scarf; a tote bag swung from her shoulder.

Fixing her eyes on his, she strolled down the driveway and yanked open the passenger door. Her butt slid into the seat.

"Good morning, ladies." She turned between the seats to look in the back. "Is this trip Daddy's idea or yours?"

"Daddy's."

"Mine."

No prize for guessing which response came from which daughter.

Sienna huffed. "Hmm, thought as much." Pinning Jack with her eyes again, she said, "Right, let's get this show on the road. If I throw up at any point, it's entirely your fault."

"You'll be fine." Jack gunned the engine. "I promise we won't be going on anything more testing than the spinning teacups."

Sienna groaned and squeezed her eyes closed. "I hate the spinning teacups."

"We need to have some fun. We're starting over."

"Theme parks are not fun. They're torture. Now, if we're talking fun…" She lowered her voice. "Last night was more my cup of tea."

At the spark in her eyes, Jack's groin flickered to life, and his imagination plunged into overdrive. Where had the man gone who didn't want all the sex? Abducted by an invisible force the moment his lips covered hers, that's where.

He coughed and shifted in his seat. "Like I said, spinning teacups are high on the list of favorites."

Her eyes lit with very sexy triumph before she slumped down in her seat, dropped her sunglasses over her eyes, and crossed her arms like Holly. "I can hardly wait."

Shaking his head, Jack pulled away from the curb as the girls' cheers bounced around the car and Sienna dropped her head to the side window.

The monstrosity that was the teacup ride rumbled to a stop under Sienna's backside. She glanced at Jack and quickly looked away. The man grinned at her with the glee of a sadomasochist. He'd pay for this in ways he didn't have a damn clue about yet. Slow, torturous, and undoubtedly sexual…

"Ah, you're smiling at last."

Sienna snapped her head around and glared at him; her betraying smile disappeared. "If only you knew why, Blue Eyes. If only you knew why."

His eyes glimmered as he quirked an eyebrow. "Sounds promising."

"Oh, it's promising, all right."

The ride gave a final jolt, and people to their left and right leapt from the teacups, apparently eager for the next installment of self-inflicted torture. Katy's small hand slipped into Sienna's.

"I want to ride the bumper cars with you." Her sky-blue eyes shone with irresistible and very practiced persuasion. "Holly can go with Daddy."

Bumper cars? Um…that would be a no. Sienna's indignation pulsed against her temples and shot a bolt through her left eye just for the hell of it. They walked down the wooden steps of the ride and onto solid and long-awaited asphalt. "I feel a bit dizzy after the teacups, sweetie. I think I'll sit the next one out."

"We never get to go on the bumper cars because we only have Daddy."

Sienna's heart turned to mush, and the fight dribbled out of her. What was she supposed to say to that?

"Fine, fine." She smiled. "Let's go find the bumper cars."

"Yay!" Katy clapped her hands and did a little jig.

Sienna looked at Jack. He mouthed a *thank you* and took off in the lead, swinging Holly—happy for once, judging by the breadth of the smile on her face—onto his shoulders. The smells of cotton candy and toffee apples suffused Sienna's senses as they walked past the food stalls. The clang of metal meeting metal and pellets being shot from dummy rifles mixed with the chorus of triumphant cheers all around them.

So this is what family fun feels like when you are an adult. Sienna pressed her free hand to the jumble of nerves in her stomach. It didn't matter how much she told herself she was in control of the situation, her nerves continued to soar. If this went wrong…if Jack walked away or something happened to him or the twins, where would that leave her?

She'd vowed never to let emotional attachment burrow through her protective walls, yet it felt so damn good being there. So good holding Katy's hand and watching Jack walk ahead of her with Holly giggling on his shoulders, his face relaxed and happy.

Sienna's shoulders slumped as her last trickle of resistance to the day dissolved. Even though her head still spun from the brutality of the teacups, she couldn't deny the satisfaction running through her veins like liquid balm. She wanted Jack and the girls to find a way for this to work for all of them—including her. She wanted their bright light in her life after existing in the semi-darkness for too damn long. Never had she felt so optimistic about her future. The time was right. Jack was right for her.

So, if further down the line, Jack did want to walk away…she'd let him go. No one should have to do anything before they were ready, and in the meantime, she could at least enjoy the time she had with him now.

Sienna squeezed Katy's hand and smiled. "After we ride the bumper cars, we'll tell Daddy we want a cheeseburger, chips, and hot apple pie to follow. What do you think?"

Katy grinned. "Okay."

"Good girl," Sienna replied with a wink.

Jack spun around with Holly screaming high above him. Maybe a kids' theme park wasn't so bad after all. If Sienna could endure this, her childfree future didn't feel so entirely set in stone. Her mother had always told her it only took one man to change a woman's mind about becoming a mother. Maybe she was right.

Ten minutes later, Sienna sat in a red-and-black bumper car, food now the last thing on her mind. Katy was securely strapped in beside her, and dance music vibrated at a hundred decibels through their eardrums. Yet Sienna's anticipated dread of the bumper cars evaporated the moment she slid into the seat. Grinning like a maniac, she gripped the steering wheel. Jack's punishment was going to start a damn sight earlier than her planned bedroom scenario.

The bell rang for lift off, and she slammed her foot on the accelerator.

Jack spun off ahead of her, and as Sienna raced after him, Katy giggled like she might pee herself any second. Sienna hesitated. Would she? She glanced at Katy and shrugged. If she peed, it was already worth it to see the glee on the little girl's face right then. Turning back, she zoomed in on her target. Now she'd show Jack who was boss. Her father had taught her a lot of things, and to ride a bumper car with aplomb was right up there with flossing her teeth every day.

A crop of Jack's glossy dark hair showed above the headrest as she neared. Sienna lined up perfectly with his rear bumper, and then *bam!* Holly screamed, and Jack cursed. Katy loved every second of the impact, judging by her yell of "Yee-haw!" Victory bubbled inside Sienna like she'd piped the post at the Monaco Grand Prix. She watched Jack tailspin to the side and gave him the queen's wave as she and Katy cruised smoothly past. Jack and Holly's shocked faces were a snapshot for the family album.

Sienna's laughter was short-lived, however. Jack's shock quickly evolved into vengeance.

"Uh-oh." Katy hunkered lower in her seat, her little fingers gripping her seatbelt as though her life depended on it.

"It's all right. It's just a game. They won't—"

Jack came at her, and Sienna slammed her foot down hard. She tried to swerve, but it was too late. Jack had her in his sights like her car was little more than a sitting duck. *Bam!* She and Katy left the seat, and Sienna's sides split clean open. All four of them — Jack, the girls, and her — sat front bumper to front bumper laughing so hard, they were a mess of nothing.

Sienna caught Jack's eye, and she accepted she was in such trouble there was little she could do but surrender. Her heart was his to do with as he would.

The bell rang, announcing the end of the ride, and she got out the car, lifting Katy into her arms without inhibition. Carrying the little girl to the edge, they stepped out onto the surrounding grass. Sienna moved to put her down, but Katy tightened her arms around her neck. She looked into her beautiful eyes.

"You okay, sweetie?"

The little girl nodded. "Perfect."

Sienna swallowed when Katy dropped her head into the crook of her neck. Jack strolled toward her, Holly on his hip, his eyes flitting from Sienna to Katy and back again. He stopped so close, Sienna could see flecks of silver in his blue eyes. Then he leaned forward and kissed her, long and lingering. Its silent meaning curled around her, enveloping her in the reassurance she craved.

They held his girls in their arms as people meandered around them — they might as well have announced by flyover they were dating.

Sienna looked at Holly, and for a split second, pleasure lit like a beacon in the child's cool brown gaze before she blinked and the habitual scowl returned.

"Ugh," Holly huffed.

Sienna smirked. "Too late, sugar. I saw the look in your eyes. You kind of like your daddy kissing me."

The girl crossed her arms. "No, I don't."

"Oh, yes, you do. Now, I'm hungry. Let's go."

Holly hesitated, then smiled. A little one. She unfolded her arms and shrugged. "Okay."

Sienna had started forward when Jack's arm came around her waist. "You should've been disqualified for that first attack, you know." His breath whispered warm across her ear.

"You deserved it for bringing me here in the first place."

"Really? You aren't enjoying yourself?"

She stopped. "Whatever gave you that idea?"

"Well, judging by the width of your smile…" He grinned.

She shrugged. "It's an okay sort of day, I suppose."

"Good." His eyes darkened with desire.

The tension between them soared, as did her need to kiss him good and hard. She cleared her throat. "We'd better…"

With words failing her, Sienna turned on wobbly legs and headed for the smells of frying onions wafting toward them on a perfectly cooling breeze. She couldn't remember ever feeling as happy or free. God, her mother would have a coronary if she could see her carrying a child around the fairground.

She laughed. "Do you know something?"

"What?"

"If my mother finds out we've shared more than one meal together *and* you persuaded me into a theme park, she's going to lock you up and never let you escape Potterford again."

Jack laughed. "It's been that long since you've had a relationship?"

"It's been so long, I think the woman already decided a year ago I was married to my multispeed G-spot, five-tongue clitoral vibrator."

Jack blanched. "Your…"

Sienna laughed again when he whipped his face from one daughter to the other. They were oblivious.

"Chill, Jack. It's all good."

"Yeah, Daddy." Holly sniffed. "Chill."

They all laughed as Sienna led them to the wooden tables and benches set out in front of one of the many burger vans littered barely more than a few feet apart around the park. She reluctantly slipped Katy from her hip onto the seat and sat down beside her. Jack put Holly down opposite them and clapped his hands.

"Okay, burgers all round?"

"Yay!"

He shot Sienna a wink that sent her stomach into a frenzied loop-the-loop before heading for the queue. God, she could sink her teeth into that ass of his every hour on the hour given half a chance. The girls busied themselves playing with the ketchup packets on the table, their giggling drowned out by the beat of Sienna's racing heart.

Jack struck up a conversation with the guy standing in front of him. His demeanor easy, his expression relaxed. There was no trace of the man who'd flipped out when he'd discovered what she planned with the shop. His face was handsome in the bright June sun, his wide shoulders relaxed, his thumbs caught in the front pockets of his jeans.

Sienna sighed. She didn't want the day to end.

Jack then raised his hand as though apologizing to the guy in front of him and pulled his cell phone from his back pocket, still smiling. Within seconds, the smile slipped.

Sienna's own dissolved. She looked to the girls. Blood-red ketchup smeared the table and their hands as the twins laughed, their eyes carefree and alive. Looking back to Jack, Sienna saw he'd left the queue and now stood alone, holding his hand to the back of his neck as he talked into the phone.

After a few minutes passed, the girls had run out of ketchup packets and started on the mayonnaise. Time stood still.

"We need to go."

Sienna jumped at the sound of Jack's voice. Anger stormed like a tornado in his dark blue eyes.

"What is it?"

Not answering her, he turned to Holly and Katy. "For crying out loud. Look at this mess."

Sienna's heart leapt into her throat. "Jack—"

"Didn't you think to stop them?"

She opened her mouth to fling back a response, then clamped it shut. Silently, she stood and snatched some paper napkins from the wooden cutlery box on the table. She wiped Katy's hands as they trembled in hers, tears wobbling precariously at the girl's bottom lashes. Holly's eyes were dry, but the dark red flush at her cheeks reminded Sienna of her own way of dealing with bad things when she'd been the same age…and now.

Jack swiped at Holly's hands, his eyes focused on his task rather than on his daughter. Holly glared at his bent head, her bottom lip quivering. Sienna looked away lest she march over and shove Jack away, telling him exactly what a jerk he was being. It wasn't her place to get involved. And it would be neither welcomed nor appreciated, judging by the thunderous expression on his face.

The day was over. Jack's daughters knew it, and so did she.

With her heart pounding, Sienna avoided looking at him as, one by one, they all rose from the table and walked through the park.

The souvenir shop stood ahead of them, and determination rose inside her. Holly and Katy weren't leaving without something good, something real and tangible to hold in their hands and remember the day wasn't about their unhappy father.

"Wait."

Jack and the twins froze. He looked at her, his eyes blazing. "What? We need to go."

"Not yet."

"Sienna, now."

"I want to buy the girls a gift."

From the corner of her eye, Holly and Katy's gazes lifted to her face, but Sienna kept her focus on Jack. Daring him to challenge her. Daring him to refuse her first request of the day. She'd done everything he'd wanted. Damn, he'd even convinced her she was enjoying herself. She'd make sure his girls went home with something good to hold when they lay in their beds later on, wondering what the hell had happened. One minute happy; the next one sad. The familiar emotion of kids with parents split apart by divorce or death.

"No," he said.

"Yes." She glanced at Holly and Katy as their heads whipped back and forth between her and Jack. "Let them buy something to keep. Today was a good day. They deserve to have something to take home from it."

His jaw clenched and unclenched. She held her nose high. Slowly, Jack's expression softened, and he closed his eyes. "Fine."

Sienna's heart ached when he leaned down and cupped each of his daughter's chins in his hands, his eyes shining with love and apology.

"Would you like Sienna to buy you something from the shop? Am I being Grumpy Daddy?"

Her eyes glassy, Katy looked at Sienna, then Jack. "Uh-huh."

Jack looked to Holly. "Holly?"

She shrugged. "Don't know."

He exhaled. "Come on. Let's go in the shop and spend Sienna's money, okay?"

They didn't rush forward as Sienna had hoped; instead, their steps were heavy…until they walked inside. The flashing lights and fluffy, rainbow-colored palette of merchandise was too much to not seduce even the most disappointed child. Sienna was delighted. The place was her shop on a different level — it supplied in kid language what she did for adults. Dare to enter and you'll leave with something you didn't even know you wanted. She grinned as the twins' hands left Jack's and they ran into the furor right along with the dozens of other kids running everywhere and giving their parents nervous breakdowns.

The moment they were alone, Sienna grasped Jack's wrist and tugged him around to face her. "Who was on the phone?"

He wiped his other hand over his face. His expression said it all.

"And?"

"I told her it wasn't a good time to talk."

"Which means what?"

He shook his head. "Nothing. It means nothing."

Sienna took his hand. "Tell me what you're thinking."

"I'm thinking I hope you've got your credit card at the ready now you've let the twins loose in that store." He pressed a kiss to her forehead and headed into the shop.

Sienna narrowed her gaze and followed. "Men."

Chapter Fourteen

Sienna was drunk. Drunk, drunk, drunk. The launch party had gone from downright rambunctious to out and out X-rated. She should've known how bad things would get when Mrs. McGill and her trio of best friends had turned up dressed in clothes better suited to girls in their twenties. With their slash-neck T-shirts worn so their fluorescent bra straps showed, skirts way too short, and fur-trimmed tiaras on their heads, Mrs. McGill had undoubtedly advertised the closing-down party as a hen night.

Sienna made an effort to focus as she collected more of the "game" paraphernalia she'd thought was such a good idea at the time. Once her mother had whipped off her top, revealing her gray washed-out bra and claiming to sporadically fantasize about Angelina Jolie in a baby-doll, Sienna had realized pretty damn quickly the party had to end. As soon as possible.

Making sure no one watched, she started sneaking the stuff out of the shop room before anyone, including her inebriated mother, could stop her. She hurried into the kitchen as fast as her rubber legs could carry her and dumped the box in a cupboard. Slamming the door, she cringed at the state of the room. It had been a party and a half—Jack had been right to pack the twins off to their grandmother's.

If he saw this, he'd have a coronary: wineglasses and streamers lined the counters. Dildos and phallus-shaped chocolate and candy bars spilled from boxes all over the kitchen table. A blow-up doll sat sentry in one of the chairs, a fake cigar sticking out of her startled O-shaped mouth.

Despite the severity of the situation, a laugh escaped Sienna as she pulled the plug at Dextrous Diana's hip. The doll deflated, looking like Sienna felt. An off-key rendition of Tina Turner's "We Don't Need Another Hero" filtered in through the open kitchen door, and she rolled her eyes. The women needed to leave. Their husbands would no doubt thank Sienna for their current state of feeling half their age when they arrived home — the women themselves probably not so much tomorrow.

Fighting the grin that threatened to break her newly emerged sobriety, Sienna pulled on her sternest expression and marched from the kitchen back into the shop room. She clapped loudly at the doorway.

Nothing. Chaos reigned supreme, no doubt causing Tina Turner to hide in her closet across the Atlantic.

"Ladies!"

Nothing.

"Fine." She strolled behind the counter and hit the *off* button on the iPod.

Everything came to an abrupt standstill, and twenty pairs of glazed eyes turned on her.

"At last." She ignored the expletives and moans and raised her hands. "Party's over, ladies. Your heads are going to be banging tomorrow."

"Hey, that's not all we'll be banging!" came Mrs. McGill's screech.

The room erupted into laughter as the women cheered and slapped each other on the back and ass. No longer able to contain it, Sienna laughed loudly, and she came back around the counter and ushered them, one by one, along the hallway. A hardworking collie rounding up a flock of errant sheep.

Another twenty minutes passed before they were a clear hundred-meter distance away from the house and their screams were at least slightly muffled. Having sobered in the light of her customers' enthusiasm, Sienna winced when her mother pulled her into a bear hug at the end of the driveway. All the while, the taxi Sienna had ordered idled behind her, the meter ticking in all its neon-digital glory.

"Mum—"

"That, my darling girl, was what I call a party." Her mother squeezed tighter, pinning Sienna's arms to her sides as their veins pulsed in outrage. "I didn't want it to end. What a laugh. God, it does the soul good."

Sienna attempted to extract herself. "What would do me good right now is the ability to breathe."

"Oops. Sorry." Her mother released her and slapped her hand over her mouth, smothering a giggle.

Sienna's heart swelled. It was so good to see her mother belly-laughing. Her eyes shimmered, and her face was flushed. She looked… happy. Sienna pressed a kiss to her cheek.

"I'm glad you enjoyed it. Now you need to get in this taxi and go home."

"Aww."

"Now."

"I wanted to meet your neighbor."

Sienna's smile vanished. "No."

Her mother wriggled her eyebrows. "I know he's a looker. Everyone's talking about him."

Sienna glanced at Jack's house. It was in darkness, but she doubted very much he was asleep considering the party had edged out into the yard up until an hour ago, when Sienna had ratcheted up the Congo music and they'd all snaked back inside number sixteen.

"What is *everyone* saying, exactly?" She arched an eyebrow.

Her mother leaned forward, wobbling precariously on her three-inch heels. Her mouth brushed Sienna's ear. "That you and Journo-Stud are an item."

"Journ…" Sienna squeezed her eyes. "God, it's no wonder I can't stop with the nicknames."

"What? Is the name appropriate? Is he as fit as they say he is?"

Sienna's eyes snapped open. "Please don't use words like *fit*. It just sounds—"

"Right? Hey, maybe if you don't want him…" She clutched her breasts and jiggled.

"Okay. That's it. You're out of here." Sienna gripped her mother's elbow and turned her around.

The woman giggled hysterically. "Hey, even I have needs. Just because you're not using your female bits, maybe it's time I started using mine."

"Hey, that's not funny. Dad—"

"Has been gone five years."

Their eyes locked. Apparently, her mother wasn't quite as drunk as she'd made out. Sienna held back from shoving the woman headfirst into the taxi. "I'm not doing this now, Mum. I know what you're going to say."

Her mother's eyes narrowed. "Do you? Do you really, Sienna Ann Lloyd? Do you really see what's right under your nose?"

"Mum—"

"No, you listen to me." Her mother snatched her elbow from Sienna's grip. "I'm told he's one fine-looking man. A man who's got a good job and two little ones. No wife. No woman. Now, what's the deal?"

Her mother was like a wild dingo when she had the chance of a meaty tale between her teeth. Sienna pulled back her shoulders. She'd no doubt go down, but damn if she'd go down without a fight. She was twenty-eight years old, for crying out loud.

"There's no deal. He's nice." She paused. "Even his kids are nice, but—"

The tight straight line of her mother's mouth arced into a smile so broad, her teeth glowed white under the streetlamp. "You're sleeping with him."

"No, I'm not." Heat flared to the surface of Sienna's cheeks. "Who the hell do you think I am? The poor man—"

"Well, if he hasn't done the deed, he's done something to get you all hot under the collar. Have you kissed?"

Sienna glanced toward the taxi, desperation making her palms clammy. Perhaps she was insane, but she felt Jack's gaze on her from his upstairs window. If she turned around to check and her mother saw him there, though, she'd have them both sitting at his kitchen table with a new bottle of wine before Sienna had time to curse.

"No, we haven't kissed. There is nothing going on. Now get in the taxi before it costs me forty quid to take you three miles down the road."

Her mother glanced toward number seventeen, and Sienna's heart picked up speed.

Please don't let him be there. Please don't let him be there…

"Hmm." Her mother studied her. "Fine, but you'd tell me if there was anything going on?"

"Yes. If I thought it worth telling."

The older woman threw her hands up in defeat. "I'll leave you to go to bed then…alone."

"Thank you."

Her mother lifted one foot to get into the taxi but then stopped so abruptly, Sienna bumped into her back on still-drunk legs. "Just one more thing."

"What?" Unease raised the hairs at the back of Sienna's neck. Her mother's eyes were demonic with undisguised glee, and Sienna automatically shot a glance at Jack's house. A curtain twitched upstairs. Damn it.

She looked back at her mother, whose own gaze lingered at Jack's bedroom window. "I was only wondering…well, if there's nothing 'worth telling' about Journo-Stud, if that means you're in the habit of letting *all* men satisfy you on your garden swing seat?"

The pavement shifted beneath Sienna's feet, and she gripped her mother's arm to steady herself. "Kelsey told you."

"Oh, yeah."

"Oh, my God. I'm going to kill her."

"What? It's great. She's so happy for you."

"She won't be so happy tomorrow when I see her. Now get in the car." Sienna covered her mother's head with her hand and pushed her into the taxi. Taking a ten-pound note from her back pocket, she shoved it in the driver's hand. "Number four Marshall Street. Whatever she says to you, don't believe a word of it."

Laughing, her mother pleaded, "Sienna—"

"Bye, Mum." She slammed the car door and stormed back toward the house once the taxi had pulled away. "I'm going to kill Kelsey. Absolutely kill her."

When she reached her front door, she stopped. A thought so ridiculous, so bad, filtered into her mind on a wine-induced haze.

Her temper melted until a warm, no, *hot* glow emanated from her body. She fanned a hand in front of her face. So what if Jack was good with his hands? What was the big deal if her mother and best friend knew she'd had a good time with him a few nights ago? Wasn't that what they'd been telling her to do for years? To get out there and enjoy herself?

Drinks and bravado edged her on as the need to have Jack back on her swing seat rose on a hungry, animalistic heat.

They'd hardly seen each other for a week. After their outing at the park had ended on such a down note, Sienna had tried to persuade him to continue their day out with the girls by having a barbecue night, but Jack had refused. He'd wanted to be alone—or alone with the twins at least. He'd explained his need for solitude wasn't a rejection of her but his automatic way of dealing with things. She'd looked at him long and hard yet only told him to let her know when he was back out of the cave.

Since then, he'd been busy with work and the girls while Sienna had been busy clearing the old shop and preparing the new one. And now, she was preparing for Jack.

Sienna stepped back and peered up at the window with the twitching curtain. Nothing.

But he was in there, and he was alone. She knew it, and he knew she knew it. What if he was up there praying she knocked on his door? What if he was waiting for her buck-naked with a rose between his teeth and petals strewn on the silken covers? Though why on earth would a single man have silken bed covers? Sienna shoved such doubt aside. Jack *would* sleep on silk, oh yeah. And he wouldn't want to be up there getting cold in those sheets, now would he?

Then she thought of the girls. *Damn.* They were gone, but he'd think of them. So, no. Not in his house. Wasn't right. But nothing wrong with them swinging from the chandeliers in *her* house, was there?

Sienna's smile bloomed once more, and hurrying inside, she raced into the kitchen and whipped around, clearing up like a woman possessed. Within minutes, it looked presentable…kind of.

Her heart thundered and her body reawakened with desire. Snatching her Blackberry from the top of the refrigerator, she dialed Jack's number.

"Do you know what time it is?" he mumbled.

Sienna inwardly snorted. Faker! He had *so* been standing at that window, watching her and her mum fifteen minutes ago. Sienna wiggled provocatively and purred (more like slurred) into the phone. "They've gone."

A moment passed. "And?"

"And you'd better get your ass over here if you know what's good for you."

Another moment. "Is that a threat?"

"A promise, Blue Eyes. So you'd better be quick before I change my—"

The line buzzed in her ear.

Sienna clicked the *end call* button and, with a trembling hand, held the phone to her stomach.

Now she'd done it.

Jack grinned and tossed his cell onto his bed. What was a man to do? He hit the bathroom at lightning speed. Ripping off his boxers, he dived into the shower, not even waiting for it to run hot. The cold water hit his bed-warm body, and he sucked in a breath, laughing. He hadn't seen Sienna for a few days, and now he wanted her with a desperation bordering on the insane.

From the slight slur in her voice, it was further evidence the party had gone well. Not that he needed to hear her voice to know. The screeching and laughter, mixed with music from every decade since he'd turned six, had boomed through his walls for the preceding four hours. He hadn't minded…but it had kept him firmly behind the safety of his closed door. Facing a group of inebriated and beyond-excited women didn't bear thinking about.

And now Sienna was alone—the tone of her voice had left little unsaid. Jack smiled. The difference between Sienna after a little wine and Martina consuming a crate-full was incomparable. Giggly, sweet, and more than a little…suggestive, Sienna got his libido soaring. Martina, on the other hand, had sent it fleeing in the other direction on a slipstream of violence, expletives, and nastiness.

Hope for a happy future knotted inside him as Jack soaped his body and washed his hair. Rinsing off, he turned off the shower and stepped out. He dried as quickly as humanly possible before grabbing some clothes from his chest of drawers. He then dressed and whipped a comb through his hair. A quick glance in the mirror and he was ready.

Ignoring the sudden leap of nerves in his stomach, Jack reached for his phone, and it vibrated in his hand. He smiled. Impatient lady.

He pressed *talk* without looking at the display. "Patience, woman."

"Hi, Jack."

He froze. Shock lodged his next breath in his throat, and eyes shut, he lowered to the bed.

"Martina." Had she sensed his momentary ease and called with the need to puncture it immediately?

"How are you?"

He glanced toward his bedroom door, his heart racing. "Fine. On my way out, as it happens."

"At this time? Wow, I guess we've both changed a lot in the last year."

Had that been intended as an insult? He tensed his jaw. Calm. "And what has *you* up so late?" Another drinking binge wouldn't have surprised him, though she did sound coherent enough.

"I know it's rude to phone at this hour, but I haven't been successful at more acceptable times of day, have I? I waited for you to ring back when it was more convenient, but—"

"Right. I'm sorry about that. Since the move I've just been…busy. Settling into the new house and job and everything. I'm guessing for you to be ringing now, you've spoken to your mother."

"Yes. She told me how reasonable you sounded on the phone when you called the other day. She thought it would be okay for me to call."

"I see." The ensuing silence bore down on him, and Jack slumped his shoulders. "How are you?"

"Good. Better."

"Your mum said you've been doing well…I'm happy for you."

Another long moment of silence lingered, and all Jack wanted was to end the call and run next door to Sienna. He'd have given a hundred pounds right there and then to be with her instead of sitting listening to Martina's breath whisper down the line.

"I want to see you, Jack. It's time."

Every nerve in his body stretched taut, and he gripped the phone. "I don't know—"

"I just want to talk. I want you to see how far I've come. It's been a year, and I don't want this impasse between us to go on anymore." She sighed. "Please, Jack."

He stared at a spot on the wall. Just days before, he'd told Sienna he'd deal with Martina when the time came, but so far he hadn't; he'd only avoided her calls. No part of him had been prepared for it to happen this quickly, but he'd delayed the inevitable long enough. Bitterness threatened to choke him, and he cleared his throat. "When?"

Her relieved sigh rasped down the line. "Whenever you want. I'm happy to come to you. Anytime. I've missed you."

Nausea swirled inside him, and he stood. "Let me think about it. I'm not sure I'm ready to do this yet. The twins—"

"I'm not asking you to bring the girls. I understand I lost the right to demand anything from you as far as they're concerned. I'd just like to see you and talk some."

Nodding through his unease, Jack said, "Okay. Give me a day or two, and we'll sort something out."

"You'll call me?"

"I'll call you."

"Thank you."

"Bye, Martina."

"Bye, Jack."

He jabbed the *end talk* button and stood immobile. The silence of the room pressed down on him, and with each passing second Jack found it harder to breathe. Loathing for the woman who'd put the twins through so much despair conflicted with his need to be a bigger man, a better man.

He used to love her. And she had sounded in control again. Normal. The anger that had laced every word she'd spoken for the last year of their relationship and afterward had gone, leaving behind the soft-spoken woman he remembered from years before.

Yet somehow she'd still just ripped out a whole piece of him, exposing it to the infection she'd not given him time to heal from.

He shook his head. No. He wouldn't let her get under his skin again, wouldn't let her crawl under his carefully erected defenses.

The twins and Sienna were his life now. Martina was outside the perimeters of what would and wouldn't happen.

Sienna.

Jack made for the bedroom door and yanked it open. All he wanted was to feel her bare skin against his. Make love to her and let the warmth of her heart and body soothe the pain and make him whole again.

Running downstairs, he grabbed his keys from a side table and stormed out into the night. The cool air hit his face, and he breathed deeply. Everything would be all right. Everything *had* to be all right.

Sienna left the front door open. An invitation (or initiation) into the unknown. She lounged seductively on the stairs, naked but for a sheer baby-doll and four-inch heels. Drunken seduction, when you had access to a room full of lingerie and toys, was pretty much full on. Otherwise, what was the point? That was what she'd been saying over and over in her head like a damn mantra for the last five minutes.

Smoothing her shaking hands over her breasts, she smacked her newly painted lips together. Where was he? Presumably, he'd hung up on her in his haste to get to her, and yet here she was, still sitting by her lonesome twenty minutes later.

Panic galloped through her sobering bloodstream. What if he'd hung up on her in distaste rather than excitement? Shame stung her cheeks and stripped away her nerve, leaving her naked and exposed. Or at least *more* naked and exposed.

No. Jack wanted her. She'd felt it in every kiss, and she'd certainly felt it in his illegally dexterous fingers during the best damn orgasm of her life. God, she wanted another one. She wanted Jack. Even with a houseful of screeching women and her mother, her thoughts had been filled with him and the fact he was alone and childless on the other side of her shop wall.

Perhaps their lives had suddenly and silently separated over the last week, but enough was enough. Hearing his deep, smooth voice tonight for the first time in days had been the flint that lit her now-raging fire. If they allowed the separation to linger, it could be hard for both of them to step back in.

The thud of footsteps approaching the open door sent her heart flying into her throat. Pulling on her sexiest heavy-lidded look, Sienna slid her legs ever so slightly apart. Praying she looked like Sophia Loren in her heyday rather than Eartha Kitt on LSD, she thrust out her breasts and casually leaned back on her elbows.

"You took your time," she purred.

Jack stepped over the threshold and kicked the door shut behind him. Sienna's heart hammered. From her position on the stairs, he looked huge. Huge, muscular, strong, and so unbelievably attractive. Her nipples reached out to him of their own accord.

She was about as in control of this situation as a mouse at a cat dance.

Why wasn't he saying anything?

Sienna's smile faltered as he strode toward her. Dressed in a plain white T-shirt and black jeans, his hair glistened damp from the shower. She felt underdressed—and underprepared. This was a bad idea. What had she been thinking? He was sober. Dressed. Clean. She was naked but for a damn gossamer nightdress, half-drunk, and no doubt smelling of wine, chocolate body paint, and a liberal application of Champagne Lick at her collarbones.

"Um…look, this seemed like a good idea—"

"It is." He cut her off as he leaned his massive bulk over her.

If this was a game, she'd already lost. She fell into the hot-blue fire of his gaze, and her entire body burst into flames. One of his hands slipped around her back and the other under her knees, drawing them together in a single fluid motion. Before she could draw another breath, Jack lifted her into his arms. She looped her own arms around his neck.

"We going somewhere, Blue Eyes?"

"Bed. Now."

"Fine by me." She settled her head in the crook of his neck. He smelled like autumn again. Whatever happened the next day, the next week, month, or year, Sienna would never forget the way Jack Beaton smelled.

As though he already knew where it was on reaching the top of the stairs, he walked straight into her bedroom. The room was dark but for the bolt of moonlight shooting across the carpet. The walls shined silver, her pictures gleaming in the half-light, and the smell from the cranberry candles flickering on her dresser was just enough to be perfect.

Silently, Jack carried her to the bed and laid her down. Sienna settled on the pillows, aware the baby-doll barely covered her lace thong. Yet all her trepidation evaporated as he watched her. He languidly appraised the entire length of her body as he yanked open his jeans and stepped from his shoes. She felt amazing. Sexy, confident, and beautiful. Her nipples ached against the sheer material.

Her gaze dropped to his crotch. His erect penis tented his boxers. A lot. Excitement quivered in her stomach, and her center throbbed.

Jack pulled his T-shirt over his head and dropped it to the floor.

Holy mother of God, the man was just…beautiful. He crawled onto the bed; thick tendons and sinewy muscles rippled as he edged toward her. When his face was level with hers, his eyes danced over her face before he closed them and kissed her. Sienna's lids fluttered closed.

For some reason, she'd expected the same frenzied possession he had exhibited when he'd touched her on the swing seat. This was different. His lips teased soft then hard, and his tongue touched tip-to-tip with hers, sending such loving sensations to every part of her, all feeling in her legs disappeared. She reached up and scored her fingers into his hair. The intensity of their kiss increased, and Sienna jumped when his hand covered her breast. He held it for a second before she relaxed, and his thumb teased her sensitized nipple.

She shivered, her arousal warm in her almost non-existent panties. She was wet already. The man was such a new phenomenon to her. For months, even years, she'd had a barely-concealed nonchalance for any guy who'd shown interest in her, but her feelings for Jack were downright terrifying. As he massaged her breast and lifted his mouth from hers to feed on the curve of her neck, Sienna sent up a silent prayer that God make him hers. That He keep him safe. Protect him from harm. And not let her sabotage this potentially fantastic relationship through fear of the unknown, of a future she had no control over.

"Hey, you're crying."

His soft whisper broke through her thoughts and jolted through her body. She lifted a hand and swiped her fingers under her eyes, waiting for the usual embarrassment and rush of nervous laughter if anyone, including her mother, caught her being vulnerable. It didn't come.

Smiling, Sienna reached up and cupped his stubbled jaw. "I'm just happy. I didn't mean to spoil the moment." She laughed. "I get kind of emotional sometimes. You'll get used to it."

The concern in his eyes deepened. "I don't want either of us to end up getting hurt."

"We won't. Make love to me, Jack."

The word *love* reverberated loud and clear in her mind, and Sienna's stomach tightened. She couldn't possibly be in love—could she? It was madness. This was too much too soon…

"I know this is crazy." His voice broke through her thoughts. "I know this isn't what either of us needs right now, but it's happening. I don't want to toss it aside just because of what-ifs."

The tension left Sienna's body, and she sank further into the mattress, her hand sliding to his neck and pulling his face to hers. She kissed him with everything she had. Branded his lips, scalded his tongue, absorbed the very essence of him.

His hand moved across her collarbones and back again, making her tremble. Then, as though giving in to the inevitable, he exhaled heavily and tugged at the crisscross of ribbon above her breasts. The baby-doll came apart. When he slid his fingers downward, the ribbon slipped from the material, leaving her exposed to her belly button. The flush of cool air against her burning skin was almost more than she could stand.

When he moved his body over hers and lay atop her, Sienna relished the crush of his broad, flat chest against her breasts. Slowly, he lifted his weight onto his elbows beside her shoulders.

"God, I want you," he said just before urgently covering her mouth with his.

The heavy, hot push of his erection pressed down on her clitoris. The scrap of lace and cotton that covered it did nothing to diminish the erotic feel of him, and Sienna's anticipation skyrocketed. She dug her nails into the rock-hard muscle of his shoulders, purposely scraping down his back, then up again and down his biceps. To her satisfaction, his body stiffened under her touch.

Jack made her feel powerful, capable, and deliciously sensuous. He was an amazing man and, God willing, her man. As she pushed against him, he ground his pelvis against her.

"Have you got anything?" she whispered against his mouth.

He lifted away and brushed some fallen hair from her face. "I've got it, but we're nowhere near ready for it."

The ache between her legs and the tingle at her breasts told her otherwise, but who was she to argue? She shivered involuntarily as his gaze stayed on hers and he eased his hand over the dip of her waist, the curve of her hip, and across her thigh. Her legs parted as his fingers played at her core through the lace of her thong.

His smile was slow, confident, and incredibly sexy. "You're soaking wet."

A bolt of stimulation struck her beneath his fingers. "You'd better take them off, then. I don't want to catch cold."

One corner of his smile stretched to a mischievous smirk, and he dropped his face to her breast. Her hand came up and held the back of his head, her eyes closing. Jack pulled her nipple into his mouth, and Sienna concentrated on her breathing as her body heated. He sucked and teased, licked and nipped. She writhed beneath him, her hands smoothing over the broad expanse of his back and up into his hair. Expectancy furled between her thighs as he journeyed lower, featherlight kisses covering her torso and stomach. Sienna curled her toes when his head disappeared out of sight.

Reaching for the headboard above her, she wrapped her fingers around the wrought-iron bars and held on. The string of her thong snapped with a single tug of his hand, and his tongue lapped like a flame of fire against her wetness. As he flicked it back and forth, her mouth drained of moisture.

"Jack."

Sliding his hand down her thigh, he eased her leg farther across the bed, his mouth still busy at her core. She moaned and tossed her head from side to side as his tongue delved deep inside her, his thumb coming round to massage her at the same time. Her body trembled; her mind scrambled.

Opening her eyes, she met his. The raw possession there sent her senses reeling, and as the pressure built, she swallowed. "I want you inside me. I want to see you come."

Ignoring her plea, he feasted further, sucking, licking, teasing, and taking.

"Jack, please."

At last, he moved away. With her eyes closed, Sienna listened to the telltale sound of a condom packet ripping open. Her body buzzing, she resisted reaching down and finishing what Jack had so expertly started. Her patience was rewarded. The bed dipped, and then his lips were on hers again as he moved over her. The heat of his skin against hers sent an electric shock of wanting straight into her heart.

A rush of panic likewise battered around inside her, but Sienna repressed it. She and Jack had the potential to be something big—something good. She wasn't about to let her recent years of reservation take over and ruin it. With her hands gripping Jack's biceps, she pulled him closer. His erection nudged at her opening, and she slid her legs wider, wanting him all.

He slid deep inside like he belonged there, natural acceptance thriving between them. They were meant to be, and now they finally were together. Nothing else mattered.

"Jesus, Sienna."

She smiled, and his baby blues shone with adoration as he stared down at her, his body moving in a slow, perfect rhythm. Scorching sensations blazed at Sienna's core, and impatience soon overtook the peace of the moment. Without a word passing between them, the measured, easy pace heightened quickly, and passion sent every fiber in her body into overdrive.

Sienna lifted her legs and wrapped them around his hips. Bolted them at the ankles. Digging her heels into his firm buttocks, she urged him deeper, faster, fiercer. Their harried breathing filled the silent room as Jack thrust harder and harder, sending her higher and higher. Sienna watched him chase his climax as hers grew with an intensity she swore would send her over the edge and into oblivion.

"Oh, God." The words left her mouth on a whisper.

Her orgasm crashed into her as Jack picked up speed. Her mind went blank as sensation after sensation spread over her body. She convulsed and held him tight. He shuddered in her arms, and Sienna watched him come, knowing it was an image she wanted to see again and again.

As her orgasm faded, she held his face in her hands. They kissed, his body weight coming down on hers, solid and strong.

Chapter Fifteen

Wide awake and with his mind buzzing, Jack went into work the next day regardless of it being eight a.m. on a Sunday morning. He stared blindly at the open laptop in front of him. Thoughts of how Sienna had felt in his arms the night before and waking with her still there filled him with resolution to get things sorted with Martina once and for all.

When their passion had settled into peace, Sienna had remarked on the time it had taken him to come over after her phone call beckoned him. But he'd played it off casually, blaming his vanity and wanting to be fresh and primed for her. Little would she know that only twenty minutes before their intimacy, he'd been speaking to Martina.

He rubbed his hands over his face as the feel of Sienna's skin under his palms came rocketing back. He inhaled as though the scent of her perfume still lingered beneath his nostrils. He'd made love to her. Twice. Three times before he'd left her bed and stumbled next door to get into work mode. She'd crawled under his skin and settled there, warm and invited.

He didn't want to regret last night. Making love to Sienna had at least temporarily banished the threat of his ex-wife, and he wanted to do it all over again. Yet he couldn't shake the feeling he'd exposed her to Martina's venom and worse.

Tapping his pen on the desk, Jack looked from his cell phone to his computer and back again until, finally, he pulled in his chair. His fingers hovered above the keypad of his laptop, and he tried to focus on typing the story his editor was expecting early Monday morning. The words leapt and jumped on the screen as his mind filled with nothing but how to deal with the vile showdown ahead of him.

He wanted Sienna as a part of his family. Holly and Katy were falling in love with her more and more each day, as was he. He owed it to them to combat the fears threatening to take over every sane thought in his head. All too aware, however, that he'd been distracted by work the first time he'd left his children open to danger, Jack worried if he became so caught up in Sienna the second time around, he'd miss the danger again.

He curled his hand into a fist. No. It wouldn't happen. He could have it all, and so could Holly and Katy. Never would he give up on the prospect of a happy future.

As his heartbeat slowed, Jack relaxed his hand. Sienna *could* make him happy. She could make them all happy. He didn't want to wage war on Martina for the rest of their lives, but if she made it that way, so be it.

He looked at his watch. Nine thirty. Snatching up his cell phone, he headed outside. It was time to make the phone call he'd been dreading. Thoughts chased through his head as he crossed the street. Rain came down in a thin sheet of drizzle, and slate-gray clouds gathered above him. Neither did anything to lighten the barrage of ugly emotions he still harbored inside.

Ducking under the overhang of a disused shop, Jack punched in Martina's number.

She answered on the fourth ring. "Hi, Jack." Her pleasure swept down the line in a breathy exhale. "I'm so glad you rang…I was afraid you might not."

"I wouldn't do that."

"When can we meet? Today? Tomorrow? I'm really desperate for you to see I've changed."

He shook his head. "This isn't just about me, Martina."

"Fine, but if you don't see me, you'll never believe I'm serious about staying sober and getting my life back the way it was."

"The way it was? How can anything be the way it was?"

"Why are you making this so difficult? You know what I mean. I was a good mum to the twins before I couldn't handle it anymore and my life fell apart. And *you* were gone. A lot."

Jack clenched his jaw. "I know, but I didn't leave the girls alone so that anything might happen to them. You did that."

"How *could* you leave them alone when you were never even…" She sucked in a breath. "Let's not do this. I've moved on. I want to start again."

Jack narrowed his eyes. The momentary hardness in her voice reminded him of Martina's potential for explosive tantrums and drew ice into his blood. It was going to take something big to thaw his distrust. "So how do you want to do this?"

"Can I come to Potterford? See where you live?"

Her excitable enthusiasm sent shivers up Jack's spine. "No, not yet."

"Jack—"

"Not yet. I'm not saying never, just not yet. I want to see you on neutral territory, and we'll take it from there."

"But—"

"Yes or no?"

Silence.

Jack gripped the phone. *Call it off. Shout, rant, and rave. Show me who you really are.*

Almost to his disappointment, she replied, "Look, I don't want us to end up hating each other again. The girls are ours. We made them, you and me. I think we should at least try to let them see that neither of us wishes it any different, don't you?"

"Yes. Of course," Jack conceded. "So how about we meet in Potterford town center? You can have a feel for the place without actually coming to the house. I don't want the girls to know about us talking until we've worked out how we're going to do this. And, if we can, I'd rather we settle it without lawyers."

"Absolutely. I want nothing more than for you and I to work through this ourselves." Her voice cracked. "I want a second chance, Jack."

The sudden emotion in her tone twisted his heart unexpectedly, and some of the tension left his body. He owed it to Martina to hear her out. If covering news stories had taught him anything, it was that people made mistakes. *He* certainly had, by not seeing what had been happening sooner — by not helping her when the depression had set in. Maybe this was a second chance for both of them to make things right. At least to make amends to their kids.

Guilt and regret circled above his head like two vultures waiting to pluck away his resolve. Glancing out the corner of his eye, he saw a young mother across the street as she pointed out to her toddler an airplane whizzing past overheard. Had Martina spent even a day with the girls like that? Would she now, if granted the opportunity?

"It's never too late," he said. "I know that. We'll take things one step at a time."

"Thank you." She sniffed. "I promise you won't regret this. We can be a proper mum and dad to the twins again. I know we can."

He nodded, accepting it wasn't his place to prevent the twins from having a relationship with their mother. "If you want to be a part of the girls' lives, we need to find a way to make that possible. Starting with a change in you…and me."

She sighed with what sounded to be a relieved laugh. "God, I am so happy you're being reasonable about this. The things that have gone through my head. I really thought I'd have to…well, none of that matters now. When can I see you?"

She sounded psyched. Edgy. It made him uneasy. And yet, if she played by his rules, there was no reason the twins couldn't grow up around both their parents.

He drew in a long breath. "How about tomorrow afternoon? Say two o'clock?"

"Great!" She gave a little squeal. "Thank you, Jack. Thank you so much."

"There's a coffee shop at the top of the high street. I'll meet you inside."

"Okay. Two o'clock. Lord, I'm so nervous now. I'll have to go and work out what to wear."

Closing his eyes, Jack tried to keep a grip on his patience. What she would wear? His belief that she'd changed at all wavered on a hair-thin line — one false move and it would snap.

"See you tomorrow," he said. He pressed the *end call* button and tapped the phone against his lip. She'd sounded so happy. But this new sobriety and enthusiasm could have just been Martina doing what she did best: acting.

Pulling back his shoulders, Jack marched back toward his office. The lines had blurred between his girls' protection and his own liberty from a woman who'd become a leaden weight around his neck. He didn't want to be the guy standing in between them, yet just then, Sienna's face came to mind right along with Holly's and Katy's. The image scared him more than he could contemplate, and Jack blinked. If he was wrong to meet Martina and any of them got caught in the crossfire…

As Jack pushed open the office door and made for his desk, he decided he ought to employ some legal protection — just in case. He needed advice, and he needed it quick.

He sank into his seat. It would probably be better having someone from Potterford represent him. The lawyer who'd seen him through the divorce had been effective, but the guy was also colder than ice. Perhaps, as far as the twins were concerned, a female argument would have better leeway with a judge. There was little benefit in legalities getting in the way of establishing good relations with Martina, but he could still ensure every loophole was covered if that didn't happen.

Looking at his cell phone again, he dialed Sienna's number.

She picked up with a sweet "Hi, you."

"I need your friend's help," Jack blurted.

"Well, hello to you, too. Are you still in work? I got your note."

"Yeah, I am."

"What's wrong?"

He leaned back in his chair. "Nothing."

"You could've fooled me. What is it?"

"I need a lawyer, and I thought of your friend."

"You need Kelsey's help?"

"If she's really a lawyer like you said. Yes."

"She's a lawyer. And a damned good one. But what's happened?"

"Martina." He brushed back the hair that had fallen across his forehead. "She rang again, and I'm going to see her. See what we can work out."

"Oh. Right."

"So does Kelsey deal with messes like mine? Is she qualified to deal with alcoholic ex-spouses who suddenly appear wanting involvement with kids?"

"She's corporate."

"Damn it." He constricted his grip on the phone. "Do you think she might have a lawyer friend who'd help me and not run a mile in the opposite direction?"

"Kelsey doesn't run from anything, so believe me, she'll find someone to help you. She's the toughest broad this side of the Thames. And yes, she'd knock me on my ass if she ever heard me call her a 'broad.' But don't worry about her finding the right person for you. In the meantime, what did your ex have to say? Or don't I want to know?"

"To be honest, she sounds good. Better. I hope she's on the way to recovery, but until I see her, I won't be convinced. She's been sober for a year, and according to the terms agreed in court, Martina is entitled to claim for joint custody, so my reluctance to see her will only make things worse if we end up going to court."

"I see."

"I need to be ready. Not just physically and mentally, but legally, too, so there's no way my girls can be exposed to risk again."

"That will never happen. We'll make sure it doesn't. I'll ring Kelsey right now. When are you seeing Martina?"

"Tomorrow afternoon."

"Okay, I'll see what Kelsey can do. If she can't get anyone to see you before then, it will be as soon as possible afterwards, okay?"

"Okay."

"And, Jack?"

"Yes?"

"Do yourself a favor and meet Martina with the mind that she's changed. I don't think it's a good idea for you go in there spoiling for a fight. Do this the right way. For the girls."

A smile pulled at his lips. "You're a wonderful woman. Do you know that?"

"Yeah, well, only certain people make me that way."

"As in me?"

"Don't flatter yourself, Beaton. I'm talking about those gorgeous babies of yours."

The line went dead, and Jack continued smiling. Once again, Sienna had made him feel fifty times better than before he'd spoken to her. It reminded him to reciprocate the support.

He pulled the envelope containing the eviction notice from Sienna's landlord from the top drawer of his desk. Opening it, he re-read the letter and dialed the number at the top. It was time to start some investigation while his mood was still elevated…

Sienna sat back on her haunches and looked around the empty space of her beloved store. Within a day or two, the door would be locked for a final time and Sienna's Sexy Solutions would operate from Marsden Place. She blinked back the stinging in her eyes. *Please, God, let everything be all right.*

Just as she inhaled a shaky breath, there was a tap at the shop door. She looked up, and her heart skipped a beat. Jack's somber face showed through the glass. With trepidation, she stood and walked toward him. Their eyes met as she turned the key and let him in. The muted sounds of the passing traffic outside seemed to emphasize the silence between them.

He focused solely on her, apparently oblivious to the see-through underwear, furry handcuffs, red-devil outfits, and oodles of lotions and potions spilling from boxes all around them. She stepped back, and he entered the store. As he strode further inside, Sienna slowly closed the door. The stress emanated from him, and she resisted the urge to shiver.

God, she'd missed him since he'd left her bed for work that morning. She cleared her throat and followed him. "Are you okay?"

His smile was forced. "Sure."

She came closer and tugged on his tie so that his mouth came to hers. Kissing him long and hard, she breathed in the scent of his skin beneath her nostrils. When they parted, she leaned her head against his chest and stole her arms around his waist. His arms came around her as well, pinning her to him in a secure embrace.

"Did you have a bad day?" she murmured against his shirt.

When he didn't respond, she frowned, easing back to look into his eyes. They were dark with worry.

"Jack?"

His arms slipped from around her, and he moved away, walking back and forth in front of the counter. Sienna's habitual insecurity enveloped her. Was this about Martina? Or something else? Was he going to call it off? Regretting the sex? The intimacy?

He stopped pacing. "Did you speak to Kelsey?"

Relief pushed the air from her lungs. Martina. External forces they could fight. It was the internal ones that caused the big problems. "A couple of hours ago."

"Good. That's good."

He slowly walked away from the counter and slumped down in one of the neon-pink chairs beside it. When he dropped his head into his hands, Sienna's heart broke for him. She eased onto the low coffee table in front of him and nudged his knees open to insert hers between. She gently drew his hands from his face and held them.

"Talk to me, Jack."

His gaze drifted over her face before he blew out a heavy breath. "I'm just getting worried again, that's all. Worried about seeing her, what she's going to say…if she's not really changed that much at all." He met her eyes. "I once loved this woman, Sienna. Loved her. I owe it to her, Holly, and Katy to make this work."

Sienna's heart kicked painfully as this external force suddenly worked its way into an internal one. Just as when they'd spoken on the phone earlier, Sienna couldn't help but wonder: Make what work? Martina and the twins? Or Martina and Jack? Emotion clogged her throat, and she coughed. "Of course you do."

He shook his head. "She sounded so…happy."

"And that's a bad thing?"

"I don't know. She just sounded more like the woman she was than the one she'd become."

"Then I'm sure she *is* happy, Jack. It seems she's got her life back on track." Sienna wilted somewhat under the knowledge that Jack knew his ex-wife better than she ever would. Still, she smiled. "This is good news, isn't it? Hopefully it means you'll be able to talk sensibly, calmly."

He glanced around the shop and at the packed boxes piled by the counter. "When do you have to be out of here?"

The change of subject further alerted her to Jack's state of anxiety. Maybe the shop's relocation to Marsden Place was still as big an issue for him as ever. The feeling that she was an obstacle loomed large in her conscience once more.

She squeezed his hands. "A week or so. But the shop shouldn't be your concern right now. The twins and Martina should." *And what about you? How are you feeling about her right now?* Sienna cursed her faltering self-confidence, her desperation for some immediate reassurance from him that their lovemaking hadn't been a mistake.

He snatched his hands from hers and stood. "If only I had some idea of what she's going to say…"

Sienna clasped her hands together, bracing for what she was about to say next. "Go see her. Listen to what she has to say before you jump to any conclusions." She paused. "You loved her once. You said so yourself. Maybe she *is* that woman again." Striving to stay above the terrifying thought that when Jack saw his ex, he might see more than the twins' mother when he looked at her, Sienna pressed on. "Where are you meeting her?"

"The coffee shop in town." He hesitated. "I'm going to tell her."

"About what?"

"About the shop."

Sienna swallowed. "The shop? Why?"

"I'm not going into this hiding things when I want complete honesty from her. If I lay all my cards on the table, then maybe she will too."

"All your cards?"

"Yes, including the fact I'm sleeping with the shop's owner."

Sienna flinched at his abrupt choice of words.

"You're going to tell her you're 'sleeping with' me?"

He met her glare. "Yes."

Hurt soared through her, and Sienna pushed to her feet. She fisted her hands on her hips. "So what am I? The big bad nymphomaniac who owns the sex shop next door? Great. Good plan. I wish you well, because when she hears that, of course she's going to be defensive."

"What else do you expect me to do? Would you rather I denied I have a relationship with you?"

"No, but…but then perhaps she could go in on the offensive and twist what's happening between us into something ugly or sordid. I don't want that for you *or* me. Just wait."

Tension pressed down on her as he stared.

He shook his head. "No. I'm sorry, but you have no say in what I do or don't do when it comes to my family."

His family. "I see. Well, listen, Jack. If you and I having a relationship, or whatever the hell it is, is going to cause you more harm than good, I'll step away myself. You won't need to tell me I have to go. I'll know."

Jack remained silent, his brooding temper cloaking the room in chilly darkness.

Eventually, he cleared his throat. "Do you know something? You're right."

"About what?"

"It doesn't look good at all," he affirmed and made for the door.

Concealing the panic for her own heartbreak, Sienna took a step after him. She couldn't make this about her. "Jack, wait."

He turned. "What?"

She closed the crater-sized space between them and cupped her hands to his jaw. "You *will* sort this out. For Holly. For Katy."

She watched his gaze brush over her hair. Then he dipped his head and kissed her so tenderly, Sienna sensed the first crack splinter across the heart. It felt as though he was already saying goodbye. After a long moment, he stepped back.

"I'll call you tomorrow. After…"

"I know. After. Kelsey said to call her whenever you're ready, by the way. She knows someone who can help, if need be."

He pressed another kiss to her forehead, and Sienna closed her eyes. She didn't open them again until she'd heard the door close on passing traffic and knew Jack had gone.

Chapter Sixteen

Jack arrived at the Potterford town center an hour early for his Monday meeting with Martina. He'd reasoned that if he was early, he was prepared. He wanted to watch *her* enter the designated coffee shop, not the other way around.

Pulling into a vacant space in the town pay-and-display parking lot, he cut the engine. The abrupt silencing of the stereo made the car feel cold. Jack dropped his head back against the seat. His heart pounded, and his mouth was dry. In less than sixty minutes, he'd be face to face with Martina again. Was it any wonder sleep had completely eluded him the past night?

Jack reached for the door handle. He'd go for a walk, get some air, and think about what he'd say and do when he saw her. The thought that she might not be alone twisted a knot in his gut; he didn't need the added stress of her latest lover lording it around like the big "I am." But, no, she wouldn't do that. He had to give her benefit of the doubt and erase his negativity.

Jack strode to the ticket machine and paid for two hours. Snatching out the ticket, he walked back to the car. Just as he tossed the ticket onto the dashboard, his phone rang. He looked at the display. It was a number he didn't recognize. His finger hovered over the *talk* button, then he pressed it, half-expecting Martina on the other end.

"Hello?"

"Is this Mr. Beaton?" a male voice asked.

"Yes."

"This is Andrew Thomas. I believe you rang my office a couple of days ago and spoke with my assistant."

Sienna's landlord. Jack shut the car door, blocking out the noise from outside. "I did. I work for *The Potterford Post* and was hoping you would be willing to answer a few questions."

There was a moment's hesitation before Thomas spoke again. "About what, exactly?"

"The reason you are finding it necessary to increase the rent of not one but three of your properties on Bourton Way."

"That's none of your business."

"Anything in the public interest is the nature of my business. There has been a lot of speculation regarding the sudden closure of businesses on that road, and I was interested to know why. Especially as I've discovered the only premises to foreclose are yours."

"How I choose to run my investment in those properties has no public interest whatsoever, Mr. Beaton. This is nothing more than troublemaking. Now, I'll bid you good day and ask that you do not ring these offices again."

"Mr. Thomas?"

"What?"

"I'll be looking into this."

A few seconds' silence ensued. Jack smiled. *Come on, come on.*

"You can do whatever the hell you want," Thomas snarled. "I've got nothing to hide."

"Good. Then I'm sure you've nothing to worry about and I'll just be wasting my time."

Jack ended the call and got out of the car. Now more than ever, he was convinced Thomas was up to no good. If Jack proved it and there was a chance, no matter how small, Sienna could keep the business at the shop and not move it to Marsden Place, surely it would be better for everyone?

Feeling optimistic, Jack locked the car and walked onto the high street, joining the throng rushing back and forth. The street was filled with workers on their lunch break, shoppers, mothers pushing strollers, and elderly men and women enjoying the freedom of retirement. Soon, he reached the painted blue and white bridge that stretched over the River Avon and served as a focal point in town.

Leaning his bare forearms on the iron railing, Jack watched a mother and child feed the ducks and swans that gathered at the bank's edge. What he wouldn't give to have the same possibility for his children and their mother. He didn't want to hate Martina. He wanted her and the girls to have a relationship, and for him and her to join forces in their girls' futures. Have equal concern and involvement in their welfare, education, and happiness.

Jack pulled his hands into fists. What he didn't want was endless arguing, questions, and accusations that would turn two innocent little girls into young women who trusted no one. If children grew up knowing their mother had walked away, abandoning them to a future without her, how the hell would they ever find it in themselves to trust a stranger, to believe a potential spouse loved them as their mother never could?

The squawk of a crow overhead jolted Jack from his dismal contemplation, and he pushed away from the railing. Drawing in a strengthening breath, he made his way up the center of the high street toward the designated meeting place.

When he reached the front of the seemingly endless queue inside the coffee shop, he smiled at the capped and aproned teenager serving behind the counter.

"Um, black coffee, please. No sugar."

She typed something into the register. "Do you want milk with that?"

Jack looked up from the change he was counting. "Black."

She smiled. "Yep, got that. Milk?"

What's wrong with this girl? Jack opened his mouth to try again, but she got there first.

"You can have it frothy, whipped, caramelized, or chocolate-injected."

He arched an eyebrow while stifling the impulse to flick her in the eye. "Chocolate-injected?"

Her smile stretched. "Cool, huh?"

"I'll just take it black."

"Black? No milk? No whip? Nothing?"

Jack silently counted to three, slapped on a wider smile than before, and shrugged. "I'm boring. What can I say?"

"You got that right." She ripped the receipt from the cash register and approached the guy who actually made the coffee before Jack could think of anything to say.

Despite the absurdity of the last few moments, he laughed and went to the far end of the counter to wait for his drink. His mood strangely lifted, and his outlook became a little more upbeat. Life went on as normal regardless; it was a lesson he kept repeating in his mind as he waited. Whatever happened with Martina happened. The world wouldn't end today. That day would come if he ever lost Katy or Holly.

His coffee was put on a tray in front of him, and he nodded his thanks to the guy before picking it up and walking through the tables of people chatting, reading, or typing on laptops. Sitting down in a leather seat so comfortable it should have been in someone's living room, Jack stared out at the people passing in front of the shop's floor-to-ceiling window. Glancing now and then at the closed door, he had an unhindered view of whoever entered.

Thirty minutes later, Jack checked his watch. Martina was late—only ten minutes past the agreed meeting time, but late all the same. His already stretched nerves tightened.

He scanned the street, looking for what, he had no idea. Would she even look the same? A decline of some sort in her appearance was inevitable, considering how she'd used to drink. Once upon a time, her hair had fallen like a golden curtain down her back, her huge green eyes happy and endlessly fascinated with the world around her…that had changed quickly and deeply within a year of the twins' birth. She'd had her hair cropped short to her head, saying she had no time to look after it. Her eyes had darkened with a depression Jack had stupidly thought he'd tried his best to help lift.

He looked down at the table. He would do better this time around. He would be focused and really see her—for better or worse. All the time he'd spent running from one place to another chasing a story and hoping to have the break of his career…it had been for nothing. What did any of it matter? What was a career, accolades, money, or drive without a family around to celebrate your successes?

He gripped his hands together. He'd been sharp with Sienna the day before. On reflection, his knee-jerk reaction to her shop moving next door had been irrational and misplaced, and the hurt in her voice and eyes would be tattooed in his memory forever. Sienna's self-preservation was thinly veiled behind a sheer curtain of nonchalance, and when he'd held her, the shaking of her body and the way her hair softly moved beneath his chin had betrayed her.

Jack drew in a deep breath. He didn't want to battle with Sienna; he wanted her to fight with him in his corner. The thing worrying him, however, was that Sienna was a free spirit who valued her independence. What if she didn't want to be tied down with a husband or family? What if she was more like Martina than he realized?

Bullshit. Not telling her how he felt had been a mistake. He'd offered her nothing in way of reassurance that everything was fine between them. Holding back never did anybody any good, but he'd closed up for *her* protection more than his own. Until he knew for sure what would happen with Martina from there on, the truth was that he didn't want to make Sienna any promises he might break.

If Martina proved a threat, he'd have no problem moving again. How was he supposed to say that to Sienna, having made love to her? He felt like crap. He wasn't the type of guy who slept with a woman and then walked away. Yet isn't that exactly what he'd already done?

He tapped his foot against the parquet flooring. Damn Martina. Damn everything she was doing to him, their children…and Sienna, a woman who cheered him with just a smile, turned him on by just a flash of her bare shoulder. More than that, he loved the slowly evolving care for Holly and Katy that glowed like candlelight in her eyes. Whether she realized it or not, the apprehension she'd looked at them with weeks ago was gone.

No, he didn't want things to end between him and Sienna before they'd even started, but Martina was back under his skin. Well, today she had a choice to make. She was either with him or against him. He hoped the former, but his gut told him his hopes of them bringing up the girls with equal responsibility were pinned on a pipedream.

The door clicked open, and Jack snapped his head up.

A mother and toddler.

Snatching his cell phone from the inside of his jacket, he punched in Martina's number. It kicked straight to voicemail; she had her phone switched off. A pulse thumped in Jack's head, and he pressed the *end call* button. Anger simmered in his blood like liquid anarchy waiting to escape and leak through his pores into the big wide world. What the hell was she playing at?

Torn between waiting and leaving, Jack decided to stay another half-hour before getting out of there. He glanced toward the door again.

Martina smiled and raised her hand in a wave as she weaved through the tables toward him.

Jack's heart stopped. He slowly put his mug on the table and stood, his eyes unable to leave her face. "Martina."

She smiled. "Hi, Jack."

They stood immobile for a long moment before Jack gestured to the chair beside his. "Have a seat. Do you want coffee?"

"I'd love some tea. White. No sugar."

"I'll be just a minute."

He walked to the counter. Martina's appearance had knocked him entirely off-kilter. He'd prepared for a lank-haired, gray-pallored alcoholic — not Martina looking together and calm, like the woman he'd first met. She was dressed in skinny blue jeans, a white T-shirt, and brown cotton jacket. Her hair was still cropped short but well-groomed and suited to her elfin face. She looked great. But she also looked like a woman in armor, ready to do whatever necessary to win in combat. The one thing she couldn't hide from Jack was her eyes. They looked no warmer than they had the last time they'd met.

Nonetheless, his mind raced as he ordered her tea. A strange sensation ripped through him that felt too much like admiration, and he couldn't weaken. Martina was clever, manipulative. He wouldn't forget that. He was ready for her. He would tell her about Sienna, about the shop, and the terms on which he would only begin to consider joint custody. Whatever Martina was up to, she had a long way to go before he would trust her with his beloved babies.

Taking her drink from the guy behind the counter, Jack lifted his chin and willed his heartbeats to slow down. A smile was impossible, but maybe something less scary than an out-and-out scowl was achievable.

As he held out the drink to her, their fingers brushed. He lowered into his seat and picked up his coffee. "So."

Martina smiled, her cool green eyes seeming to appraise him. "You look great, Jack."

"Thank you." He put down his mug. "So do you."

She huffed out a laugh. "It's been a long, hard road, but I think I'm back in the driving seat again."

He nodded. "Good."

Her smile diminished, and her eyes turned somber. "I'm so grateful to you. Really grateful. I was so scared you would cancel. That you'd change your mind and not see me."

"I keep my promises, you know that."

"I know." The skin at her neck shifted. "And I won't ask you to make any promises today, tomorrow, or next week. I'm willing to do whatever it takes to get to know you again, Jack. Whatever it takes."

"Get to know me, Martina? What about the girls?"

She laughed and picked up her tea. "Well, of course the girls." She met his eyes over the rim. "Surely that goes without saying?"

"It would still be nice to hear you say it. This meeting is about them, after all."

"Of course." She looked away to the window and studied the passersby.

Jack watched her profile, noted the way her cup ever so slightly shook in her hand. The glaze of makeup she'd applied and the sheen of the silk shirt she wore did nothing to disguise her nerves.

He cleared his throat. "So, what happens next? You have me here. What is it you want?"

"I want my family back." She faced him. "I want you and the twins to look at me and know I'm not going to disappear again. To let me say sorry for the mistakes I made and move on. I want to be a part of your life again."

"It's going to take a long, long time before that happens. Did you really think I could forget what you did to them? That I'd forget you haven't written or rang them in a year? You knew where we were. You knew, but you didn't even send a damn birthday card, for crying out loud."

Her cheeks flushed, and her gaze turned cold. "I knew where you were until a month ago, you mean."

Jack shook his head and dropped back in his seat, disbelief pushing a wry laugh from his throat. "And what happened to the other eleven months? They don't count, I suppose. It's just the month I moved here, is that it?"

"I'm trying my best to make this work *now*, Jack."

Leaning forward, he put his elbows on his knees. "And that is what concerns me. Why now?"

Their eyes locked for a moment before she looked to her lap. "Because when you disappeared, it frightened me. It made me realize you might not always be where I can reach you." Her voice cracked. "I've made some terrible mistakes. I don't blame you for hating me, but please, don't punish the girls. Let them see me. Let them make the decision whether they want me in their lives."

"They're four. Not fourteen. How do you expect them to know what they do or don't want? You're their mother; they'll love you no matter what you've done."

"So let me see them." A tear slid over her lower lid. "Please."

Apprehension slashed behind Jack's ribcage like a million knives.

"I can't," he said. "I just can't. Not yet."

She swiped her finger under her eyes. "And I understand that. I do. How about I come and see where you're living at least? I'll come when they're at daycare."

Jack's mouth drained dry. Martina in his home. The twins' home. The home next door to Sienna. Sienna and the shop. He drew in a long breath and exhaled. "There's something you should know."

She lifted her eyebrows. "What?"

"I'm seeing someone."

Time stood still as she stared. The apparent unexpectedness of his confession drew the color from her face and lit a wariness in her eyes. "I see."

"Do you? Because it's still brand new to me."

"And does this someone have a name?"

"Sienna. Sienna Lloyd. She's a lovely woman, Martina." Jack tried and failed to keep the warning from his voice.

"How long?"

"A couple of weeks. She's my neighbor."

"I see," she repeated, looking to the window. "And this is a problem for us? For me coming to the house?"

"No. But if you do, I want you to understand Sienna is a part of my life now, which means she's a part of the twins'. In fact, I want you to meet her."

He could see her jaw clench, and he waited. Surely the idea of another woman judging her, accessing her, would put her off this idea of coming to his house? Back into his life?

Yet, she answered, "Okay."

Jack gave a curt nod and leaned forward to pick up his coffee. "Good. Then I'll set it up."

The silence was heavy. He had nothing else to say to her, nothing to discuss until the next day. It was Sienna he wanted to speak to now. He drained his coffee cup. "Right, well, I'll call you tomorrow, then."

"You're going?" She widened her eyes. "But I've only just got here."

Jack pushed to his feet and whipped his jacket from the back of his chair. "I've got to be somewhere. I'll see—"

"I'm guessing this *somewhere* involves the neighbor."

There was a sneer to her tone, and Jack held her stare. "Tomorrow, Martina."

He strode from the coffeehouse and out onto the street. Releasing his breath, he marched unseeing along the high street toward the parking lot. People passed in a blur as Jack's thoughts battled with his inner demons. He'd already been scared to death by his pull toward Sienna; a relationship was the very last thing he'd needed or expected when he'd moved there. And from the way his meeting with Martina had just ended, there was no longer any question Sienna could complicate matters. Which could mean complicating life for his girls.

If he *did* turn away and didn't pursue her, would he regret it? Would his backtracking be based on nothing more than how Martina could potentially cause more heartbreak to more people than she already had? For all either he or Sienna knew, it could be a once-in-a-lifetime opportunity wasted, right when something that had started so badly had been turning into something so damn good. But that didn't mean it wasn't also something happening sooner than he could properly deal with.

Sliding into the car seat, Jack pulled out his phone. He needed to speak to Sienna. Set things straight as best he could and tell her how he felt. He dialed her number. The line was busy.

Chapter Seventeen

Sienna cut the line on her cell again and put it beside her coffee cup on the balustrade surrounding her back yard. The morning was bright and warm; not even the slightest breeze ruffled the trees, the opposite of the storm raging through her heart and mind. How could everything look so stunning and peaceful in the world when she had no idea what she was doing?

Since Jack walked out of the shop the day before, the prospect of going to London no longer felt like the completely wrong thing to do. It actually felt like an open door waiting for her to escape through. Of all the things she'd thought would never happen to her, it was to be an obstacle in someone else's relationship. Yet how could the Beatons work out what they wanted to happen next if she was a factor in that decision? A factor living next door, where they would see her every day.

Family mattered to Sienna more than anything. She was a grown woman yet would have still given anything to have her parents together again. How would Katy and Holly feel one day if they knew she'd been the reason their father had never given their mother a second chance? Sienna wiped away a tear that had fallen onto her cheek. She couldn't do that to them.

She picked up the phone and dialed. Her friend and businessman extraordinaire, Ian Archer, picked up.

"Sienna Lloyd! How the devil are you?"

Despite her despair, Sienna smiled. "I'm fine. How are you?"

"Great. Really great. Busy as always and wondering when you were going to ring and ask me for a job."

She pressed her eyes closed. "Well, today is your lucky day, then."

"What?"

"I said—"

"Are you serious?"

There was no denying the smile in his voice, and Sienna's stomach knotted. "Yes. Well, I'm at least considering it."

"You want to come to London? You're finally realizing Potterford won't collapse without you?"

"Very funny. You know why I didn't take you up on your offer before…but the time feels right now. I'd at least appreciate you seeing me."

"Of course I'll see you! I'd love to see you. How's your mum doing?"

"Better." Sienna stared out across the yard. "A damn sight better than me, anyway."

"Are you okay?"

She gulped. "It's time for me to move on. I've had to move out of the shop. Maybe it's a sign that I should be doing something different."

"A sign that's all good for me. When did you want to come?"

She glanced toward the fence separating her yard from Jack's. "As soon as possible."

The sound of papers being shuffled and keys being tapped on a computer filtered down the line. "I can fit you in first thing on Thursday. Is that too soon?"

Three days. "That's perfect."

"God, Sienna, I am so glad you called. I have got the most perfect vacancy for you. It's as though you damn well knew."

Sienna forced a smile she hoped would reflect in her voice. "I'm looking forward to hearing all about it. See you soon."

She cut the line, her hand shaking and her heart racing. There was no going back now. She would hear what Ian had in mind for her, and if it was good enough, she'd leave Potterford. Things happened for a reason. If she and Jack were meant to be…she wouldn't be a million miles away if he wanted her.

Picking up her coffee cup, she walked back into the house and put it in the sink just as her phone vibrated on the counter. Jack. She let the phone kick to voicemail and pressed to loudspeaker:

"Sienna, it's me. I need to speak to you. The meeting with Martina went well. It looks as though she's going to play nice. She looks…good. Different. I'm on my way into work, but I'll try you again in a while."

The line went dead, and Sienna stood paralyzed looking at the phone. *Martina looks good. She's going to play nice.* But no apology for how he'd acted the day before. Her breath caught in her chest and pulled. How could she have let him in this way? She hadn't wanted to want anyone ever again, hadn't wanted to feel this pain ever again. She had to get out of there.

Through her tears, she snatched up the phone and dialed Kelsey's number. For the time being, she'd only let Kelsey know her plans. Until she took the job, there was no need to worry her mother…or allow Jack the opportunity to stop her.

"Kelse? It's me. I've got some news. Can you meet me at the shop?"

The bell above the shop door rang, and Sienna looked up.

In swept Kelsey, looking more poised and together than Sienna had any hope of achieving in this lifetime or the next. Sienna had just moved to come around the counter to greet her when her phone rang. She looked at the display, and her heart kicked. She pressed *talk*.

"Hi, Jack." Her eyes briefly met Kelsey's before her friend walked over to one of the few displays left to pack up.

"You didn't return my call."

"Things are hectic at work. I haven't got much time left to sort things out."

"I've been thinking. Don't you think the best thing would be for you to meet Martina?"

Sienna sucked in a breath. "You want me to meet her? Why?"

"It's better this way. Like I said yesterday, I'm not hiding you away from her. I'm not hiding you or the shop."

"But what if that makes her angry?" His silence down the telephone line spoke volumes. "See? You don't have to do this, Jack. Now isn't the time to introduce me to your ex-wife." Sienna glanced at Kelsey as her friend continued wandering around the shop room, randomly picking up and discarding items. Kelsey have would bought the whole lot if doing so wouldn't label her Sex Fiend of the Year. "I don't understand why you'd want to…especially after what you said to me about your *family*." He needed to know he'd hurt her, that he couldn't make her feel wanted only to push her away.

"I want you there. Beside me."

"Why? What's changed since you saw Martina?" *Say it. Say what you're really thinking.*

"I shouldn't have said those things to you. I'm sorry. But before I met with her, I didn't know what to expect. Now that I've seen her, I just want to move forward."

"Which means what?"

"Which means I want you to meet her. I want Martina to see I have someone new in my life who is a part of this whether she likes it or not."

"I won't be used, Jack." Sienna's pulse beat hard, and her protective walls slammed back into place.

"I wouldn't do that."

She pressed her lips firmly together. Even above her defensive barriers, self-doubt hovered like an invisible and toxic cloud.

Jack sighed. "Sienna, you matter to me. You matter to the twins. I want to know what you think of Martina, this situation, everything. If this stands a chance of working, it's only fair you see my life as a whole, with and without the ugly."

"Well, we've all got a bit of that going on." She smiled softly. *God, please don't let me regret this.* "Fine, I'll meet her."

"You will?"

Her mouth was parched as she nodded. "Yes."

"Thank you. You have no idea—"

"So, what can I expect?"

His exhale blew down the line. "Well, first and foremost, you need to know Martina's changed. A lot. She's got herself together. But the coldness is still there. It's deeper under her skin than it was before, but it's still there." He cleared his throat. "Which is why I was so apprehensive about you…us. If I think for one minute she's going to drag you or what you do into the middle of this, then I'll have no choice but to step back."

Her heart sank. "From us or Martina?"

"Both."

Then, more than ever, Sienna knew she'd made the right decision by ringing Ian. Jack didn't know what he wanted, and she wasn't the type of woman to wait around while he figured that out.

"This doesn't feel very fair to me, Jack." Her jaw tensed. "I'm already in this whether you realize it or not. The girls matter to me… so do you. And I vowed no one would ever dictate what happens in my life after what happened to Dad. Don't you think you should do the same?"

"I know what you're saying, but that doesn't stop me from worrying about how this is going to affect you. The last thing I want is to hurt you."

"Then don't."

"Sienna, please."

She shot another glance toward Kelsey, who, thankfully, was engrossed in a lingerie magazine, her back turned to the counter where Sienna stood.

"Please what, Jack? I'm not the sort to beg. If you want out, that's fine. But for God's sake, make sure it's for the right reasons and not because of your ex-wife."

"Of course it's because of her. Until this is sorted out, you have to trust I'm doing the right thing for you, the girls, and me."

He sounded so sincere, but in her heart, she knew she'd been a fool to fall in love. A fool who'd fallen in love with a man she'd started to picture in her future until yesterday. Now she pictured him working at a future with a woman she didn't know.

She dropped her head into her hand. "So what's the plan?"

"I want to stay in Potterford without looking over my shoulder all the damn time, but I can't do that without knowing once and for all how Martina will react to me moving on. So I'm going to do something about it. Now I've seen she's doing her best to get her own life straight, I can't abandon the mother of my children on top of all the other bad decisions I've made. The girls are going to grow up. They're going to ask about their mum, and when that happens, I want to be able to look them in the eye and know that I acted in their best interests. Not mine. Do you understand that?"

Sienna slumped against the counter, clutching the phone tighter in her hand. "Of course. But—"

"It's for the best. Please, Sienna. Will you meet her? I can set something up for tomorrow. She wants to see the house. See where we're living. She agreed to come over when the girls aren't here."

It all still seemed inappropriate, but Sienna nodded. She would soon leave for London and, while there, be able to make an informed decision about Jack and the job. "Fine. But I'd like to see you before that happens. Why don't you come over after work tonight? Bring the girls. We'll have something to eat and talk about it."

"I'll come over now. I had some interviews scheduled, but I've managed to put those off. I need to be at the primary school at four o'clock, though, so I can't stay long."

Sienna looked up. Kelsey was watching her with an eye not unlike like that of a bald eagle zooming in on its unsuspecting prey.

"Okay, fine." Sienna kept her gaze level with Kelsey's. She couldn't show weakness in the face of a woman who could throw a dart at eight feet and still hit the bull's-eye. "I'll see you soon. I have to go. I have a million and one things to do if the shop is going to be open for business at Marsden Place any time this century." *Or if I'm moving to London.*

Sienna ended the call and slid her phone under the counter. Kelsey strolled slowly toward her, carrying a boxed dildo and a pair of gold handcuffs. "So…what's going on?"

"Jack's coming over."

"Why?"

Sienna looked past her friend's shoulder. "To talk."

"About what?"

"Martina."

"And?"

"And nothing." Sienna whipped from the counter some unwanted Dracula outfits that left little to the imagination and brushed past Kelsey.

"You can run away from me all you want," Kelsey said, blowing out a theatrical sigh, "but *you* asked me over. And now I want to know what's got those tears popping into your eyes like little glass beads."

Sienna squeezed her eyes shut and kept her back to her friend. If she looked at Kelsey again, her last shred of dignity would abandon her.

"Sienna?"

Sienna turned around and fisted a hand on her hip. "He wants me to meet Martina. Tomorrow. And now I'm worried I'm the woman who stands between him and a reunion with the twins' mum."

"Don't be daft." Kelsey laughed, but then her smile vanished. "Did he say that?"

Sienna flung the outfits into a plastic box. "No, but he seems to be pretty obsessed with how good she looks now."

After studying her for a moment, Kelsey shook her head. "So? The last time he saw the woman she was an alcoholic slut. Any improvement would make her look amazing."

Normally, this type of Kelsey response would extract a smile from Sienna, but nothing came. "You know, I can't help thinking Martina showing up now isn't anything to do with the twins. From what Jack's told me, this woman couldn't give a damn about them. I have no idea what this is about, but it could be something like money, pure and simple. She might only use Holly and Katy like a double-edged sword to continually stick in Jack's heart."

"Well, that can't happen." Kelsey pushed herself bolt upright from where she'd been lounging against the counter and whipped her cell phone from her bag. "Right."

"Who are you ringing?"

"The bane of my life, of course."

"Mike."

"Who else?"

"Kelse, wait. There's more."

Kelsey raised her hand, cutting her off while holding the phone to her ear. She tapped one spike-heeled foot on the floor. "It's me. I'm at Sienna's. I need to see you. I need your help…What? No, I am not buying, I'm browsing…Will you forget what I'm doing and meet me at the office later? I need some advice…This is about Sienna,

Mike." She glared at a spot on the wall. "For crying out loud, will you reel it in?" Kelsey scowled. "Fine. I'll buy you dinner next week as a thank-you." She hesitated and then jabbed her hand in the air, clearly frustrated. "Fine. Tomorrow, then."

Sienna laughed as Kelsey snapped the phone shut. "That man has got you just where he wants you."

Kelsey sniffed. "The hell he has."

Quirking an eyebrow, Sienna said nothing.

Kelsey stepped away from the counter and pointed her cell at her. "Enough. We're talking about you, not me. Come on, let's get the kettle on and think about a plan of action before Jack-O gets here."

The need to defend Jack rose like a tidal wave in Sienna's heart, despite her reluctance to meet The Bitch from the Black Lagoon. "You're making him sound like he couldn't fight Martina on his own."

Kelsey raised her hands in mock surrender. "Hey, I'm not saying that at all. The way that man is built, I don't doubt for one minute he can handle himself." She walked closer and pressed a kiss to Sienna's forehead. "It's his feelings for you and those girls that are going to make him do something stupid."

Kelsey disappeared into the back-room kitchen, her high heels clicking on the tiles.

"I'm scared he's already done something stupid," Sienna said, following Kelsey. "And what do you mean Jack's 'feelings'? His feelings for me have nothing to do with this; he's doing the right thing by the girls."

Kelsey turned from filling the kettle and raised her eyebrows. "Is that what he told you?"

"Yes…No…Well, he said he's doing it for all of us, but this can hardly be for *my* benefit."

"Well, that may be true, but getting you to meet this Martina bitch has a lot to do with Jack-O, too. A big dose of this is for him, my friend."

"Why?"

"Because he wants you by his side."

Sienna shook her head. "Haven't you forgotten something?"

"What?"

She jabbed her thumb over her shoulder toward the door. "The shop? I think he wants me to meet her so I can defend to her what I've been defending to him."

Kelsey shrugged. "Well, that's fine. You can defend what you do for a living forever."

"Maybe. But I can't defend why I'm in the middle of a family that might have a second chance at making it work."

"What? Are you serious?"

"Yes, I'm serious. I don't want that on my conscience, Kelse."

Kelsey put the kettle on to boil before taking Sienna's hands in hers. "That man has it bad for you and bad for those girls. I saw the look in his eyes when we were standing at your door. He's falling and falling fast. Don't walk away from this. Please. These past couple of weeks, you've been happy with him. Really happy."

"But what if I'm right?"

"You're not. Jack is doing the honorable thing. He's not hiding you away like a dirty secret. He's bringing you to the forefront, letting his ex see who you are and saying 'deal with it.'"

"But—"

Kelsey leaned forward and kissed her cheek. "No buts. Trust me." She turned and took two mugs out of an overhead cupboard and spooned in coffee and sugar. Filling the mugs with boiling water, she added milk then handed Sienna one. Together, they walked back into the empty shop and sank into comfy chairs in the seating area.

"All we need to do is think this through so when Jack arrives, we can listen to his plans." Kelsey blew across the top of her mug. "That way, by the time I see Masterful Mike, he can advise the best way forward."

Sienna smiled and lifted her mug to her lips. "Are you sure this isn't just an excuse so you can see him?"

Kelsey glared. "Shut up."

Sienna drank as Kelsey scowled into her coffee. Her smile wavered, however, and she said, "I'll meet her, Kelse. Talk to the woman who put so much pain in Jack's and the twins' eyes that all I want to do is smack her in the face." Sienna gripped her coffee mug and took a deep breath. "But I'm also going to explore other alternatives."

Kelsey frowned. "With Martina?"

"With me. I've called Ian. I'm going to meet him in London on Thursday."

"What? You're thinking about taking a job with him?"

"Yes. *Thinking* being the operative word. I just want…I just want to know what my options are."

Kelsey tapped her mug to Sienna's. "Well, I'm all for a girl exploring options." She grinned. "This is good, Sienna. Really good."

Doubt weighed heavily in Sienna's mind, but she nodded. "I think so too. Just do me a favor and keep this to yourself. I don't want Mum finding out until I know what I'm doing."

"My lips are sealed. And as for Martina, you see that woman — but with Jack and Jack only. I'm worried she'll come after you."

Sienna huffed. "I'd love to see her try."

The tinkling of the shop door made them both jump. Jack. Sienna put down her coffee as he came toward them. He threw a quick smile to Kelsey, but Sienna could tell he would have preferred them to be alone. Strangely, she didn't want that to happen. It was safer to have Kelsey there so Sienna wouldn't risk losing her resolve to explore London.

"Hey, come and sit down," she said, gesturing toward an empty seat. "Kelsey just got off the phone with *your* new best friend, Mike Scott, if you need his advice."

He looked at Kelsey. "Is he any good?"

Kelsey nodded. "Yes."

Sienna looked at Kelsey's face and laughed. "Good? Jack, Mike's the best family lawyer in the southwest. He gets things done. And wait until you see the guy. Any female jurors have his vote before he even opens his mouth. The judges aren't keen on that fact, nor are his adversaries, but that's the way it is."

Jack raised an eyebrow. "That hot, huh?"

"Put it this way, any woman with blood beating through her veins gives Mike what he wants, when he wants it. Well, apart from Kelsey — "

"Hey!" Kelsey glared.

Sienna grinned. "Believe me, any other woman would fall on her back with her legs wide open if there was any hope he'd notice her."

Jack looked from her to Kelsey and back again. "What does that mean? Is he gay?"

Sienna's burst of laughter was loud, but Jack maintained his somber expression. "What?" he asked.

"Mike is about as gay as Don Juan. He's got eyes for one woman and one woman only." She nodded toward Kelsey, who'd developed an intense interest in her coffee cup.

Jack smiled and then blew out a breath. "I can't help thinking you shouldn't have asked him to get involved yet. There's nothing for him to do."

Sienna looked at him in disbelief. "Jack, you asked me to contact Kelsey about this. What's changed?"

He lifted his shoulders. "All I'm saying is involving lawyers is the last resort."

"But I thought you didn't trust Martina, that you wanted all bases covered."

"I do."

"Then —"

"I'm doing my best here, you know."

Sienna took a calming breath and looked to the floor. His contradictions were maddening. How could they go on like this? She looked up and met Kelsey's steady gaze, widening her eyes to silently ask for some backup.

Crossing her arms, Kelsey cleared her throat and shifted her focus to Jack. "Just because I've contacted Mike, it doesn't mean you've hired him. It would just be good for him to know what you've got planned. Regardless, if you need anyone in your corner now, it's Sienna. She's a one-woman machine when it comes to looking out for other people." In a murmur, she added, "Not that you aren't clearly talented when it comes to taking care of *her* needs…"

Kelsey strikes again. "Haven't you got somewhere you should be?" Sienna asked her.

"Fine." Kelsey stood and hitched her bag onto her shoulder. "I'll go and leave you two alone. I need to speak to Mike about it anyway. The one thing you need to learn about us, Jack, is we rally around our friends. You move in next door to Sienna, you get my friend all gooey and happy for the first time in years, then you're a friend to Mike and me now, whether you like it or not."

Sienna wanted the floor to open up and a monster to take her by the ankles and drag her under. She closed her eyes rather than risk meeting Jack's. "Kelse?"

"What?"

"Go."

Silence.

"Now," Sienna sighed.

"I haven't finished."

Sienna popped her eyes open. "Yes, you have."

"Look," Jack intervened, "there's nothing for either you or Mike to worry about at the moment. Of course, that might well change in the not too distant future. Just tell him possibilities, nothing more."

Kelsey flashed Jack an encouraging smile. "Mike's a pain in the ass most of the time, but even I can't argue how skilled a lawyer he is. He'll look after you if the time comes."

"I'm still hoping it doesn't come to that."

His gaze then locked with Sienna's, his eyes softening as they lingered over her face. In spite of herself, Sienna had the urge to slide onto his lap and kiss his neck to make him smile in the way she'd come to love. But she wouldn't do anything so careless…not now. There was far too much at stake. Like her heart, for a start.

She cleared her throat. "Leave it to us, Kelse. Everything will work out."

Kelsey raised her hands. "He's all yours. Look after him." She left the shop, the door closing behind her.

The abrupt silence was disconcerting, and Sienna debated whether to get up and resume her work or slide her hand across the rigid expanse of Jack's neck and kiss away their worries.

"Jack?"

Nothing.

Drawing strength from the endless reserves she'd accrued since her dad's passing, Sienna pressed on. "Talk to me, Jack."

His dark blue gaze locked on hers. He opened his mouth, closed it, and opened it again without saying anything. Shoving his fingers into his hair, he held them there. Sensing he wanted to be alone right then, Sienna resisted going to him and wrapping her arms around him. "What is it you hope is going to happen tomorrow?"

"I want her to see we live in a nice place," he began, "with nice people. But I won't forget she gave up on Holly and Katy. Everything has to work out the way I want it because over my dead body can she just come back and call the shots."

Frustration tip-tapped up Sienna's spine, making her want to cry for him, for her. She didn't know what it meant to have children, to have been married, but his emotions were clearly all over the place, and the torture in his eyes was undeniable.

Jack dropped his hands from his hair and sighed. "I haven't wanted to see her for these past two years. Moved away so she couldn't find the girls. So what kind of man does that make me? She's their mother, for crying out loud."

"But she hasn't been a mother to them," Sienna consoled him. "Not in the sense of the word that means anything. And if she wants to try now, you have options, and you have support. Look, I'm a stronger person than you're giving me credit for."

Jack stood, and the unexpected tenderness in his gaze took her breath away. Unable to even breathe, much less move, she allowed him to take her hands and pull her to her feet. Tugging her close, he stared deeply into her eyes. So deep, Sienna was rocked from her trance-like state as he kissed her, taking another piece of her heart. London suddenly felt so far away.

Chapter Eighteen

Sienna glanced at her watch for the fortieth time in the last hour as she stood at Jack's living room window. The familiar sounds of coffee percolating and crockery being taken from cupboards filtered through from where Jack worked in the kitchen. Martina was due to arrive any minute.

Her stomach lurched with trepidation. She and Jack had barely exchanged a word for the last hour as they waited for his ex-wife's arrival. What would Martina be like? Would she behave as Jack had described? Would she maintain this new persona of sweetness and light—or upon sight of another woman turn defensive? Ever since Sienna's father had been killed, she'd had an uncanny knack for worrying about things before they happened, silently hiding her fears behind the usual optimism and enthusiasm.

Neither of those traits filtered through her mind or heart right then.

Sienna had never been more aware that, once upon a time, Martina had been Jack's wife and the twins' mother. They'd been a family. She couldn't afford to lose sight of that. And though she'd been so swept up in the moment, it hadn't been lost on her that Jack's kiss the day before hadn't sealed the deal that he wanted Sienna as a permanent fixture in his life. It could have been as much out of gratitude—or pity—as passion.

She drew her folded arms tighter around her body, then froze as a black taxi pulled to a stop in front of the house.

"Oh, God. Here goes."

She fled the room and hurried along the hallway to where Jack stood staring out the kitchen window into his back yard. Sienna coughed. "She's here."

When he spun around, his gaze bore into hers. But rather than wrap her arms around him and tell him everything would be all right, Sienna knew he had to take the lead; he had to do what was best for his family.

The doorbell rang and kicked them from the silent stupor. Jack came toward her and squeezed her hand. "Let's do this."

He marched past her, and Sienna turned to look after him. *Do what, exactly? I haven't a damn clue what I'm even doing here.* Nonetheless, she pulled back her shoulders and followed him along the hallway. Exchanging a final glance, they faced the door just as Martina pressed the bell a second time.

Jack opened the door. "Martina, you made it."

Sienna stood stock-still as Martina leaned forward and pressed a kiss to Jack's cheek. "I did. The drive through this little town showed me why you chose to bring the girls here. It's quite lovely."

Before he could answer, she turned her attention to Sienna. With her heart beating hard and fast in her ears, Sienna moved forward to greet the woman who had no idea she held Sienna's immediate future in the palm of her hand. Their eyes met, and Sienna internally shivered. A wide smile spread across Martina's face, but her eyes were like two dull pieces of gray stone.

Sienna offered her hand first. "Hi, I'm Sienna. Jack's new neighbor."

After another moment's appraisal of her entire face, Martina clasped Sienna's hand. "And girlfriend, so Jack tells me. Sienna. Such an unusual and lovely name. I'm happy to meet you."

Sienna continued to smile as she eased her hand from Martina's clutch. Jack broke the heavy silence. "Okay, well, why don't we go through to the kitchen? Have some coffee?"

Martina stepped over the threshold. "Sounds good to me." She walked inside Jack's home without a second glance, her high-heeled sandals tapping along the hallway toward the kitchen.

Sienna looked at Jack and released her held breath. "She's pretty," she said.

"Pretty what? Unpredictable? Untrustworthy?" He pressed a kiss to her cheek. "You did great. This will soon be over."

As he followed Martina into the kitchen, Sienna tipped her head back. With short, dark-blond hair, pixie features, and slender figure, Martina didn't come close to the femme-fatale image Sienna had conjured up in her mind. The twins had taken Jack's dark hair and blue eyes, but she could see their picture-perfect features were entirely Martina. Drawing in a strengthening breath, Sienna walked into the kitchen, hoping for one single second everything wouldn't scream at her to get the hell out of there.

To get the hell out and let this family have a second chance.

"Why don't we all take a seat, and I'll pour the coffee?"

Jack's voice had cut through her thoughts, and Sienna blinked before slapping on a smile so forced it hurt her cheeks. "Good idea. Martina?" Sienna gestured toward the table.

Martina smiled and slid into one of the chairs around Jack's kitchen table. She placed her bag on the floor beside her and her elbows on the table, casually lacing her fingers together. "So what is it you do, Sienna?"

Oh, God. Sienna looked to Jack as she sat down. "I, um…I run a shop in town."

Jack's gaze changed from apprehension to cool resolve. The coffee pot rattled as he thumped it down on the table. He took a step back, choosing to remain standing, leaning against the counter.

"A shop?" Martina smiled. "How lovely. What sort of shop?"

Jack cleared his throat. "You know, don't you. You already know what Sienna does for a living."

Sienna looked from him to Martina.

The woman's eyes shone with triumph, her cheeks flushed with… excitement? Embarrassment? Sienna didn't know the woman well enough to hazard a guess—but from what Jack had told her, she'd say the former.

Martina laughed. "Oh, Jack. You know me so well. When you told me you had a girlfriend and she lived next door, what else was I supposed to do but a little digging? I didn't mean anything by it."

She looked at Sienna. "You understand, don't you? From one woman to another. From one mother to another…oh, but sorry, you don't have any kids, do you?"

Sienna's chest burned as her survival mechanism clicked into place. All thoughts of doing the right thing and keeping up appearances for Jack during this meeting were obliterated by her core belief in self-respect. If this woman thought she was going to play with her, she could think again.

Smiling, Sienna replied, "No, I don't. But I understand perfectly. Of course you want to know who I am. After all, I've been spending time with Holly and Katy. I'm sure their welfare is at the forefront of your mind right now."

Martina's smile broadened. "Absolutely. And that's why when I found out that your little shop will be moving next door, I was even more excited to meet you."

"And why's that? Does it bother you?"

"Not at all. It might well bother a judge, though."

Sienna opened her mouth to respond, but Jack got there first.

"I knew it." He splayed his hands on his hips. "What exactly is it you've got in mind to do now you're here?"

Martina looked at Sienna. "I only—"

Jack moved forward and slapped his hands on the table, making Sienna flinch. "Talk to me. Not Sienna."

Martina rolled her eyes and pinned him with a hardened glare. "What I've got in mind is coming to see you. That's it. I want to talk to you and work out the best way for us to do this."

"Do what? A damn custody battle?"

"Of course not." She laughed. "Does this have to be a battle? It's you who seems to want that, Jack. Not me."

Sienna touched his hand. "Jack, maybe—"

He snatched his hand away as though her skin burned. "What do you want, Martina?" he demanded. "I'm trying to build a life for our daughters. Once I'm convinced you deserve to see the girls, I'll tell you. Until then, at least respect their right for a happy, secure future."

She stared at him, her eyes wide. "You've absolutely no idea how hard I've worked to stay sober. And you can't keep me away from them, so you might as well come up with a better plan than running away from the fact I'm here and their mother whether you like it or not."

Martina's tone struck a nerve in Sienna, and she sent up silent prayer of gratitude for Kelsey's insistence that Mike be aware of Jack's possible situation before it began. Every hair on her body stood to attention. Martina was going to come after Jack and the girls, one way or another. Sienna moved forward and pressed her hands on the table.

"This has nothing to do with me, but both of you need to think about Holly and Katy…regardless of what you'd like to see happen from here. They're the ones that matter."

Martina whipped her head around. "You're right. This has *nothing* to do with you." She turned and faced Jack once more. "I came here to be civil. If you can't do the same, then the next time we speak, it will have to be through our lawyers."

Jack pushed the hair back from his face, and Sienna saw that his hand trembled. "I've got representation whenever you're ready."

The tense atmosphere hitched up a notch, and Sienna wished for some invisible force to come in and airlift her out of there. The sooner Thursday and London came, the better. Her shoulders and neck ached; her hands itched to claw Martina's hair out. Instead, she merely pressed her lips tightly together. The ball was in Jack's court, not hers. He had to decide what happened next.

For a long moment, Martina said nothing, until her eyes glazed over with tears. "This is ridiculous. I don't think either of us wants that. I'm not here to kick up a fuss about a few bits of lingerie next door." She dabbed a fingertip to the corner of her eye. "Despite what you might think, Jack, as long as my girls and you are happy, so am I."

Not wanting to lower her defenses just yet, Sienna eased back into her chair. "Well, that's good. Jack's been worried—"

"About the fact you haven't changed." Jack's gaze focused entirely on Martina. His arms crossed. "And I'm still not convinced I'm wrong."

"You are wrong." Martina stared at him. "Wrong to even think I would start throwing my weight around as soon as I see you for the first time in a year. As long as the shop isn't a problem for the twins, then I'm fine with it."

For want of something to do, Sienna picked up the coffee pot. Filling their cups in turn, she, Jack, and Martina each added milk or sugar as the silence closed in on them.

After a moment, Jack pulled out a chair and sat. "You'll have to give me more than that to convince me you mean it."

Martina shook her head. "To cause trouble is the last thing I want. I want you — *all* of us, to be okay with me being here. I've made mistakes, but I want a fresh start, a new chance to make things right." She looked into his eyes. "To make you happy."

Sienna gripped her cup. The woman hadn't referred to the twins in her *need* to make things right. Shouldn't the twins be all she spoke about? Sienna noticed Jack curl his hand into a fist on his knee.

Martina slowly returned her coffee cup to the table. "Why don't I answer your question and tell you what I want, and then we can discuss what we're going to do so we're all happy?"

Sienna slowly counted to ten in her head. This conversation was for Jack to navigate. She had no idea why she was there. Did he want her as a witness? Protection? If Martina lashed out or used something against him in court? Doubt that she was anything more than a pawn in a custody battle tasted sour on her tongue.

Martina stood and walked to the window. Sienna glanced at Jack. His jaw was set, and his study focused on Martina's back.

"I've messed up, but I'm back and know exactly what I want: what I had."

"It's a little late for that, don't you think?"

"I want back into the girls' lives, Jack. I want joint custody." She turned and leaned up against the counter. "But I don't want to have to fight for that right."

"That's a long way down the line as far as I'm concerned."

She glanced at Sienna before turning to Jack. "I've contacted my lawyer. He says I've got every right to make an appeal for joint custody whenever I'm ready. I'm sober, and I'm ready to see my children. You might as well know, I've told him to go ahead and make the request."

"I need more time before I can even think about you seeing them. I'm sorry."

"How much longer?" She gripped the counter. "What am I supposed to do to prove I'm recovered unless you let me spend time with you?"

The room fell into silence. *Time with you.* Sienna looked from Martina to Jack and back again. Their bodies were held in stiff defense. She shouldn't be there. Sienna drained her cup and stood. "Look, I think I should go. This is something you two need to sort out for yourselves."

"Stay." Jack touched her hand.

Sienna shook her head. "No. As I believe we established before, this has nothing to do with me."

She squeezed his fingers before pulling her hand away and leaving the kitchen. She was barely halfway along the hallway when the telltale clicking of Martina's shoes sounded behind her. Praying for the strength to bite her tongue, Sienna turned.

Martina smiled. "I wanted to walk you out. I don't want any bad feelings between us, Sienna. I appreciate this can't be easy for you."

"There's no need. I'm absolutely—"

"Of course there's a need. Here." She opened the door. "Let's go outside. I think Jack needs a moment alone."

They stepped outside into the warm mid-summer sun and walked toward Jack's open gate. When they reached it, Sienna saw Martina visibly shook. God, was she crying?

"Hey, are you—" Sienna touched her elbow, and Martina flinched as though she'd struck her. Sienna held up her hands. "Sorry. Look, are you okay? Why don't you go back inside with—?" Her voice dropped off when she noticed the woman wasn't crying but—laughing.

Martina faced Sienna straight on with a grin, her shoulders still dancing with contained laughter. "No, *I'm* sorry. It's only that…well, I can't believe you're setting up a sex shop in your *home*. Are you mad?"

Sienna smiled back, though it felt strange at her lips. "Not mad. Determined."

"Determined?"

"I love what I do. Due to circumstances beyond my control, I've had to leave my shop in town and move the business home. But it's no big deal."

"No big deal…I'd say it's a huge deal." She glanced toward Jack's house. "Especially for someone with as much ambition as you seem to have."

Sienna stared; she didn't care for the derisive tone in Martina's voice. "My ambition won't stop if—*when* I move my shop to Marsden Place. I don't understand what you're—"

"Won't it stop for Jack, though?"

Sienna swallowed. Jack? What did Jack have to do with her ambition? "What do you mean?"

Martina shrugged. "Jack's the kind of guy who likes a woman to be at home looking after his babies. Surely he told you that? I'm just wondering if you're happy knowing you'd have to give up what you've worked so hard for if you and he…you know, had a future."

Heat seared Sienna's cheeks. "What happens from here on with me and Jack hasn't been discussed. I'm sure we'll iron things out. In time."

"Hmm…Jack is very set in his ways. I remember so many times when he told me things…you know, when we were lying in bed, the babies between us…" Martina sighed and glanced toward Jack's house once more. "He's a wonderful father. I realize that now. All he wants is a woman to mother his children. I'm so glad I can be here now."

Sienna's primal instinct rose up, and her hands itched to smash Martina right in the middle of her snidey-sneering face. Words stuck in her throat as animosity writhed inside her like a wakening cobra desperate to strike. Focus. She needed to focus for Jack, for the twins.

She plastered on a smile, her teeth grinding. "Me too. The girls need their mum."

Martina nodded. "Absolutely. And now that I'm back, you don't have to feel burdened with them. I can take care of them while you and Jack…do whatever is it you do without the twins." She paused, her forehead creasing. "He does want to spend time with you alone, doesn't he?"

Sienna swallowed the nausea that rose bitter in her throat. "Of course."

Martina patted her hand. "I'm glad to hear it. I'm sure everything will work out just how he wants it. After all, the twins come first, don't they?"

"Absolutely."

"Good. Then we'll have no problem convincing a judge you feel that way if it comes to it, will we?"

"Hey, what's going on?" Jack's voice shattered the tension, and both women turned their attention to him as he walked toward them, his arms moving like pistons at his sides.

Sienna waved her hand. "Nothing. I have to go. See you later."

Lifting her chin, Sienna exited Jack's yard and strode into her own, anger pulsing with each step. The humiliation of having to endure

Martina watching her retreat into her own house instead of standing and defending herself was more than she could tolerate, but she was out of there. This was between Martina and Jack. Sienna opened her door and slammed it behind her.

She leaned her forehead against the adjacent wall of her entryway as foreboding weighed like lead on her chest. How would getting into a catfight with their mother help Holly and Katy? Martina's words about Jack doing anything to keep his girls rang loud and clear in her mind—echoing what Jack himself had said. Hadn't Martina already won?

Sienna was losing Jack to her…Holly and Katy, too. She slapped her hand to her mouth as a sob escaped.

I can't do this anymore.

Suddenly, Sienna felt her dad standing beside her. Soon she'd been in London. Maybe she should've been there all along.

Chapter Nineteen

Two hours later, Jack sat with Holly and Katy on the sofa as Big Bird shared his seeds of sensibility with the kids gathered at his feet. Shame he didn't have any for the adults watching him on TV, too.

It hadn't been until Katy and Holly had bounded through the doors of their daycare and into his arms a half-hour before that Jack had been able to breathe again.

Martina had left promising not to do anything more toward filing for joint custody until Jack had time to think. Time to decide what to do and how to do it. The twins came first—even though his mind constantly drifted to a certain woman next door as well. He couldn't imagine for one minute wanting to leave Sienna alone with an ex-husband if she'd had one, yet she'd done just that—she had gone home, leaving him with Martina. And her ensuing silence had spoken volumes.

He'd leave her be for tonight, but come morning, he would make sure she knew nothing had changed between them. He still wanted her. Was scared by the strength of his feelings and frustrated with his inability to adequately convey them during this mess.

"Daddy?"

Katy's voice broke his thoughts, and Jack fought the scowl from his face when he saw the concern in her eyes. "Yes?"

"Where's Sienna?"

"At home, I think. Why?"

"Can she come round and play? I want to show her how to play Snakes and Ladders."

Jack pressed a kiss to her hair. "Not tonight, sweetheart. Maybe tomorrow."

Her pretty brow creased. "Why?"

"Because she's probably busy. We don't want to bother her."

"You could try." On his other side, Holly slipped silently from the sofa. She looked around the room, her face a mask of concentration.

Jack shifted Katy to the side and moved forward, carefully watching Holly. "Holly? What's wrong, Pud'?"

"Where's your phone?"

Uh-oh. If Holly wanted his phone, she wanted to make a phone call. And if Holly wanted to make a phone call, it meant she wouldn't be swayed until she'd done exactly that.

"Who do you want to call?"

She picked up the cushions on the sofa, searching beneath them. "Sienna."

Jack raised his eyebrows. "*You* want to call Sienna?"

"Uh-huh."

"Why?"

She straightened and looked him directly in the eye. "Because Katy wants to see her."

Jack saw the underlying yearning in her eyes, the slight crack to her voice. "So do you."

Holly glared. "No, I don't."

"Yes, you do. You like Sienna, huh?" He smiled.

She lifted her shoulders, the color at her cheeks darkening. "She's okay. It's Katy who likes her best."

Hope wound into Jack's gut. Surely, there was nothing Martina could do in court that would detract from what Holly and Katy wanted? But his smile slipped as Holly continued her search. What if they also wanted Martina when they saw her? Sooner or later, the twins *would* want to see their mother. He knew that—and so did Martina.

"Found it!"

Jack looked up. Holly marched across the room and held out the phone. "Call her."

"I really don't think—"

The ringing of his doorbell cut Jack off mid-sentence. He looked to the living room door and back again. He stood and tucked his phone into his back pocket. "You two stay put. I'll see who that is."

Holly climbed onto the sofa next to Katy, instantly glued to the TV. Even so, she instructed, "And then you can ring Sienna. She'll like that."

Smiling, Jack left the room and entered the hallway. Flicking on the porch light, he opened the door. Dressed in satin pajamas with her hair tied in a messy knot atop her head, Sienna was beautiful in the golden glow of the light.

She held up a bottle of red wine and two glasses. "We need to talk."

Jack's heart turned over as he gestured for her to come inside. "Are your ears burning?"

"What?"

He closed the door and moved his hands to her waist, the slippery sheen of her pajamas giving a whisper of a barrier between his palms and her skin. *God, she is stunning.* He stared at her open mouth. "The girls were just in the process of insisting I call you and ask you over when you rang on the doorbell."

"Really?" She smiled. "I'm pleased."

"How are you feeling?" He could barely think with her huge brown eyes staring up at him and the hungry need to feel her skin on his lips.

"About Martina?"

"About everything."

They stood staring at each other for a moment before Jack glanced toward the living room.

"Do you want to go and see them?"

"Sure. In a second. It's because of Martina I'm here, Jack. I've spoken to Mike."

He took a step away from her. "Why? I thought you left earlier because you felt it was better I dealt with Martina alone. What's happened to get you worried enough to call Mike without speaking to me first?"

"I wanted his advice. I wanted to know how much credence there was to Martina's claim that she has the right to appeal for custody. I'm just worried. That's all."

Jack studied her for a moment. Concern stormed in her eyes and anxiety creased her brow. He nodded and pulled her into his embrace. "I know you are."

"I think we—*you* should meet with him and Kelsey tomorrow. Hear what they have to say."

Jack pulled back and looked into her eyes. "That bad, huh?"

"No. I just don't want her putting in an attack before you're prepared, that's all."

He frowned. "What did she say to you, exactly? When you were outside with her."

She looked to the floor. "Nothing. Particularly. I just don't trust her after everything you've told me."

"I know there were moments the old Martina showed up today, but she was also surprisingly cooperative after you left. No chance in hell I'm granting her joint custody, but I do think I should give her benefit of the doubt where visitation goes. At least for a while."

"I see."

He touched his finger to her chin and lifted her face. Her eyes shone beneath the light above them. "Do you?"

She nodded.

"I've known Martina a long time. We have kids together. I don't want to make any mistakes by keeping my bitterness at the forefront all the time. That's going to be no help to the girls whatsoever. I have to put my emotions aside and think of theirs. If Martina's trying, I'm going to try too."

She shrugged. "You're right. I'm sorry."

"Nothing to apologize for. I like that you care this much."

"I don't want to get in the way of something good that could happen if I wasn't slap-bang in the middle of all this, Jack."

"You won't."

"I will. If it's not the shop, it could be me physically punching the woman."

Jack laughed.

"Look, let me go and say hi to the girls." She thrust the wine and glasses at him. "You go open that, and I'll see you in the kitchen in a minute."

She moved to walk away, but he gripped her wrist. "I don't want my problems troubling you this much."

"They aren't. I have…the shop to think about."

Her wrist slipped from his hand. Of course it was about the shop. Why would it be about anything else other than her own life? Four weeks they'd known each other. How could he expect her to think solely about Holly and Katy like he did? The shop was her lifeline, and he had no right to expect more from her so soon.

Head held high, she walked into the living room. Jack watched her plaster a smile on her face and step over the threshold.

"Hi, girls. What are you watching?"

"Sienna!"

Jack started as Katy's delighted greeting cut a slash straight across his heart.

He walked into the kitchen and put the wine and glasses on the table. His mind whirled with scenarios of what Sienna was about to tell him—each one worse than the last. He took a corkscrew from the drawer, sat down, and opened the wine. Filling the glasses, he then stared ahead out of the open patio doors.

A few minutes later, he sensed her hesitating at the kitchen door. "Are you coming in?"

She stepped into the room and slid into the vacant chair opposite him.

"Are the girls okay?"

"They're fine."

"Good." He turned back to the yard.

They sipped their wine in silence for a few moments. "Jack?"

"Uh-huh?"

"When all is said and done, the most important thing is Holly and Katy, right?"

"Of course."

"Then that's what you should focus on. Nothing else."

He turned. Her eyes were dark with something he couldn't name. Anxiety. Guilt. Maybe even nervousness. "What's wrong?"

Her smile was too quick, too wide. "Apart from what's going on with you and Martina? The shop?"

The sarcasm was obviously meant as a distraction, and Jack reached across the table to take her hand. "Well, the good news is, I think we might be able to do something about one of those things sooner than I thought."

"Oh?"

"The shop."

"What about it?"

He smiled. "I've been looking into your landlord. I'm more convinced than ever that the rent increase had nothing to do with good business or recession-sense. In a few days, I think I'll have everything I need to get to the bottom of it. If what I suspect is happening, you'll get the shop back."

"Right." She looked to the patio doors.

Jack watched her profile. The set of her face had not been the reaction he'd expected. "Don't you want to keep the shop and not have to move it to Marsden Place? Wouldn't that be ideal?"

She lifted her shoulders. "I suppose."

"Sienna?"

She met his eyes. "The shop is not the end of the world. Concentrate on the twins. Not the shop…or me." Draining her glass, she abruptly stood, her chair scraping against the tiles. "I have to go."

What is going on here?

Jack reached for her, and then dropped his hand when he saw her tears. "Sienna, please. Talk to me."

She shook her head. "I'll say goodbye to the twins on the way out."

He leapt to his feet. "Wait."

"Jack —"

In his desperation to keep her there, Jack said the first thing he could think of. "Is Mike expecting me tomorrow, then? Wasn't that what you came here to talk about?"

Her shoulders slumped. "Mike thinks Martina might have a valid case to bring in front of a judge as far as visitation goes, with or without your consent. You need to be prepared."

Jack's gut knotted. "Fine. Then I'll go see him. For all I know, Martina was bluffing about custody to antagonize me, but it's worth knowing how things stand with visits before the inch I give her becomes a yard."

"Good."

"But I'd like it if you came too."

"But you don't need me there."

"I do. I respect you. I trust you…I need you."

She closed her eyes. Jack waited.

"Fine," she conceded, finally looking him straight in the eye. "I'll come with you. Then I leave."

Jack released his held breath. "Thank you."

"Don't thank me. You have no idea what it's like to sit in the room with those two yet." She looked to the door. "I have to go. I'll tell Kelsey we'll see her at midday tomorrow. Is that okay?"

He nodded and pushed his hands into the pockets of his jeans to stop from grabbing her. "That's great."

She smiled. "Okay, I'll see you then."

Jack stared after her as she left the kitchen without initiating any sort of goodbye embrace. Picking up his glass, he finished his wine in one gulp as he listened to the muffled sounds of Sienna and the girls talking in the other room. Seconds later, the front door slammed behind her, and Jack dropped his head into his hands, wondering what the hell had happened to put such a look of utter despair in Sienna's eyes.

The following day, Jack glanced at Sienna sitting next to him in the outer lobby of Kelsey's office. His leg bounced of its own accord upon the oatmeal carpet tiles beneath their feet; Sienna's fingers tapped the same beat on the handbag in her lap. It was the first time in a while they'd seemed remotely in rhythm with each other.

All night he'd tossed and turned with the possibilities of what the future might hold. Sienna had asked nothing of him, yet he felt he asked so much of her. The words telling her how he felt stuck like barbed wire in his throat; each syllable, each letter of what he should say drew blood, leaving his flesh raw and unbearably sore. It didn't matter that the prospect of turning away from what they had set his heart pounding and made his stomach sick.

The emotion in her eyes was in his mirror's reflection every damn day. They were good together, and they were already in deeper than either of them could have anticipated. Jack swallowed the bitter taste in his mouth.

He looked at his watch. Time ticked by as they waited for Kelsey to come out of her office. Sensing Sienna watching him, Jack turned.

She smiled. "What are you thinking?"

Nodding toward the frosted glass door of Kelsey's office, he said, "I'm wondering what they're talking about in there. And hoping Kelsey will come out and tell me my worries are over." He gave a wry smile. "What else?"

Sienna looked to the door as well. "I can't promise you that, but I can promise they'll do their best for you if the time comes."

He took her hand. It lay there, warm and soft in his grip. He pressed a kiss to her knuckles. "That's enough. For now."

"Jack, I really hope everything works out as you want it."

"I want *you*."

She lowered her gaze to her lap. "Sometimes things —"

The frosted glass door flew open with such force, it banged against something solid behind it. Jack leapt to his feet.

Sienna merely blew out a heavy breath. "Here we go again."

Kelsey and the man Jack assumed to be Mike Scott walked out. Kelsey's face shone white; her mouth was set, and her hands hung in fists at her sides. Mike grinned as he stepped forward and offered his hand.

"You must be Jack. Mike Scott. Nice to meet you."

Looking from Kelsey, whose glare bore into Mike's temple, Jack took his offered hand. "Same to you."

Mike dropped his hand and slid an arm around Kelsey's shoulders. She stood ramrod straight beside him. "If what Kelsey has told me is true, you're hoping I'm going to do something about keeping your ex-wife from causing you and your girls any more trouble, right?"

Jack glanced at Kelsey, who'd stiffened to the point her face looked like it was about to crack into a million pieces, her spine right along with it. Jack hesitated before looking at Mike. "I certainly hope so."

Sienna stood up. "Hey, what's a girl got to do to get a hug around here?"

Mike's arm slipped from Kelsey's shoulders, and he moved forward, pulling Sienna into a bear hug. "Hey, you."

After a moment, Sienna pulled from Mike's embrace. "So? What do you think? Can you help?"

Mike smiled, showing perfectly white and, no doubt, very expensive teeth. "Depends what the deal is. How much do you like him?"

The intensity of Jack's worry lightened ever so slightly, and he grinned. Turning to Sienna, he saw her own smile slip as a bright red flush stained her cheeks.

Kelsey snorted.

Sienna turned to her best friend. "Do you really want to go there?"

"I'm not saying anything."

"Good. Don't." Sienna faced Mike. "Well?"

Laughing, Mike gestured toward the door leading outside onto the high street. "I thought I'd treat us all to lunch at The Barge. We'll talk business there. What do you think?" He turned to Jack. "Jack?"

Jack returned his smile as the first whispers of trust seeped into his blood. His instincts were rarely wrong…apart from the catastrophic case with Martina. Something told him Mike Scott would be his saving grace. "Sounds like a plan."

"Great." Mike rubbed his hands together. "Do you want to bring your little ones along? They're more than welcome."

Kelsey clicked her tongue. "This is a business meeting, Scott. Not a family day out."

Mike's eyes darkened, and his grin vanished. "Excuse me, Jack." He turned toward Kelsey. "Tell you what, Cruella, why don't you stay here and spend the rest of this sunny day hiding behind your desk like you always do?"

Her cheeks now a deep red, Kelsey's eyes shot lasers of rancor. Mike glared straight back, a vein pulsing at his temple. Jack subtly cupped his hand to Sienna's elbow and steered her toward the door.

"We'll…um, meet you outside."

He propelled her firmly out the door.

As soon as they were outside, she rounded on him. "What did you do that for? It's so much fun watching those two rip ten bales of crap out of each other."

"Yeah? Well, I don't think Mike would appreciate a brand new client standing there to witness it."

Sienna chuckled. "You seriously need to get to know him ASAP. He's the only guy I've ever known who can get my Rottweiler of a friend under control. Although, she'd never agree with me in a million years."

"Are they…"

"Lovers? Dating?" She laughed again as they walked to his car. "Nope. But I have a funny feeling they will be one day in the not-too-distant future if Mike has anything to do with it."

He smiled. "When there's that much tension between two people, they either hate each other or want to rip each other's clothes off. I guess it's the latter."

She arched an eyebrow. "Is that so?"

"Uh-huh."

Her eyes flashed with silent suggestion before she hurried away from him and opened the passenger door of his car. He watched the length of her bronzed legs disappear inside the car and regret wound tight inside him. It was clear she had just checked her flirtation, wanting to dismiss her slip. Why did it have to be this way? Why did their closeness of a few nights before have to be yanked away from them before it had even begun?

Jack cursed his bad luck he hadn't met Sienna before Martina. Yet if he hadn't met Martina, he wouldn't have had Holly and Katy. He wouldn't have had the life he had now.

The tip-tap of stiletto heels behind him clutched fingers of distaste around his gut. The sound was a cold memory of Martina. He turned around. Mike strode out in front of Kelsey, his smile wider than Buckingham Palace as Kelsey jogged behind trying to keep up. Her face was a picture of shock. Mike had either just given her a kiss she wouldn't forget or slapped her ass. Jack didn't want to contemplate which, but he liked Mike Scott already.

Sliding behind the wheel, Jack gunned the engine and stole a glance at Sienna as she looked out the side window. God, he wished things were different.

He faced the windshield just as Mike passed him in his car to lead the way to the pub. He pulled out of the parking space and followed on behind.

"If your ex-wife does want to fight for custody, Jack, there's only so much she can do at this stage."

As they sat in The Barge pub garden, Jack turned from watching the canal boats pass beside them and looked at Mike. "Which means?"

Mike blew out a breath. "First of all, her sobriety needs to be confirmed, whether by talking to her AA counselor, her sponsor, or whomever else I decide I want evidence from. Plus, we need to see where she's living, where she intends to stay with your kids if she's allowed access. She'd been missing in action for twelve months, made no effort to contact them. With all that and what you've told me of your ex-wife's reputation in the community where she lived before she disappeared, this is will be a lengthy process—despite her claim that she can have her daughters back because the year is up. It doesn't work that way."

Jack shook his head and pushed his half-eaten ham, eggs, and potatoes away from him. The food was delicious but sat heavy in his stomach.

"I'd be a lot happier if you said there's a good chance she won't get joint custody, period. I don't want her even visiting the girls without my supervision." He curled his hand around his pint glass. "You need to know something."

Mike, Kelsey, and Sienna turned to face him as though bound by invisible strings. "Martina *might* no longer have an alcohol problem nor live a life jumping from one bloke's bed to the next…" Jack inhaled a heavy breath. "But she always did go after what she wanted with single-minded determination. I can't imagine that has changed."

Mike narrowed his eyes. "Meaning?"

"Meaning perhaps she could still get out of control. Her violence was always directed at me and was usually carried out under the influence, but the day she struck Katy was the day I wanted her out of my life for good."

Sienna sucked in a breath. "You never told me—"

He looked at her. "I'm not proud of the fact I was too preoccupied to notice just how bad things were."

Mike sat back in his chair and picked up his pint of beer. "I have more than enough reason to believe no judge in the land would grant her preference over an award-winning journalist who gave it all up to be there for his four-year-old twins. It's a done deal."

Hope flickered, albeit dully, in Jack's heart. He wanted to believe that if Martina didn't play ball, it would be cut-and-dry in his favor. But he dared not go there. Not yet. "We'll see."

"There's no 'we'll see' about it, my friend."

Kelsey tutted loudly, and Jack looked at her. "What?"

Her cool green gaze met his. "As much as I hate to admit it, if Mike says you have nothing to worry about, you don't. He always delivers on his promises. Always."

Mike's face split with a wide grin. "Thanks, Kelse. That must've hurt."

"Shut up," she said, scowling.

Sienna spoke up beside Jack. "Oh, God, don't you two start again. Jack's going to run for the hills if you carry on much more today."

Jack smiled. "So, in the meantime, I should at least see Martina again and hear what she has to say, right? Because as of now, she's neither done nor said anything that I can argue with." He took a drink. "Long may it continue."

Mike bobbed his head. "Frankly, the courts would prefer that you and your ex-wife sort out visitation arrangements on your own. But if you can't resolve it between yourselves, my hands could be tied unless she does something that constitutes breaking the law. It's within her rights of parental responsibility to apply for child access; then it's in the judge's discretion to administer a formal assessment of what is in your children's best interests."

Sienna squeezed Jack's fingers, and he turned around in surprise. She smiled, but worry was clear in her eyes. "Just be careful, okay? I want the twins to be happy. And you. Everything else is insignificant. You're doing your best without exposing the twins to anything. If this gets to court, Mike will make sure they understand that."

Everything else is insignificant. Did she mean him? Her? Them? For a moment, Jack just stared at her, willing his heart rate to slow. None of this was her fault, and he hoped to God Sienna was out of Martina's firing line if the time came for his ex-wife to show her true intentions.

He covered her hand with his. "Thanks."

She kept smiling but eased her hand from his and sipped her wine. Jack sat back in his chair as the lawyers started discussing something else, their conversation fading into the background as he focused on Sienna's pretty profile. She'd been putting on a good enough show for her friends, but Jack knew she wasn't altogether herself. Hadn't been ever since Martina had reentered his life…and was now infiltrating Sienna's. The weight hung around him like a heavy dark cloud. One too difficult to shake off, no matter what she — or Mike, for that matter — said.

He watched her put her wineglass down on the table with a seemingly decisive clunk. When she looked back at him, her eyes shone with fervor, and her cheeks flushed.

Jack firmly held her gaze, then looked at each face around the table. They all turned to look at him. "I'd be okay about Sienna's shop, you know, as long as I didn't think Martina wouldn't use it against me — or her."

"Don't worry about me," Sienna said. "I don't let anything happen to the people I care about. Not anymore."

Inscrutable tears shined in her eyes, and she looked past his shoulder. He drained his glass. Why now? Why did a woman like Sienna Lloyd, who wore her heart on her sleeve, who was more honest than a damn monk, have to be dragged in the middle of Martina's reappearance? All that he'd put her through, yet here she was. Still by his side, still trying to help.

"So…first things first," she continued. "You let Martina say what she needs to say. Once you know what you're dealing with, you'll take it from there. Deal?"

"*You*," she'd said. No mention of "we" this time. Unease rippled through Jack, but he pushed it away. No more running. No more waiting. He already knew what he was dealing with when it came to Sienna, and it was time to finally cut the string he'd been dangling her from and do right by her.

He nodded. "Absolutely."

Chapter Twenty

"Gotcha."

"Got who?" Seated at the desk across from Jack's, Steve raised his eyebrow.

"The landlord who owns three side-by-side properties along Bourton Way," Jack replied.

"You still looking into that?"

"Yep, and now I'm glad I did." He slapped his notepad down on the desk. "The son of a bitch has plans for those properties I'm pretty sure were not fully disclosed when he applied for planning permission."

Steve scooted forward on his chair. "Yeah? Do you want tell me about it?"

Jack grinned. "Not yet. There's someone else I need to speak to first."

"That someone wouldn't happen to be Sienna Lloyd, by any chance?"

"Might be."

Steve laughed. "You ol' dog! Should've listened to those rumors that you two had a thing going on. The last time you stormed out of here after Sienna, I thought things were going to get messy…not down and dirty."

Jack laughed and reached for his cell phone. "You, my friend, are a bad man. She's a real lady who doesn't do down and dirty."

"I believe you…" He winked. "Millions wouldn't. Fair play to you, mate. You two go for it. That girl deserves some happiness."

Jack shook his head and dialed Sienna's number. It kicked to voicemail.

He frowned at the phone. He hadn't managed to reach her all morning, and her car had already been gone from the driveway when he'd left for work. Tension knotted his shoulders, and he glanced at the wall clock. It was now close to noon. The more he thought about it, the more he realized how little he'd seen or heard from her since the pub lunch with Kelsey and Mike. As far as he knew, she'd have been at the shop as usual on a Thursday morning. Then again, didn't he know less and less of what Sienna was thinking and doing?

Steve got up from his desk, leaving Jack alone. Making a snap decision, Jack dialed Kelsey's number. The phone rang four times, five times…

He cursed and was about to hang up when she answered. "Hello, Kelsey Morgan speaking."

"Kelsey, it's Jack."

"Hello."

Her tone was cool, aloof. Jack frowned. "Did I catch you at a bad time?"

"No."

"Right." Something was different with Kelsey. The usual teasing tone of her voice was gone, leaving pure business attitude in its wake. "Is Sienna with you by any chance?"

"No."

"She's not answering her phone."

"Oh."

What the hell is going on here? "Kelsey?"

"Yes?"

"Where is she?"

"Why?"

Jack's shoulders stiffened. "Has something happened? I didn't see her car this morning—"

"She's gone away for a few days. See you soon."

"Wait! Where? Where's she gone?" Jack gripped the phone, a horrible sense of foreboding stealing through him. "Kelsey?"

She huffed out a sigh. "London. She's in London. Just let her do this, Jack."

"Do what?" He glanced toward the office door, willing himself to stay seated and not run through it and straight into his car.

"She's in London looking at her options. She has a friend—"

"Who can give her a job. She mentioned something about him to me a while ago."

"Good. Then you know everything you need to know."

"Bull…" He closed his eyes. "Why now? Why is she looking into a job in London now when she's decorated the shop room, sent out fliers, and told every single one of her customers she'll be opening again soon?"

Silence.

"Why now, Kelsey?"

"Jack, don't do this to me, okay? Sienna is my friend. I'm not going to sit by and let her get her heart broken when it's taken this bloody long to get her to realize a date won't kill her."

Jack's heart picked up speed. "Get her heart broken? What…is it because of me that she's left?"

"Of course it is. Why else would she ever leave Potterford if it wasn't that the prospect of staying here filled her with more heartache than going? You've got to sort your stuff out and leave Sienna out of it. You're not hers to have. Not yet. When you are, you go find her, but don't you dare mess up what she can find in London. Don't you dare."

The line buzzed dead in his ear.

He tossed the phone on the desk, frustration blurring the edges of his vision. "Goddammit."

"Hi, Jack. Bad time?"

He snapped his head up. "What are you doing here?"

Martina stepped closer and brushed her red-painted lips across his before he could stop her. "I thought I'd treat you to lunch."

Jack pulled her hands from his face and held them in a firm grip. "Don't."

She glanced around her, her eyes gleaming with triumph. "What? Don't you kiss hello?"

Jack stood, looking around to see the curiosity etched on his co-workers' faces despite their best efforts to feign interest in the papers in front of them or their phones or the damn photocopier.

"You shouldn't be here." He gripped her elbow and marched her toward the exit. They walked outside, and he spun her to face him. "What do you want?"

She smiled and lifted her hands to his lapels, moving across to his tie…

Jack snatched her hands away and held her at arm's length. "Martina, for crying out loud. What do you think you're doing?"

"There's no need to be like this. I just want us—"

"There is no *us*. Now, what do you want?"

A slow blush spread from the low V of her shirt up to her neck, covering her face in reddened anger. Her eyes turned from puppy to predator in seconds.

"You owe me this, Jack." She glared. "I mean it. I can't lose you a second time."

He released her and pushed his fingers into his hair. Held them there. "I don't believe it."

"You'd better believe it, because I'm deadly serious. I want my family back. It's time for me to settle down."

"For God's sake. I'm in love with another woman, I—"

"You're in love with her?" Martina mouth twisted. "How can you be? You barely know her."

He dropped his hand then raised it, palm up. "I know her enough to know she's good for me, Martina. She makes me believe in things that I thought you'd forever tainted."

She narrowed her eyes. "*I'd* tainted? I was struggling, Jack. How can you say that to me?"

He closed his eyes. "You're right. We *both* hurt each other enough to whittle love away beyond recognition. I'd lost faith in whether it could ever exist again for me."

"So, you agree—"

He opened his eyes. "But what have I ever said or done to make you think there would ever be a second chance with *us?*"

"Maybe it was too much to hope it could happen straight away. But I know in my heart it's only a matter of time before you'll want me back. To be a mother to your children. Especially now your precious *lover* from next door has gone missing." Icy laughter burst from her mouth.

He trembled with rage, his mind whirling. "Sienna hasn't gone 'missing.' She's away on business. It will take more than the likes of you to scare a woman like her."

"How about the likes of her shop? Nothing could have been more perfect than to find out you're sleeping with a woman who intends to run a sex shop from her damn living room. Who in their right mind is going to let four-year-old children around that stuff? I should find Sienna myself and thank her for making this so damn easy."

Jack gritted his teeth. "Just get out of here. If you want to shake someone down, go hassle your damn lawyer because now you're getting nothing from me. Absolutely nothing."

She stared at him, her cold green eyes boring into his. "One way or another, I will. You have a simple choice: you either bring them up with me or you lose them. You decide." She moved to walk away toward her car.

Jack's heart thumped inside his chest; his head ached. He couldn't wait for lawyers and red tape. His damn ex-wife was a silent virus, buried deep in his blood. He had to flush her out of his system once and for all.

"Martina."

She halted. "What?"

Now that he had her attention, the words didn't come.

This was Holly and Katy's mother. What good would it do to continue hating her for abandoning them? What message would it send to his precious babies and their future relationships? He swallowed the lump of indecision in his throat. He had no idea if he would live to regret letting even an inch of his guard down, but this had to end.

"It doesn't matter what goes on or what's said once this goes to court. You can do your worst as far as I'm concerned, and I'll come back fighting. All that matters to me are Holly and Katy. I suspect the same isn't true of you."

She sauntered back toward him, saying nothing.

Anger struck afresh inside him. He could barely look at her. "I'm neither blind nor stupid. You've started a war here you'll lose. No more games or I swear to God this isn't going to end the way you think it is." He met her ultimatum with one of his own: "You either work with me for the sake of Holly and Katy or you become enemy number one. Which is it?"

"I've lost everything, Jack." Her gaze lingered on his lips. "I've lost everything, including you. I gave you two kids, and I won't walk away with nothing."

"That doesn't mean we have to go through the courts. You don't have to do your hardest to infiltrate the girls' lives before you're truly ready to be a mum to them."

"What else can I do? I've no money. Nowhere decent to live…" Her eyes darkened, and her mouth sneered. "Do you really think I want to be here? Living on your perfect little street, with your perfect little house? Do you?"

And there it is. Jack curled his hands inside his pockets as the truth finally started to rear its head. "Which is it, Martina? Are we going to do this civilly or not?" He shook his head. "You weren't a perfect mother then; you won't be now."

"What were you? The model father? I don't think so."

He looked to the sky. "No, I wasn't, and I've still got no idea what I'm doing." He dropped his chin. "Can't we at least try and start making a change? Both of us?"

She looked into the distance. "I can't."

"Why?"

"I just can't."

"Do you really want this? To be threatening me? Sienna? Our children?"

She faced him once more, her shoulders slumping. "I don't stand a chance in court of even visiting the girls unless you help me get straight and reconcile with them. But why should you?" She shook her head. "My life's a mess, Jack."

"You can still make a better life than you ever could've with me. You can still see the girls…though you've barely even asked about them."

She lifted her hand in defeat. "What is there to know? Holly and Katy are with you. I know they're okay. I know you're doing everything for them. My mum loves telling me how much they love you, how you're doing such a great job. She tells me they don't need me. My own mother tells me to leave them alone. You have no idea how that feels."

She made for her car again, and Jack cursed before chasing after her. He gripped her elbow. "Listen to me. I want to try to work this out so they have both of us. Both of us doing our hardest to rectify our mistakes. To make them see a good marriage isn't a hopeless aspiration. Do you really want them growing up bitter and resentful like you did?"

"I did not—"

"Yes, Martina, you did. I can't believe I haven't seen it all this time. This is a cycle. Your mum never had any time for you, did she, until I came along and she saw the prospect of money and children. She used me in the hope we'd last, that I'd look after you because your dad walked out on her. Don't you see that? Because I do."

"That's psychological bullshit."

"Last chance. Do you want to be a part of your daughters' lives or not? With you or without you, I'm going to love those girls for the rest of their lives. I hope Sienna will too."

She glared. "She has nothing to do with this."

Pride filled his chest as he felt a weight lift. He could do this. A sense of liberty permeated through him. "Yes, she does. Because I love her. Now, do you want to be a part of my new family or not?"

For a long moment she said nothing, and then she swiped at the tears spilling down her cheeks.

"What the hell am I supposed to do, huh? I'm living in a tiny apartment with a man I can't stand. I've no job, no money—"

"I can help you get back on track. But I won't give you money."

Anger swirled in her dark green eyes. "I can't do anything without money. Why can't you understand that?"

Jack took a deep breath. "Move home."

She huffed. "With my mum? No chance."

She yanked open her car door, and this time Jack made no move to stop her. "Fine. Then go. But if you come back here again asking for a single penny from me, there will be no more phone calls. No more chances to make things right with Holly and Katy."

She stopped. Jack's heart thundered in his ears as he waited for her next move. When she met his eyes, she blinked, and a tear rolled down her face. "I don't even know where to start with them."

Jack took a breath in an effort to harden his heart. "You have to at least take the first step."

"But my mum's, Jack? She'll drive me insane."

"You'll tolerate it. You'll live with it. If you want a relationship with Holly and Katy, you'll do anything. I did."

She hesitated, then asked, "You'd actually help the girls find a way to forgive me?"

"If you go to your mum's," Jack said, nodding, "clean up, find a job."

"You'll have to give me time. It may take a while."

"And Sienna?" Just the thought of her lit a fire in his stomach, just like every time he saw her.

Martina's lips curved into a wry smile, and she straightened her posture. "I guess she's in and I'm out. Sooner or later I'll have to accept I can't fight against the way you look at her when she's near you. How you look at *me* every time you even say her name."

He nodded again. "I guess you will."

"More than that," she said after taking a breath, "you trust her to be around the twins. That couldn't have been easy for you considering the way their own mother was with them." Her eyes softened. "I'm sorry, Jack."

Jack returned her smile. "We can do this if we take one day at a time. No promises. No saying things we're not sure we can guarantee. Okay?"

She hesitated and then sighed. "Okay."

They stood for a moment before Jack slowly offered his hand. She looked down at it for a moment before a soft smile curved her lips. "Goodbye, Jack." She shook his hand.

"See you soon."

Their hands slipped apart, and Martina turned and slid into her car. The door slammed shut, and she pulled away without looking back.

Jack stared after the retreating car. He'd figure this out. He'd find a way to fix it. For all of them. He just prayed what he dreamed would come true, because right then, not a single person he cared about was happy.

Having spent two nights exploring her options in London, Sienna was back at Marsden Place. She watched the realtor pull out from her driveway before turning to face her house. The "For Sale" sign was a wooden placard challenging her to a new life.

Inhaling a shaky breath, she walked inside the house she loved and through to the shop room. She lifted the lid on a box of furry handcuffs and nipple tassels and smiled. God, she'd miss every aspect of what she'd built since her father was killed, but deep inside, she'd changed.

And she'd be forever grateful to Jack for making that change possible. He'd broken down her concrete wall and given her the gift of release. The possibility of love, of laughter, of having a family of her own one day wouldn't have come unless she'd met him. A firm believer in fate, Sienna knew Jack had been meant to enter her life. She was now equally confident that leaving was the right thing to do; otherwise, things would not have happened as they had.

Her front doorbell rang, and Sienna stiffened. She didn't want to see anybody, but avoiding Jack over the next few days while she packed her things for London would be impossible.

She stepped forward and peered through the window.

Damn it. She'd been just in time to see Jack glance back at the "For Sale" sign and ring her doorbell a second time.

"Okay." Sienna stepped back and took a deep breath. "Okay, let's do this."

Marching from the shop room into the hallway, she opened the front door before she could change her mind. "Hi, Jack."

He stood silent, staring. Sienna felt her body respond to his muteness, and then there it was—that appraising gaze of his that penetrated her own before wandering over her face, neck, then down to her breasts and back again. The one that made her feel like the loveliest woman in the world.

She cleared her throat. "Do you want to come in?"

"I've missed you."

Having expected a question about her selling up, the softly spoken statement caught her off-guard. Denial was futile. "I've missed you too."

He stepped inside, and they stood facing each other, the atmosphere heavy with unspoken questions and accusations. Sienna gestured toward the kitchen. "Let's grab a cold drink and sit outside. Are the girls with your mum?" *Please say they're not with Martina.*

"Yes."

"For the weekend?"

"No, they'll be here soon. I've texted my mum to tell her where I am. But can we put the girls on the backburner for now and talk about that sign stuck in your front garden?"

Heat struck her face, and she cast her eyes downward. "Why don't you go and sit outside? I'll bring out some drinks, and we'll talk. Diet Coke?"

"Sure."

He held a newspaper so tightly in his hand, Sienna could've sworn his fingers would soon snap.

"What's that?" she asked.

He glanced down at the paper. "News."

"News?"

"Yes." Without another word, he walked away.

She followed behind and stopped short in the kitchen as she watched him step out the back door. Opening the refrigerator, Sienna's heart raced and her hands shook. The way he'd looked at her when he'd mentioned the sign had been intense. How could he look at her that way when he'd forgiven Martina? On her return from London, Mike had told her about Jack's and Martina's intention to work things out for the sake of the twins—and their newfound amicability.

Nausea knotted inside Sienna as she pulled two cans of Diet Coke from the fridge. She winced against the pain in her heart that had become a habitual thing since the previous week. Grabbing two glasses from a cupboard, she walked outside on unsteady legs.

Damn. He'd chosen to sit in the swing seat, *their* swing seat, rather than at her small patio table. Pulling back her shoulders, she forced her feet forward and lowered onto the seat beside him.

"Here." She passed him a glass and can.

They snapped open their drinks, and the sizzle of filling their glasses permeated the tense silence. When they simultaneously leaned forward to put their cans on the table in front of them, their thighs brushed. The jolt of awareness caused Sienna's breath to catch. She didn't doubt the electricity between them would've lasted forever if her and Jack's circumstances were different.

"So you're leaving."

Sienna shifted sideways in her seat to face him, and her heart ached at how sad he looked. Exhaling, she said, "I don't know if it will be forever, but I've been offered a great job managing one of the biggest lingerie stores on Oxford Street. It's an amazing opportunity."

"Better than working for yourself?"

No. Nothing is better than working for myself. Here. In Potterford. With you next door. The twins. My mum and Kelsey just a few streets away. "It's certainly something I haven't tried in a while."

"I see."

He stared ahead, a muscle working in his jaw. Sienna could tell he knew she wasn't happy; he had an uncanny knack of making her feel completely exposed. How could she lie to him? She sighed. "Look, Jack, I have to go and let you work out what's best for Holly and Katy. Martina is their mother."

"And that means what? I give her access to them regardless? I don't think so."

Sienna surveyed his profile, her stomach tight. "I thought things might be working out for you."

He turned his face to her, his forehead creased. "How can anything be working out for me if you're moving to London?"

"Mike told me."

"Told you what?"

"Told me Martina was prepared to back down and do things your way."

With him looking at her mouth as though he wanted to kiss her, her strength faltered. A sudden neediness lodged in the place her heart had been moments before. She could no longer deny she'd fallen in love. Was no longer sure she even wanted to.

"Jack?" she asked when he'd still said nothing.

Uncertainty shone in the deep blue depths of his eyes. What was he thinking? The shake of his head was barely perceptible, but it was enough to knock the wind from her lungs. What else did he want her to say?

The steady thump of a headache snaked across her furrowed brow. "I don't want to come between you and Martina giving your relationship a second try. If Holly and Katy have any chance of their parents being together—"

"I'm sorry, Sienna."

Sienna blinked hard against the tears burning like wildfire behind her eyes. "You don't need to apologize. That's why I left."

He gave a wry smile. "You really don't get it, do you?"

"Just because I haven't had children, it doesn't mean I don't appreciate the importance of parenting as a unit. I might not be a mum, Jack, but I've been a child. And I've loved my mum and dad dearly."

He lifted his hand to her jaw and kissed her. She didn't push him away; she didn't demand he stop and tell her what the hell he thought he was doing. Like a masochist, a starving woman, she met his tongue, slid her hand across his thigh. Deeper and deeper he took her until Sienna could feel herself drowning in the cruelness that he wouldn't be hers.

They parted, and he brushed the hair from her eyes as he traced his tender gaze over every inch of her face. "I'm sorry," he repeated, "that I put you through going to London and finding a job because you didn't know what else to do."

"I just want you to be happy, and if—"

"I'm sorry…because you've had a wasted trip."

His eyes gleamed, and Sienna's heart raced. He was happy—no, smug. Elated. Goddammit, he was grinning. She frowned. "What's going on?"

He lifted her hand and pressed a kiss to her knuckles. "I'm sorry for not making you see what you meant to me. I'm sorry for making love to you and not doing it in such a way it was clear I was yours no matter what happened next. I'm sorry I risked losing you. And I'm sorry I didn't learn my lessons a damn sight quicker as far as fatherhood is concerned, but I've learned them now. The twins need us all to work this out, Sienna. You, me, and Martina. I want you to stay. Right here, with us."

"I don't understand—"

"I've let it go, Sienna. I've let go of the guilt and fear. I've let go of my anger toward Martina. It's true that she and I are going to try. One step at a time, without lawyers so we can get the trust back and she can be a part of the girl's lives. But not mine."

Hope sparked in Sienna's heart, but it was nothing against the fire of doubt there. "But you're part of what she wants. She won't accept —"

"Then she won't see Holly and Katy. She knows that." He leaned forward and kissed her lips, her jaw, then lifted her hair and kissed her neck. "You mean the world to me. I'm happy when I'm with you. I don't want that to end."

She shivered as his fingers brushed over the curve of her breast and down to her waist. "I don't know, Jack. What if farther down the line this changes and you walk away."

"I won't."

"You can't promise that."

He pulled back and looked deep into her eyes, his hand holding hers. "I can. I know I can because of what I feel for you, what the twins feel for you. Please. You have to trust me. Trust life. Please."

The excitement of possibility lodged Sienna's words into her throat. Could this really be happening? In a matter of weeks, she'd gone from being scared to look a child in the eye to longing to care for the two little girls next door.

In the midst of her elation, however, she slowly put her glass down on the table.

"It won't work, Jack. If I stay here, I'll still have to open the shop in my front room. And you were right: Holly and Katy shouldn't be around that." Sienna hesitated. "What are you smiling about? I'm serious. I have to work, and I don't want to do anything other than what I'm good at. What I love. The move to London makes more sense than you seem to understand."

Jack picked up the newspaper lying behind him on the seat. "Read this."

"What is it?"

"Read it."

Dragging her gaze from the power of his, Sienna looked at the front page of *The Potterford Post*. Emblazoned across the page was a photograph of Sienna's Sexy Solutions and the two shops on either side of it, along with the headline:

LANDLORD'S PLAN FOILED — TENANTS OFFERED
RENT FREEZE AND LOST EARNINGS

Sienna stared at Jack. "You…"

Beaming, he nodded. "Yep, while you were gone, I found out exactly what Thomas has been up to. Did you know he owns that entire block? The man has more money than he knows what to do with but still wanted more."

Sienna glared at the newspaper with a mixture of shock and anger. "So, he raises the rent, and then what? The shops remain empty until someone can afford to pay what he's asking? That doesn't make very good business sense to me. It's better to get something than nothing, surely?"

"But if you're lying to the council and have plans for those shops, big plans — plans that will make you a fortune if you can pull it off…"

Sienna looked at him. "What plans?"

"He wanted to renovate the whole lot into a wine bar cum night-club. Thought by the time the town council found out what he was up to, he would be committed to surveyors and all, and they wouldn't want to waste the money going to court — "

Sienna laughed. "The man's an idiot."

He kissed her temple. "Yeah, an idiot who has to give you lost earnings for any days you closed the shop to prepare its move, plus keep your rent as it was for the foreseeable future."

She tossed the paper onto the coffee table, then stood and strad-dled Jack's lap. "I can't believe you did it."

"Did what?"

"Fixed it. Fixed everything."

He smiled and gripped her waist. "I love you. I'd do anything to keep you near me, because you fixed *me*. So, do you want to stay here? With me?"

She grinned, her heart swelling with love for him. Did this mean they actually stood a chance? They could be together? The twins too? "Jack, I — "

"We can do this. All four of us."

Daring to hope, Sienna laughed. "My God, I can't believe this is happening."

"It is. It's going to be okay."

Unable to think of anything past kissing him, Sienna leaned forward and lowered her lips to his. Tentatively, she savored the delicious taste of his mouth, stroked his tongue with hers before seductively shifting forward. "I want to stay right here more than you would believe."

"Thank God."

They kissed again, and the fire came alive. Sienna threw all the loss and love that had been mixed up inside her into that kiss. She'd missed him so much.

Pulling her mouth from Jack's, she looked into dark blue eyes almost black with desire.

"Upstairs," she commanded. "Now."

He moved his hands under her buttocks and stood, lifting her with him. Sienna locked her ankles around his waist and her lips to his mouth. He carried her inside. But just as they started into the hallway, the front doorbell rang.

They froze. Gaping at each other wide-eyed, their voices merged into one:

"The twins."

Abruptly, Jack put Sienna down. "What shall I do? Oh, God." He looked down at the front of his jeans.

Sienna laughed. "They won't notice that."

"My mother will."

Her face dropped. "Your mother?"

His smile was gleeful. "Of course. She won't just deliver the girls to your porch like a parcel. Seeing her isn't a problem, is it?"

"No. Yes. No."

"Well? Which is it?"

The doorbell rang again.

She strode past him. "No. It's not a problem." With her heart pounding and her hands clammy, Sienna swallowed. She'd show him. She'd show him she wasn't scared of anyone.

Fighting the impulse to flee in the opposite direction, she marched to the door. By the time she pulled it open, Jack stood beside her.

There was no mistaking from whom Jack got his looks. Although Sienna hazarded a guess his mother must be in her fifties for Jack to be thirty, the woman looked closer to mid-forties and beautiful. Blinking out of her temporary paralysis, Sienna thrust her hand forward.

"Mrs. Beaton, it's so nice to meet you. I'm Sienna."

Ignoring Jack and the twins as they ran into Sienna's home like they belonged there, Mrs. Beaton grasped her hand, her eyes shining and her smile wide. "And it's lovely to finally meet you too. There's no need to tell me your name; Jack has spoken of little else but you for the last three weeks."

Sienna glanced at Jack. "Is that so?"

He merely shrugged. "And you're surprised?"

Overflowing with love, Sienna faced Jack's mother once more. "Would you like to come in?"

"Thank you, but I'm not staying; I have some errands to run. And please, call me Lorna." She grinned. "'Mrs. Beaton' makes me sound like his grandmother." She stepped forward and pressed a kiss to Jack's cheek. "Look after those babies of mine. I'll expect you all for Sunday lunch. Two o'clock."

With a wave and a wink at Sienna, Jack's mother turned and walked back over to Jack's driveway and into her car. As Sienna watched her leave, she became aware of the twins beside her and smiled at them. "Hey, you two."

Jack leaned down and effortlessly lifted Holly and Katy onto each of his hips. He then fixed Sienna with a look so determined, she was trapped like a rabbit in a snare. Albeit a six-foot-three-inch snare she loved more than life itself.

She opened her mouth to fill the silence, but Jack got there first. "I want you, Sienna. So do my daughters." Stepping closer with the girls in his arms, he pressed a lingering kiss to her forehead. "Your father meant everything to you. I know that. This will be different. This will have a happy ending. I promise. Let us make you happy."

Sienna looked at Holly and Katy and realized this was one fight she didn't stand a chance of winning. A smile pulled at her mouth.

"Fine."

"Fine?"

"Fine. I want you too. I love you too. All of you. We're meant to be a family, Jack. I know we are."

She opened her arms and wrapped them around him and the twins. The girls embraced her, and leaning between Holly and Katy, she and Jack kissed, long and deep.

"Ugh," the twins groaned.

Parting from Jack, Sienna laughed, knowing nothing would make either of them afraid to love again.

The End

Acknowledgments

Once again, the people I have to thank most of all are my amazing husband and beautiful daughters for putting up with my endless grumpiness and glazed looks through the writing of this book. I promise one day you'll see what I look like without a laptop strapped to my person!

Also, to my wonderful agent, Dawn Dowdle—I couldn't have written this book without her endless enthusiasm for Sienna and Jack. She convinced me to turn off my internal editor and get it finished.

Finally, my thanks also go to my fabulous editor, Colleen Wagner, who held my hand through revisions and edits as I honed *16 Marsden Place* uniquely for Omnific Publishing. It was worth every drop of blood, sweat, and tears!

About the Author

Rachel lives with her husband and two young daughters in a small town near Bath, England. She started writing short stories about eight years ago, but once her children were in school, she embarked on her first novel. It was published in 2007. Since then, she's had several books published with small presses and secured her first contract with Harlequin Superromance in May 2012.

Rachel is a member of the Romantic Novelists Association and Romance Writers of America. When she isn't writing, you'll find Rachel with her head in a book or walking the beautiful English countryside with her family. Her dream place to live is Bourton-on-the-Water in South West England. And in the evening? Well, a well-deserved glass of wine is never, ever refused…

www.rachelbrimble.com

www.rachelbrimble.blogspot.com

Twitter: @rachelbrimble

◄ ──►Young Adult◄──►

Shades of Atlantis and *The Ember Series: Ember* and *Iridescent* by Carol Oates
Breaking Point by Jess Bowen
Life, Liberty, and Pursuit by Susan Kaye Quinn
Embrace by Cherie Colyer
Destiny's Fire by Trisha Wolfe
Streamline by Jennifer Lane
Reaping Me Softly by Kate Evangelista

◄ ──►Historical Romance◄──►

Cat O' Nine Tails by Patricia Leever
Burning Embers by Hannah Fielding

◄ ──►Erotic Romance◄──►

Becoming sage by Kasi Alexander
Saving sunni by Kasi & Reggie Alexander
The Winemaker's Dinner: Appetizers & Entrée by Dr. Ivan Rusilko & Everly Drummond
The Winemaker's Dinner: Dessert by Dr. Ivan Rusilko

◄ ──►Anthologies and Singles◄──►

A Valentine Anthology including short stories by Alice Clayton, Jennifer De-Lucy, Nicki Elson, Jessica McQuinn, Victoria Michaels, and Alison Oburia

It's Only Kinky the First Time by Kasi Alexander
Learning the Ropes by Kasi & Reggie Alexander
The Winemaker's Dinner: RSVP by Dr. Ivan Rusilko
The Winemaker's Dinner: No Reservations by Everly Drummond
Big Guns by Jessica McQuinn
Concessions by Robin DeJarnett
Starstruck by Lisa Sanchez
New Flame by BJ Thornton
Shackled by Debra Anastasia
Swim Recruit by Jennifer Lane
Sway by Nicki Elson
Full Speed Ahead by Susan Kaye Quinn
The Second Sunrise by Hannah Downing
The Summer Prince by Carol Oates
Whatever it Takes by Sarah M. Glover
Clarity by Patricia Leever
A Christmas Wish by Autumn Markus